MURDER ON THE HIGH SEAS

A HARLOWE & FITCH HISTORICAL MYSTERY

ELIZABETH ROSE

OLIVERHEBERBOOKS

A Note to My Readers:

Dear Readers,

The **Harlowe & Fitch Historical Mystery Series** is ongoing with a main thread that continues to develop throughout the entire series. Mixed in with each story is a new murder mystery that is solved before the book is finished. While every installment can be read as a stand-alone, it is advised, and also ideal, to start from the beginning with **Murder at Mablethorpe Castle**, Book 1, and to read them in order. If not, there could be surprises ruined along the way.

There might be cliffhangers, but never for the current murder. And while these are murder mysteries and not romances, there is still a romantic thread woven in as well.

See more notes at the end of this book, but for now, welcome to the world of Harlowe & Fitch where investigations into murders in Mablethorpe and the surrounding areas are underway. A headstrong noblewoman searching for justice, and a stealthy sheriff trying to secure the safety of his town, team up to uncover that which is hidden but needs to be brought to the surface.

A Note to My Readers:

Elizabeth Rose

Chapter One

Mablethorpe, Late 1300s, England

Sheriff Zachariah Fitch stumbled out of bed after having heard a strange noise. He hurried out of his room and to the stairs, rubbing his eyes and trying to remember if he'd locked the front door. There had been a murder in town recently, and this gave him great concern. Living so close to the bad part of town, Rotten Row, he needed to do all he could in order to keep his young daughter, Starah, safe.

Something just didn't feel right. He couldn't help but think there was something he'd forgotten to do. But at this time of the morning, he couldn't think straight or remember anything. Then again, he actually found it hard to think at all with the loud, obnoxious noise that seemed to be coming from downstairs.

At the bottom of the landing, he stubbed his toe in the dark, hopped on one foot, and cursed softly to himself. Too bad he hadn't thought to bring a candle with him, but it was too late now. Zachariah was in a hurry to check the bolt on the front door.

He took one more step and this time he tripped on something, landing hard and ending up prone on the floor.

"God's eyes, what just tripped me?"

"It's just me, Brother," came a male voice from the dark.

"Isaac." Zachariah pushed up to a sitting position and groaned. "Now I remember," he mumbled, cursing the fact he'd agreed to let his brother stay with him until he could find a place of his own. Isaac had been a mercenary, but just gave up the profession. To make matters worse, Zachariah also vaguely remembered offering his brother a job. A job, training as one of his deputies! What the hell had he been thinking? He already regretted that decision.

"Light a candle, will you? I almost broke my neck in the dark," complained Zachariah, standing up and brushing the dirt from his hands. "And why the hell are you sleeping on the floor at the foot of the stairs in the first place?"

As soon as Isaac lit a candle, Zachariah had his answer, able to see the room completely now. His jaw dropped, not able to believe what he was looking at, right there in his own home.

The floor was filled with sleeping...pirates. Men lay sprawled out with their arms thrown over their faces, and most of them were snoring loudly. Now he knew what that awful noise had been. They were dirty and smelly, and certainly didn't belong in his home! These men were the crew members of Bear, or Nairnie's husband. They had all been pirates at one time, but supposedly now they all worked for King Edward III. Zachariah wanted to believe this was true, but in his business he knew that people didn't change. And they lied often. Once a pirate, always a pirate, as far as he was concerned.

"Why are these men sleeping in my home instead of bunking down on their own blasted ship?" spat Zachariah. "When I went to sleep last night, I made damned sure that they knew they were not welcome here overnight."

"They were going to leave, but then a bad storm blew in," answered Isaac with a big yawn. "Nairnie thought it would be safer for them to stay right here until morning."

"She did, did she?" He'd have to have a word with the old woman who served as nursemaid to his young daughter. Nairnie needed to know her place, and accept that *he* made the decisions in his own home, not her. She was such an old, crusty woman that even these pirates feared her. He rubbed the back of his neck, thinking it was more than likely the heavy ladle she swung that they feared. The one she wielded that kept them all in place. Including him.

"Och, I didna ken ye were up already, Sheriff." Nairnie stood at the top of the stairs in her nightrail, clutching her robe for additional modesty. She held a lit candle in her free hand. "It's early and I didna think ye'd be up for hours yet. I'll get the food started to break the fast, anon." She waddled down the stairs, her entire round body jiggling with each step she took.

"Nay, it's fine," he told her in a soft voice, holding up a halting hand. "Just go back to bed. There is no need to start your day yet."

"Nonsense," said the old woman, kicking at one of the men sleeping at the bottom of the stairs. "Move it, ye big lunk. Canna ye see I am tryin' to get by?"

"Mmmph," mumbled the crew member rolling over the other way to let her pass.

Zachariah shook his head, not able to believe this motley crew was taking up room in his abode. This was the last thing he wanted Starah exposed to. He hurriedly made his way over to Nairnie who was digging in a cupboard for something.

"Nairnie, I never said your husband's crew could sleep here last night," he said softly, trying not to be heard by the men.

"Ye didna say they couldna either. I told them they should." She pulled out a pot and a big wooden spoon and placed them on the counter.

"Actually, I'd like to have a talk with you about that. I don't

3

think having these ex-pirates in the same house as my young daughter is a good idea at all. I don't like it."

"What are ye sayin'?" She turned toward him and squinted one eye. "That my husband and his crew are no' good enough for ye, Sheriff?"

"Well...nay. I didn't mean that at all."

"Then ye're sayin' ye dinna trust them since they used to be pirates."

"I...didn't say that either." Although the thought had crossed his mind. He wondered how many of his belongings the pirates already had pilfered during the night.

"I can tell ye dinna want them here." Her hands went to her hips. This was never a good thing. Especially since she was still giving him the evil eye. He felt a cold shiver go through him.

"I have to admit, that I'm uncomfortable with this situation. Why couldn't they have just stayed on their ship last night? After all, they are used to living on the ship."

"Ye'd let them risk their necks goin' out in a bad storm, tryin' to make it back to the ship? After all, there was a rip snortin' storm last night, Sheriff."

"Nairnie, they're sailors," he said with a nervous chuckle. "I am sure they are used to not only bad weather, but also stormy waves on the sea. It is a way of life for them." Zachariah couldn't help thinking that mayhap the rain would have cleansed these men if they went out in the storm, and it would have at least washed some of the stench and filth from their bodies.

Almost as if Nairnie could read his mind, she took it upon herself to make the next decision without consulting him. Again. "Boys, get up!" she shouted at the top of her lungs.

"Nay, Nairnie, don't," he said with a flinch, not wanting to deal with angry pirates in his home, especially this early in the morning.

"The sheriff doesna want ye here, so ye'll have to leave."

Zachariah groaned. "Nairnie, really! Why did you have to say that?"

"These boys deserve the truth, Sheriff. If ye dinna want them in yer home, I am no' goin' to keep the fact from them." Next, she picked up the metal pot and the wooden spoon with the long handle, banging the spoon hard against the pot, waddling around the room, kicking at the sleeping men as well. "Ye heard me, get up!"

"Bid the devil, old woman, what are ye making all the ruckus about?" Her husband, Bear, who was built like a castle's retaining wall, sat up at the other side of the room, glaring at them.

"Bear, ye need to take the boys back to the ship and wait for us to join ye there," said Nairnie. "The sheriff doesna want them here."

"Leave? Now?" Bear scratched his beard. "But what about some food to break the fast first? I've got a powerful hunger, old woman. I am sure the boys do as well." Bear yawned and stood up, stretching his arms high over his head.

"Well, I planned to make some food for ye and the crew, but since the sheriff is actin' so arrogant this mornin', ye'd best leave now before he complains again."

"I wasn't complaining. Not really," said Zachariah under his breath.

"Oh no?" Nairnie gave him the evil eye again.

"I'm going upstairs to change." Zachariah picked his way through the horde of men, wanting nothing more than to get out of here right now. He stumbled and almost fell when one of the pirates stuck out his wooden leg, right in his path.

"Careful there, Peg Leg Pate," said Bear in his deep voice that echoed off the walls. "Ye almost tripped the sheriff, and he's already cranky this morning."

5

"I was just trying to get up off the floor, Cap'n," said the man with a shrug. "It's not easy with one leg you know."

A sense of guilt filled Zachariah. He wasn't so coldhearted as to not have a little compassion for a man who had lost his leg. "Let me help you," said Zachariah with an outstretched arm, not sure he believed the man's story and thinking that he'd really been trying to trip him all along. However, not wanting to come across as arrogant as Nairnie had already accused him of being, he decided to keep quiet.

Pate took Zachariah's hand and Zachariah pulled the man upright. The pirate wore a dirty and tattered headscarf and seemed a little more seasoned than some of the other crewmen. It was as if he'd been living on the sea for a long time. Standing close, he smiled, showing his broken and blackened teeth. It was almost enough to make Zachariah gag, but he tried his hardest not to flinch at the sight and smell.

"Ye don't want us here, Sheriff?" asked Pate. "That's an odd thing to say since ye and yer family will be joining us on our journey aboard our ship today."

Damn. That was the thing Zachariah had forgotten! Now he rather wished he hadn't been reminded of it. "I was just surprised to see everyone still here, that's all," he answered.

Bear and his crew had all shown up at his door last night, having supposedly just finished a mission for the King. Of course, Nairnie invited them all to stay for dinner, and then her husband invited Zachariah and his family, as well as Lady Vivienne and her family, to join them on their ship today as they sailed to Whitstable to pick up some fresh oysters.

"Ye didna change yer mind about goin' along on the journey, did ye, Sheriff?" asked Nairnie, finally putting down the damned pot but still clutching the spoon. "Because if so, Starah is goin' to be mighty disappointed. Especially since Martin and the others will still be joinin' Bear and his crew when they set sail."

The old woman certainly had a way of getting what she wanted. Not unlike Lady Vivienne, he decided. Even if he did back out and keep Starah from going, he knew Vivienne would still take her son Martin, as well as her handmaid Maleine, and that rat-catcher boy Wymond with her on the ship for the day's journey. That would truly break Starah's heart. It was the last thing he wanted.

"Nay, I didn't change my mind," he told Nairnie, trying to convince himself silently that it was only a day trip and would be over with soon. "I just worry about Starah's safety, since I am her father. After all, she's never been on a ship before and doesn't even know how to swim, should she fall overboard."

"Don't worry, my crew and I will watch over the little girl like she was our own," Bear assured him, wiping his nose with his sleeve. The man's words didn't give Zachariah any sense of confidence at all that this wouldn't be a horrible trip.

"Bear! Dinna do that! Have some manners around here," snapped Nairnie, hitting her husband with the wooden spoon. "Wipe yer nose on a cloth instead of yer sleeve. Ye are actin' no better than a dirty bilge rat, I swear."

"Don't hit me, old woman," said the man, grabbing on to the wooden spoon so hard that when Nairnie tried to pull it away from him, the handle snapped in half. "I might not have manners, but I do live with bilge rats so what do ye expect? Plus, I'm a sailor and spend most of my time at sea with the lousy lot of them who have less manners than me." He jerked his head toward the rest of his crew who were slowly standing up.

The crew heard his words and suddenly they all started to straighten out their wrinkled clothing. One of the pirates pulled his dagger from his belt and turned away to pick his teeth with the tip of the blade. Another man picked up a metal cup tied to his belt, breathing on it, and then shining it with the torn hem of his tunic. Peg Leg Pate took off his head scarf and bent over to buff the wood of his fake leg.

"Go on! All of ye. Shoo!" Nairnie waggled her fingers in the air. "Quit stinkin' up the sheriff's hovel." She herded the complaining crew toward the door.

None of this felt good to Zachariah. Did she have to call his home a hovel? Zachariah realized it was just a simple, two-story wooden home in town, with a thatched roof, but it certainly wasn't a hovel. Or was it? Mayhap he had been a little too harsh or perhaps judgmental toward these men, after all. If King Edward trusted them enough to hire them to work for him, then perhaps he should accept them too.

"Nay, wait," he said, letting out a deep sigh. The pirates stopped and turned to look at him, and he couldn't help but notice the hope in their eyes. For all he knew, the only decent meal they ever got was when Nairnie cooked for them. "You can make them something to eat first, Nairnie."

"Ye sure about that, Sheriff?" asked Bear, looking put out. "After all, we wouldn't want to be a big problem to you."

"No problem," said Zachariah, hurrying to the stairs. He heard his brother from behind him, talking to Bear.

"I bet it's exciting being on a ship out on the sea with the wind in your hair, and feeling as free as a bird," said Isaac, fishing for an invitation to join them today.

"It is," Bear answered.

"I've never had the pleasure," said Isaac.

"Really. Well, then why don't ye come with us and see for yerself?" said Bear, plopping down atop a bench at the table, obviously wanting to be the first one to get at any food that Nairnie put down.

"Nay, he can't," Zachariah broke into the conversation. "Isaac volunteered to stay here in town and help Constable

Dorson until I return." Zachariah looked down the stairs, over his shoulder.

"We'll only be gone for the day," Bear pointed out. "Can't yer constable handle things by himself for that short time?"

"That's right. Just a day. Plus, you do have another constable here in town as well as Constable Dorson, right?" asked Isaac, sounding as if he really wanted to join them on the ship.

"Well, aye. But he's more of a clerk, really," mumbled Zachariah, making it to the top of the stairs. When he turned back to look at Isaac, not only his brother, but also Nairnie, Bear, and the entire crew were all staring a hole through him. That damned shiver swept through him for the second time this morning. He couldn't ignore the fact that Nairnie had her hands on her hips and was giving him the evil eye yet again. "What the hell. Why not. Come along with us, Isaac," Zachariah told his brother. "Ask the entire town to join us while you're at it. Mayhap go down to Rotten Row and bring all of the whores and drunks, too."

"Sheriff!" snapped Nairnie.

"What is it, Nairnie?" he asked, challenging her, since he figured she was scolding him in his own home once again.

"Bear's ship isna nearly big enough for all those people." She turned around and busied herself preparing food as all the pirates talked and bellied-up to the table. His table. In his home. Not to mention, he'd paid for the food they were all about to consume.

"Bid the devil, I hope this day is over with quickly," mumbled Zachariah, heading to his room to dress, just wanting to get back to his normal life.

~

9

LATER THAT MORNING, Lady Vivienne Harlowe stood on the docks with Martin, Maleine, Wymond, and Grunt, as they prepared to embark on their exciting journey.

"Be careful, and don't let the children stand too near the railing of the ship so they don't fall off," called out her Aunt Ellen from the wagon, waving to them. She and Vivienne's uncle started back to Castle Mablethorpe, leaving them at the docks, waiting for the others to arrive.

"We will. Thank you!" Vivienne waved back, but noticed that her uncle was still sour about the fact she was going on this trip when he had warned her not to. He didn't even acknowledge her at all this morning, or wish her well. She wasn't sure if his grouchiness came from not getting his way, or perhaps it was just from being overprotective.

Gripping the King's ring hanging from a chain around her neck, Vivienne stared up at the *Falcon*, the ship that she and the children were about to board. She had just recently been claimed by King Edward publicly as being his bastard daughter. Now she didn't need to keep it a secret any longer since everyone knew. Although she'd worn his ring hidden beneath her clothing for the past seven years since her dying mother had said not to tell anyone, there was no longer a need to be discreet. Still, she felt funny about exposing it, and often still hid it beneath her clothing, out of habit.

"Move aside. Out of the way. Coming through," came a gruff voice. She moved quickly as three of Bear's crew headed to the shuttle boat that would take them to the ship that was anchored farther out in the water. Some of the bigger ships weren't able to pull right up to the pier to dock. The waters weren't deep enough. So small boats were used to shuttle people and supplies back and forth to the ships as needed.

The crewmen carried what looked like heavy bags over their shoulders, throwing them down into the shuttle boat before climbing in afterward. The bags were filled to the brim with items she couldn't see. These men were rugged, dirty, and foul-smelling. Most seafaring men were no different she supposed. But no matter what this crew called themselves now, to her, they still seemed to be pirates through and through. She couldn't push the thought from her mind that perhaps the contents of those bags included stolen items. Mayhap even some of the sheriff's things since they'd been in his house last night. She certainly hoped she was wrong. The sheriff didn't deserve that. If this were the truth, she'd feel awful about it.

Suddenly, she wasn't so confident anymore that going on this trip had been a good decision. Reaching down, she quickly took the gold and ruby ring she wore, hiding it under her bodice once more. Part of her warned her not to go. That part was her stomach churning again, the way it always seemed to do when trouble was about to happen. She supposed she could cancel the trip and just stay in Mablethorpe, but if she did that, she was afraid she would disappoint Nairnie. The old woman was so sweet and Vivienne didn't want to lose her trust. Nay, they just had to go on this trip as planned. There was no way around it.

"Lady Vivienne, I'm scared," whispered her handmaid, Maleine, who was joining them on the journey today at Vivienne's request. "Will we be safe on the ship with ex-pirates?"

Even Vivienne's bloodhound, Grunt, whimpered softly as he sat at her side. When she had accepted the invitation last night, things didn't seem so foreboding. But being here now, standing next to the ship and seeing the tall masts and the rugged crew in the daylight, she was starting to have her doubts. Still, she needed to stay strong for the sake of the children. She couldn't show any fear or doubt.

"Everything is fine," she told Maleine, releasing a deep breath and forcing a smile. At least the sheriff would be there with them, so that brought her a sense of comfort.

"Don't worry, Maleine, I'll protect you," said her seven-year-old son, Martin, patting his wooden sword that he wore at his side. He was a castle page and in training to someday become a squire. Vivienne had lost her baby boy seven years ago and thought she'd never see him again. But by a miracle of God, she recently found Martin...her lost baby. Once more, they were together, and she vowed they would never again be apart.

"I'll protect you too, Maleine," said Wymond. Wymond was once the rat-catcher's assistant on Rotten Row. He worked for the man called the Pied Piper who had been terrorizing the town. The boy was the same age as Maleine, at six-and-ten summers. He glanced down and fussed with something in the pouch hanging at his side.

"There is no need for anyone to be frightened," Vivienne assured them, even though she was also feeling rather nervous this morning. "After all, this is Nairnie's husband and his crew. They're friends...I hope." She added the latter part under her breath.

Another two pirates walked by cursing and spitting on the ground near their feet. Vivienne quickly turned away from them and pulled Martin to her, holding him tightly against her body. Grunt shot out of their way as well.

The hound walked over and sniffed Wymond's bag that hung from a long strap on the boy's shoulder. Then the dog whimpered and pawed at the pouch. Grunt was a bloodhound and good at tracking. He'd also been beneficial in every murder investigation so far. She knew that look and action from the dog, and Grunt didn't do it for no reason.

"Wymond? Did you by any chance sneak Chomp and Snuff into your pouch?" asked Vivienne knowingly, speaking about the boy's weasel-like pets.

"Well...mayhap," he responded, and looked up at her with a shy smile.

"You heard the sheriff say no pets except Grunt on this trip."

"I'm sorry, Lady Vivienne. There was no one to watch over them back at the castle," he told her. "Besides, if there are any rats on the ship, the ferrets can hunt them down. They'll be an asset."

"Rats," repeated Vivienne, her gaze going back to the ship once again. It was big and foreboding as it swayed back and forth with the movement of the water, the staves making odd creaking and squeaking noises. "Yes, I am sure the ship is loaded with rats." A shiver ran through her as she remembered all the rats she'd seen recently while helping the sheriff with a murder investigation that happened in the bad part of town, on Rotten Row. "Well, mayhap you're right about that, Wymond. Just keep a good hold on the ferrets, and perhaps you might not want to mention them around the sheriff until we are out at sea."

"Yes, my lady." Wymond smiled from ear to ear. "Thank you."

"Wymond, are you sure you'll be able to keep your balance aboard the ship with your hurt leg not being fully healed yet?" asked Maleine in concern. The two admired each other greatly.

"Yes, Maleine. I'll be fine. It is almost back to normal now." In one hand, Wymond clutched a walking stick that he used for support. "I'm only bringing this along in case I need to get the ferrets out of a tight place. Or to ward off a pirate."

"Of course," said Vivienne with a grin, knowing the boy didn't want to seem weak around Maleine and still used the walking stick since he wasn't quite back to normal yet. "It is a beautiful day. I am sure this outing will do every one of us some good, especially after all the murder investigations lately."

"Don't be fooled, my lady," said Bear, coming up behind her. "The weather on the sea can turn bloody bad in the blink of an eye, so do not trust her. She's not a kind lady in the least."

"Who's not a kind lady, Mother?" asked Martin, making a face and seeming confused.

"I believe Bear is talking about the sea, Martin," explained Vivienne. "And he is right, so we all need to stay together and keep away from the railings on the ship if the wind starts to pick up."

"Ah, this is going to be fun. I can't wait." Isaac walked up, taking a deep breath of air and releasing it, puffing out his chest and holding his face up to the sun with his eyes closed. He seemed more excited about this trip than the children right now.

"Isaac? Are you coming with us?" asked Vivienne in confusion. "I thought you were going to stay behind and help Constable Dorson today."

"Nay. I mean, yes. I mean, I was, but not anymore," answered Isaac, opening his eyes to look at her. "Zachariah agreed that I needed a day to relax as well, so here I am." He held out his arms and couldn't stop smiling. She supposed for an ex-mercenary, this trip might be a dream of a lifetime. She wasn't really sure.

"Brother, I don't believe those were my exact words. Or my words at all, actually." Zachariah walked up with a large canvas bag over one shoulder. He held his daughter Starah's hand.

"Starah!" Martin ran over to greet the little girl. "I'm going to protect you from the pirates today. I have my sword."

Vivienne loved the enthusiasm of her young son, not to mention his courage. At such a young age, the boy never seemed frightened of anything.

"Protect me? Will I need protecting, Father? And won't you be here to protect me?" Starah's dark eyes turned upward to look at Zachariah. "After all, you are the sheriff."

"Of course, I'll be here, sweetheart," he told his daughter.

"Martin is just excited, but there's nothing to be frightened about," Vivienne told the little girl. "Right, Sheriff?"

By the exasperated look on Zachariah's face, Vivienne thought he was about to disagree. Thankfully, he didn't.

"Yes, that's right. It is perfectly safe." Zachariah adjusted the bag on his shoulder, looking back at Nairnie who was hobbling along behind them. "Nairnie, this bag is heavy. What could you possibly have in here?"

"Just some things we'll need today, Sheriff," she answered, edging right past him and down the pier to wait for the crew to return with one of the shuttle boats to take them to the ship.

"We're only going to be gone a day," he called after her, but she didn't turn around. "And why couldn't one of the crew carry this instead of me?"

"The crew was in too much of a hurry to leave the house since they knew you didn't want them there," Nairnie called back to him.

"Well, I guess it's time to board so we can start this adventure," said Isaac, taking a step to go, but Zachariah stopped him by clearing his throat. "Is something wrong?" asked Isaac.

"Yes," said Zachariah. "You take this. I need to carry my daughter." The sheriff pushed the heavy bag at Isaac and scooped up Starah, settling her on his hip. Starah smiled, liking the attention she was finally getting from her father.

At last, they arrived at the ship, having to climb out of the shuttle boat and up a rope ladder to get aboard. Bear was with them in the shuttle and had to carry Grunt up the ladder, holding him with one arm and using his other to climb. Vivienne found it challenging to use the rope ladder while wearing a long gown, but the children seemed to love it. And after seeing the way Nairnie climbed up without faltering, it gave her confidence to do the same. After all, Nairnie was an old woman and quite overweight. She truly did seem comfortable around the ship, and now Vivienne didn't doubt that her many stories about living on a ship with pirates were true, and not made up at all.

"All hands on deck," called out Bear once his men were aboard and the cargo had been loaded and the shuttles had been hoisted up and secured to the ship's side. He quickly pulled up the rope ladder, looking directly at Vivienne and the rest of the guests. "We're ready to weigh anchor. I keep a tight schedule and it is time to take to the sea."

"We're ready," said Vivienne, reaching down to grip her son's hand, then looking up to the ship's high masts. She couldn't help feeling that twisting sensation in her gut, hearing the lines hitting against the masts in the wind. It was odd. She had the same feeling she'd had the night her family was attacked on the road and when her parents were murdered by bandits. It was also the night that the spooked horses took off with their wagon that held her newborn son and younger brother, Adrian, in it. She'd never seen either of them again, until she'd recently found Martin after so long. Adrian, however, was still missing.

"Lady Vivienne? Are you all right?" Zachariah had his daughter happily riding atop his shoulders.

"I...yes. I'm fine, Sheriff," she answered, flashing him a smile.

"Come on, Mother, let's watch from the railing as the ship pulls away," Martin urged her, pulling her to the side of the ship with Grunt leading the way. "We don't want to miss a thing."

"Nay, we can't have that, can we?" She looked up to the masts again and got a really sick feeling now. It was too late to back out of the trip, and she'd had no choice but to board the ship. After all, the last thing she wanted was to disappoint the children after promising them a ride on a ship out at sea. But by God, if she didn't know any better, she had the feeling that something bad was about to happen. Again. She could only pray that if her instincts were correct, that whatever happened wouldn't involve those that she cared about...or loved.

Chapter Two

Vivienne watched in awe as Bear gave orders to his crew, and the process got underway to prepare the *Falcon* to sail. She held tightly to Martin's hand, while the sheriff also watched with his daughter still sitting atop his shoulders.

"Bosun, anchors aweigh. Cast off," called out Bear. "Crew, raise the sails. Stitch, man the helm," Bear told an older man who looked to possibly be his quartermaster.

"Aye aye, Cap'n," they all answered, going about their jobs with no discussion at all.

The sound of the anchor chain lifting out of the water rattled the air as the ex-pirates scurried up the lines like monkeys, climbing and swinging from vines. The sails were unfurled, and the wind filled them, making them flap wildly in the breeze before they billowed out, enabling the ship to move across the water. The *Falcon* swayed and slowly started to sail away from the dock as they embarked upon their journey.

"Sweat the lines," ordered Bear. He grabbed the lines to help. He leaned his body inward with all his weight, tugging on the already tight ropes that led up to the top of the masts of the ship. Then he pulled them back as far as he could, removing every bit of slack from them.

"What is he doing, Mother?" asked Martin.

"Shhhh," she told her son. "We don't want to distract them from their work."

She watched the men's muscles bulging as they worked the lines. Then she saw Bear fasten a line around the short wooden pin that served as an anchor so the rope wouldn't slip. Once that was done, he handed the excess rope over to a young man, one of his crew members, to coil it properly so it wouldn't become tangled. Vivienne noticed the young man look over at Maleine and he smiled.

"Ramble, keep yer mind on yer work," commanded Bear. "There will be time for visiting once we're sailing."

"Aye, Cap'n," said Ramble, his attention quickly returning to his job.

"Fair winds and following seas," boomed Bear's voice, in what Vivienne realized was some sort of nautical blessing or said for good luck on a voyage.

Martin broke out of Vivienne's hold and ran over to the young man called Ramble. "What's up there?" asked Martin, shading his eyes and looking up to the top of the center mast.

"That's the lookout basket," explained Ramble.

"What's it for?" Martin wanted to know. He was a curious boy and always wanted to learn all he could about everything and anything.

"The lookout basket is used so we can keep a lookout for other ships, or bad weather," Ramble told him.

"I want to go up there," said Martin excitedly, with a sparkle in his eyes.

"Nay, you don't, Martin." Vivienne's stomach lurched at the thought of her son being so high up. She shot forward to pull Martin back into her arms for protection. Something about the masts was proving to be very unsettling to her, although for the life of her, she didn't know why.

ZACHARIAH TOOK Starah off his shoulders and set her feet on the deck of the ship. He knew a little about sailing vessels, and the *Falcon* was a large ship and a really nice one, too. It was clinker-built with lapstrake boards and high sides. It had an aft and forecastle, which were usually only on warships, since they were raised decks at the front and back of the vessel and used for men to stand on to fight. This ship also had more than just one sail, which was unusual. The *Falcon* actually had three! It also seemed as if it had a captain's quarters that was tucked away at the back of the ship. Near the front was what looked like a small enclosed quarters, too. Possibly something like a galley.

This ship wasn't a normal fishing ship with a flat bottom that could dock at any shore. This one was made for the open sea. Yes, he was sure it was one of the fastest ships on the water, with the power of the three sails and the strength it had behind it.

"Starah, hold on to Maleine's hand," instructed Zachariah, wanting to go over to talk to Vivienne, but at the same time needing to see to the safety of his child. Vivienne seemed to be upset about something and he needed to find out what that was.

"Yes, Father," said the little girl, taking the hand of Vivienne's maid.

Zachariah hurried over to Vivienne, pulling her aside. "I know that look. Something is wrong. What is it?"

"I don't know what you mean," she answered.

"Don't lie, Vivienne. We have a pact to always tell the truth to each other, if I must remind you."

"You're right," she said softly so the others could not hear. "I just have a bad feeling. In my gut. Like something is going to happen."

"Well, just push that feeling away right now," he told her, not liking to hear this since she was usually right. "We can't afford for anything to go wrong today. Not with the children along."

"I agree," she told him, letting out a deep sigh and forcing a smile. "We are here to have a good time and to find some relaxation. I suppose I am worrying about nothing. We'll only be gone for the day and we're on a ship, not Rotten Row. I am sure there is nothing to worry about at all."

"Not at all," agreed Zachariah, not wanting to let Vivienne know that he, too, had a bad feeling about this trip.

Grunt started barking and jumping up on Isaac, who was still holding the canvas bag that Zachariah had given him.

"Down, boy! Leave me alone," commanded Isaac, trying to swish the dog away with his foot. Isaac lost his balance when the ship listed, and he ended up on his back with Grunt's paws atop his chest.

"Grunt, nay! What are you doing?" Vivienne ran over to help Isaac. Martin followed right behind her.

"That dog doesn't seem to like me," snorted Isaac, pushing up to a sitting position. Grunt sniffed the outside of the bag.

"I'm so sorry, Isaac," apologized Vivienne. "My hound doesn't usually act this way."

"Not unless he's got the scent of something that riles him." Zachariah reached over his brother, opening the top of the bag. Just as he thought, a little nose and whiskers stuck out, sniffing Grunt back. "God's eyes, Starah!" spat Zachariah. "Did you really have to sneak that damned cat on board?"

"Midnight!" Starah ran over and dropped to her knees, gathering up the cat in her arms, snuggling her face up against Midnight's black fur. "She's scared, Father."

"She's a cat on water, of course she's scared," grumbled Zachariah. "What the hell were you thinking to have brought her along? I said, no pets except the hound."

"Sheriff, stop cursin' around the wee ones." Nairnie hurried out of the galley, thankfully not having her ladle in her hand. "What did ye expect, without Isaac there to watch the cat? The girl couldna leave Midnight all alone."

"That cat used to live on the streets with a rat-catcher," Zachariah pointed out, holding Grunt back by the collar. "Midnight can survive anywhere alone."

Almost as if he'd brought on a curse by saying *rat-catcher* aloud, the next thing he heard was Wymond.

"Chomp, Snuff, get back here!" The boy used his walking cane as he hurried across the deck, trying to catch the ferrets as they headed for the galley. Maleine rushed after him.

"Och, dinna let those weasels near the food I have in there that I'm preparin'!" Nairnie hurried after them, waving her hands above her head. The pirates all laughed, their deep bellows filling the air.

"Still think this was a good idea?" Zachariah asked Vivienne.

"Well...mayhap it won't be quite as relaxing as I'd hoped. Or not yet, anyway," she answered.

Zachariah shook his head, counting down the minutes until they were back in town.

"Everyone, gather around," came the shout of Bear a little while later, after things had calmed down and they were sailing south toward Whitstable. The bad feeling that Vivienne had felt in her gut had receded, and she was loving watching how excited the children were to be on a ship and out at sea. And they were extra thrilled to be sailing with pirates, even if these men were not pirates any longer.

"Hurry up, all of ye," yelled Nairnie. "Yer cap'n wants to introduce ye to our guests."

"We're going to meet all the pirates?" asked Maleine, looking more than nervous now. They had already seen the crew at the sheriff's dinner, but hadn't personally been introduced.

"Yes," said Vivienne. "Nairnie asked me, and I said I thought it would be nice to know all their names."

"My lady, it is a big crew and we're only going to be with them a short time," said Zachariah. "Do you really think this is necessary?"

"It is, if we're going to feel at home."

"But we're not at home," said Zachariah, shaking his head and not liking this idea at all.

"I could very easily make this ship my home." Isaac leaned his elbows on the side rail, gazing out to sea with a smile on his face. The sun beat down and the smell of the sea rose up around them. The waters were vast and a bluish green. The sails billowed, filled with air, and the ship, even as large as it was, sailed smoothly across the waters.

"Isaac, you going from being a mercenary to being a pirate is not a step upward," Zachariah told him, almost making Vivienne laugh aloud.

"All right, listen up," said Bear. "This here is Lady Vivienne and her son, Martin."

"And Grunt," said Martin, whipping out his wooden sword. "I have a sword too. Mayhap someday I can be a pirate like all of you."

"Arrgh," bellowed one of the men, and they all burst out laughing.

"Nay, you can't be a pirate so just get that idea out of your head right now," said Vivienne. She reached out and lowered Martin's arm before one of these men took it as an act of aggression that he waved a wooden sword at them. "You're going to be a squire and then a knight. Remember?"

"Oh, that's right," said Martin, finally getting his mind back on track. "Mayhap I won't be a pirate, after all. Sorry, everyone."

"Mayhap, I'll be a knight someday," yelled one of the crew, once again making them all laugh. Men hung from the lines watching, while some leaned on the railing or loitered on the main deck. They all seemed amused by Martin.

"This is Wymond, and Maleine, who is Lady Vivienne's handmaid," Nairnie introduced them.

"Nice to meet you, Maleine. I'm Ramble." The young pirate who looked to be about the same age as Maleine stepped forward to greet her. He had seemed to have eyes for the girl ever since they stepped aboard the ship. Wymond scowled, his disapproval evident.

"Get back," said a big man, pushing Ramble behind him. "I'm Goldtooth. I'm the bosun of the *Falcon*." He smiled, showing off his front gold tooth.

"What's a bosun?" asked Martin.

"I am in charge of the crew," Goldtooth explained.

"Oh, kind of like a steward or captain of the guard," said the boy.

Goldtooth seemed to think about it and then smiled pleased at the comparison. "Aye, that's right," he said, standing straighter and throwing back his shoulders.

"This is the sheriff of Mablethorpe, Sheriff Zachariah Fitch and his daughter, Starah," Nairnie continued. "I'm sure all of you remember them since you stayed at the sheriff's house last night."

"Not all of us," one of the men called out who was grungy-looking and had thinning hair. He was skinny and tall, but bent over. His head stuck out almost horizontally from his neck, reminding Vivienne of a vulture. "Remember, there were some of us left on the ship to guard it. Like always. Tyne and me didn't get to feel the comforts of a pillow beneath our heads or a bowl of pottage in our stomachs like the rest of you."

"That's right," said another of the crew members standing next to him, who was obviously Tyne. This man was short and seemed small for a grown man, especially a pirate. "Next time, we get to go to town instead of staying here."

"This is Scythe and Tyne," said Goldtooth. "They're always complaining so just ignore them."

"They're not part of the original crew of the *Falcon*, like the rest of us." It was Peg Leg Pate who spoke up. "You know I'm Pate, and this is Coop," he said, nodding to a broad-chested man who kind of looked like a barrel.

"Nice to meet all of you," said Vivienne with a nod.

"Don't forget us." Two men stepped forward. "I'm Jax and this is Grouse," said a dark-haired man, nodding at his friend who was much taller.

"Grouse? Like a bird?" asked Wymond, holding the bag that contained his ferrets, trying to keep them from running off again.

"I like birds and I like to whistle," said Grouse, pursing his lips and making a bird noise. Immediately, a gull dropped down from the sky, landing on the railing next to him.

"Everyone calls him Birdman," explained Jax.

"I see why," said Vivienne, impressed by his bird call.

"Want to see him get a bird to land on his shoulder and not just the railing?"

"Nay, not a good idea," Zachariah spoke up. "After all, we have a cat, a dog, and two ferrets on board. No birds needed. They'd only chase them."

"Oh, then ye'd better leave now," said Birdman, waving his hands at the gull, making it fly back up in the sky.

"Father, does Midnight really have to stay locked up in the captain's cabin?" asked Starah.

"Yes," said the sheriff. "Unless you want her falling overboard."

"Nay, I don't want that," answered Starah, frowning.

"This man is Stitch," said Bear, introducing them to the man who was steering the ship. "He's the eldest and the most experienced among us."

"I started off as the ship's navigator," explained Stitch.

"Can you use the stars in a night sky to navigate in the dark?" asked Vivienne, always having been interested and fascinated with stars.

"I can," he answered.

"I love stars," spoke up little Starah. "My mother named me after the stars. Did you know that?"

"Really?" asked Stitch. "How nice. Is your mother here too?"

"Nay. She's dead." Starah looked as if she were about to cry. Everyone became silent.

"How about a little somethin' to eat?" Nairnie finally spoke up. "I've got some pickled herring and some cheese to be served with brown bread."

"Fresh bread? Not just hardtack?" asked Pate, referring to the hard, dried flat bread that sailors usually ate while at sea. Simple fare that was more like a cracker and very dry.

"That's right, no hardtack. For now," said Nairnie.

"Then we'll take double," said Scythe, nodding to his short friend. "To make up for what we missed out on last night."

"Let's eat," said Goldtooth, and the men all started to move toward the galley.

"Wait. We haven't met everyone yet by name," said Vivienne.

"Och, just call them whatever ye like, and I'm sure they'll come runnin'," said Nairnie, waving her hand in the air. "Everyone, follow me over to the galley."

"Can I go to the galley too, Father?" asked Starah.

"I suppose. Just stay with Maleine and Wymond, and keep away from the sides of the ship," answered the Sheriff.

"Wait for me and Grunt! Come on, Grunt. Nairnie might have some food for you, too." Martin ran off with the hound right behind him.

Once everyone had left, Vivienne found herself standing alone with the sheriff. " What do we do now?" she asked.

"I say we take this blessed, quiet moment for ourselves and look out at the sea and try to find that serenity, after all." He held out his arm to escort her to the rail. "My lady?"

"Yes, I like the sound of that. I'll take you up on it, Sheriff." Vivienne took his arm and they walked to the side rail, looking out at the big fluffy clouds in the sky and listening to the waves hitting against the hull of the ship in a rhythm pattern. The ship suddenly lurched and she almost lost her balance, having to grab on to Zachariah tightly in order to keep standing.

"Don't worry, Vivienne," said Zachariah, not using her title. "I won't let anything happen to you." Their eyes met. He looked so handsome with the sun on his face and his deep brown eyes drinking her in. Vivienne had been good friends with Zachariah ever since childhood. But since she was a noble and he wasn't, they had remained friends only and nothing more. Now, they had both lost their spouses, and each had a child to raise on their own. Even though they were so different, parts of their lives were very similar indeed.

"How long do you think it'll take us to get to Whitstable?" she asked, trying to make conversation. She had started to have romantic feelings toward Zachariah lately, but she pushed them away, knowing it wasn't right.

"I'd guess we'll be there soon. Mayhap in a few hours or so. Why? Are you in a hurry?" He was still staring at her, and she swore she saw him look at her lips. That only made her stomach flutter.

"Nay. Are you?"

"I'm not sure. I do want to get back home, but I have to admit that it does feel nice to be out here, away from all the problems in town."

"You mean away from all the murders lately."

"Yes, that too."

"Well, I would take this time today to relax, if I were you, Sheriff."

"Why is that?"

"Because you don't often take time for yourself or away from work long enough to spend any quality time with Starah."

"I suppose you're right." He glanced down to her touch, and reached over and made lazy circles atop her hand with the tips of his fingers. "We don't take time anymore for us to spend time together either."

"What do you mean? We've been together a lot lately, Sheriff."

"Mayhap I should have said, when a murder wasn't involved. After all, trouble always seems to follow you, Vivienne, wherever you go. Or haven't you noticed?"

"Oh, I noticed. Believe me," she answered, and they both chuckled. "However, today will be different."

"How so?" he asked curiously.

"We're away from everyone, so trouble will not be able to find me."

"Let's hope you're right, sweetheart. For all of our sakes, let us hope you are right."

Chapter Three

"My lady, I'm going to be gone for a little while and have to ask you to watch Starah for me until I return, if you don't mind," Zachariah told Vivienne as soon as the ship had docked in Whitstable.

"What? Why?"

Zachariah could see the disappointment on Vivienne's face immediately.

"I won't be long."

"We just arrived in Whitstable and you planned to spend time with your daughter, Sheriff. To spend time and relax. With all of us. What could possibly be so important that you're willing to leave?"

"Before you say anything else, let me explain."

"There's no need to explain," she answered, reaching down to pet Grunt. "You have more important things to do. As always."

"Nay, that's not it at all."

"Then what is it? I thought we were taking today to relax and have fun and spend time with our children."

"I am. We are. I will." Zachariah blew out a deep breath. "It's just that Nairnie wants me to go with Bear to pick up the shipment of oysters and I couldn't say no. Not after all she's done for me regarding Starah."

"You pay her for that. You don't owe her any favors." Vivienne looked at him as if she thought he were crazy. "I'm sure some of his men can go with Bear instead. Why does it need to be you?"

"It seems they've all been promised some well-needed time off. They won't return to the ship until tonight."

"Well-needed time off for you is just as important." She wouldn't back down from trying to make him feel guilty. "Besides, I'm sure all the crew members didn't leave the ship."

"All of them left except those two named Scythe and Tyne." He nodded to the two men standing near the boarding plank but still on the ship. "They are being left back to guard the ship again. And by the sound of it, they're not happy about it."

"Why can't Bear go by himself to pick up the shipment of oysters? I'm sure he can handle it. Plus, no one will give him trouble since he is so big and fierce."

"I'm sure he can take care of himself, that's true. However, it seems that Bear has a habit of stopping in the taverns along the way and forgetting to come back. Nairnie wants him to return as soon as possible."

"And you're going to do that? Really."

"Well, I...I didn't want to turn Nairnie down." He rubbed the back of his neck. "Believe me, I'm not excited to go with a pirate down to Rook Row."

"Rook Row? What is that?" she asked him.

"If I understand correctly, it isn't much different than Rotten Row back home."

"Oh, Zachariah," she said, knowing how dangerous a place Rotten Row was back in Mablethorpe. "Nay. Please, don't go."

"I have to go. Nairnie has done so much for me. Not only by caring for Starah, but she cooks and cleans, too. Vivienne, I honestly feel as if I owe it to her. It's the least I can do to show my appreciation."

"I don't feel good about this. It doesn't sound safe at all."

"You're not talking me out of it, so don't bother trying."

"Then at least take someone with you. Besides Bear, I mean."

He knew she was going to suggest herself next, and that is why he'd already made other arrangements. He said the only thing that would stop her from tagging along with him.

"I asked Isaac to join me."

"Isaac?" She looked at him and blinked several times in succession. "You're going to the bad part of town with an ex-pirate and an ex-mercenary? Why doesn't that make me feel any better?"

"You worry too much, my lady. Now, please take the children and Nairnie with you and have a fun day on the beach. We'll be back before you know it."

She watched him from the side of her eye and raised her chin. "You promise?"

"Yes. I promise. I'll keep Bear from stopping in any taverns, just like Nairnie wants me to do. We'll come right back to the ship after he receives the load of oysters."

"All right, then. But hurry back. Starah wants to spend time with you, so don't forget that."

"I know. I didn't forget. So do I," he said under his breath. He reached out and gently caressed her cheek with his hand. "Thank you." Their eyes interlocked and he found himself slowly getting drawn into the depths of her beautiful bright blue orbs. Damn it, she was just a friend. So why in the hell couldn't he stop thinking about kissing her lately? He'd had a weak moment and kissed her when she was out cold recently, but thank goodness she'd never known about it. After all, they had an agreement. That is, an arrangement that was best for both of them. They were good friends and nothing more. He wasn't about to ruin that relationship between them. "Ah, here they are now. We'll see you later," he said, seeing Bear and Isaac coming in his direction.

"Shall we be off, Brother?" asked Isaac, still smiling. "I can't wait to visit Rook Row, see the women, do a little gambling, and taste the fine wine."

"What?" gasped Vivienne.

"He's only jesting." Zachariah grabbed his brother by the shoulder and yanked him in the opposite direction, walking away from Vivienne.

"Zachariah, what the hell is the matter with you?" asked Isaac, pulling out of his grip and scowling as he straightened out his tunic.

"I don't want you saying things like that. Not in front of Vivienne," he answered.

"Why not? It's just Vivienne." He shrugged. "We've known her since we were children. She's like a sister to us."

"Nay. She's nothing like a sister."

"It sounds as if he's got a longing for the girl," said Bear with a deep guffaw.

"He does?" Isaac turned toward Zachariah. "You do? Is there something going on between you and Lady Vivienne that I don't know about?"

"Nay. Now stop with all the questions. Let's quickly get to town to pick up this shipment of oysters and then head back to the beach right away. I really need to spend some time with my daughter. Like I've promised."

"All right, all right, just calm down," said Isaac. "So, Bear. Where are we picking up these oysters? Is there a fishmonger shop on Rook Row, or is it directly from a traveling vendor on the street?"

"Neither," said Bear. "I'm to meet the man at the Blue Mermaid."

"Blue Mermaid?" Zachariah already didn't like the sound of this. "Please tell me that is the name of a proprietor's fish shop on the row and not a tavern."

"Why do you sound so worried?" asked Bear. "The Blue Mermaid is a place I haven't been in a while, but every seafaring man knows and loves it."

"That's what I was afraid of," said Zachariah, feeling his jaw tightening.

"Oh, so it's a popular spot then?" asked Isaac.

"Damn right, it is," said Bear with a toothy smile. "The Blue Mermaid is the best tavern on the entire coast."

"A tavern. Of course," said Zachariah to himself, wondering how in the hell he was going to keep his promise to both Nairnie and Vivienne now.

"Hurry up, Starah. Grunt and the others are waiting for us in the shuttle boat," said Vivienne, talking to the sheriff's daughter but at the same time keeping her eye on the crew member named Tyne who seemed to be following her on the ship everywhere she went.

"Lady Vivienne, I'm worried about Midnight and I want to check on her."

"I'm sure she's fine. Midnight is in the captain's quarters."

"But I don't know if she has enough water and food." Starah hadn't been happy when she heard her father wouldn't be joining them right away. Since Vivienne had given her the news, Starah seemed to be stalling. Vivienne's heart went out to the girl. If seeing her cat once more would give her peace of mind and get her to smile, then mayhap it was worth the few extra minutes.

"All right. But we need to check on her quickly. Martin and the others are waiting to play in the sand and in the water with you."

"I know." Starah released a big sigh. "I just wish Father was joining us."

"He is. He'll be here shortly."

"Really?" she looked up with hopeful eyes.

"That's what he said. Now, I don't think you want me to tell him that you were sulking around the ship and not going to the beach as planned, do you?"

"Nay, my lady. Let's go."

Vivienne led the way, opening the door to Bear's cabin. She stopped abruptly when she saw someone in there, although she was expecting it to be empty, except for the cat.

"Oh, excuse me. I didn't know—" She stopped talking when the man turned around and she saw it was Scythe. Something about this man made her feel cautious.

"I was just checking on the girl's cat," said Scythe, grinning devilishly. He picked up the cat from the hammock that hung from the low rafters. Midnight hissed at him and squirmed out of his hold, landing on the floor.

"Midnight!" Starah bent down, scooping up the cat and holding her to her chest. "She doesn't like you." She spoke to Scythe in a tone and with words that Vivienne had rather she wouldn't have.

"Nonsense. Everyone likes me," said the man. "I'll watch your cat for you while you're having fun on the beach. After all, Tyne and me are stuck here again as always."

"Nay. Thank you, but we're taking Midnight with us," said Vivienne.

"We are?" Starah looked up at her with wide eyes. "Father won't like that."

"Your father is the sheriff, right?" the man asked Starah, slowly making his way toward them.

"Yes, he is," Vivienne answered for her, stepping in front of Starah to protect her.

"And you're the memorable Lady Vivienne Harlowe. Bastard daughter of King Edward III, I hear."

"That's true. My father is the King, so you'd better treat me right." Something made her say that, although she wasn't feeling overly brave at the moment. Mayhap, she hoped, her words would scare the man off. She wasn't really sure. All she knew was that she didn't like him.

"Your family was murdered on the road seven years ago. And you lost your baby as well as your brother."

Vivienne gasped, surprised to hear her personal life events spilling from this stranger's lips. "How do you know that?" she asked, feeling as if this man were reading her mind. Or possibly stalking her.

"Lady Vivienne found Martin again," said Starah. "He's her son."

"Yes. I know."

"You do?" Vivienne asked, wondering how he'd come across all this information and so quickly. She hadn't said anything about it to any of the crew, and was sure Zachariah didn't mention it either. Perhaps it was Nairnie or maybe even Isaac who had revealed her personal life events that she would have rather remained secret.

"Your brother is still missing, isn't he?"

This was getting just a little too odd. Vivienne folded her

arms over her chest and narrowed her eyes. "Do you know something about my brother, Adrian, and his whereabouts? Because, if you do, you'd better tell me."

Scythe laughed heartily. "Or what?" he asked, his shoulders still hunched over with his neck sticking out, holding up his bony head. "Are you going to send your king father after me? We work for him, don't forget."

"Starah, I think it's time we go," said Vivienne, reaching back and guiding the little girl to the door. Midnight was still in her arms.

"Lassie, what are ye doin' in here? I thought everyone was already in the shuttle." Nairnie stepped up to the door of the cabin. "Och, Scythe, ye shouldna be here with the lassies. Out! Out with ye, I say." She pointed a demanding finger, outstretching her arm.

"I'm going, I'm going," said the man, brushing past them out the door.

"What was that all about?" asked Nairnie.

"I'm not sure," said Vivienne, not wanting to say too much in front of Starah.

"We don't want to leave Midnight here with that scary man," the little girl informed her.

"Well, ye canna bring the cat to the beach," said Nairnie with a huff. "It's already bad enough that Grunt is comin' along. The beach is no place for animals in my opinion."

"But Lady Vivienne said Midnight can come with us," protested Starah, sticking out her bottom lip in a pout. She seemed to always do that when she didn't get her way.

"I don't feel comfortable leaving the cat in the cabin now," Vivienne admitted. "Not after just finding Scythe in here."

"Then ye can leave Midnight in the galley instead," offered Nairnie. "I'll even give her some extra food to keep her happy.

Scythe wouldna dare go in there, because he kens there would be hell to pay with me if he did."

"Chomp and Snuff are in the galley, aren't they?" asked Starah.

"Blethers, that's right." Nairnie put her hand to her chin in thought. "But they are rat-catchin' weasels and used to work alongside Midnight," she pointed out.

"It's a small area, and I'd rather not take the chance that Midnight will chase Chomp and Snuff. They might ruin your things."

"Aye. That wouldna be good. Well, I'll put the weasels in the hold until we return then. They can hunt rats while they're down there and make themselves useful."

"They're ferrets, not weasels, Nairnie," said Vivienne. "And do you think the pets will be safe here. I mean, with Scythe on board?"

"Dinna ye worry yer head about him. I told ye that he'll have to answer to no' only me and my trusty ladle, but also Bear and his temper if he even thinks of touchin' them." She clenched her jaw and smashed a fist into her hand to prove her point.

"Are you sure, Nairnie?" Vivienne didn't know what to do, since she'd basically already made Starah a promise. However, taking a cat to the beach wasn't a good idea, that much she knew.

"If I say they'll be fine then they will be. Now follow me and let's get these animals where they belong so we can all go have a little fun in the sun." Nairnie led the way and they followed.

∾

"And I thought Rotten Row was bad," Zachariah mumbled to his brother as they followed Bear down the street in the bad part of town that was referred to as Rook Row. With every step they took they had to be sure not to step into a mud puddle, human excrement, or the remains of smelly fish guts buzzing with flies.

"Egads, it stinks around here," said Isaac, with his hand half-covering his face. "No wonder everyone looks to be deep in their cups."

Whores stood in every doorway trying to lure them over. Beggars sat right in the filthy street and were half-clothed, holding out their hands and asking for a penny from passersby.

"Don't give the beggars anything, if ye know what's good for ye," warned Bear. "And keep anything of value close to ye, unless ye never want to see it again." The man spoke over his shoulder and kept moving forward. "There is a band of misfits that works this street and I swear they will steal ye blind before ye even know anything happened."

A young boy ran up to Bear with an open hand. Bear looked down at the boy and wrenched his face and growled. "Be gone, ye filthy bilge rat! Go!" The boy turned and ran in the opposite direction. The beggar was just a child and couldn't have been much older than Starah and Martin.

Zachariah almost felt sorry for the child.

"See what I mean?" said Bear with a grunt. "They just don't leave ye alone."

"Thanks for the warning," said Zachariah, still thinking about the beggar boy. Not any sooner did he say the words than he felt someone knock into him hard. He stumbled and had to catch himself from almost falling into a pile of dung. "Dammit," he spat, realizing his money pouch was gone. Sure enough, the thief who just bumped him, stole it. Zachariah looked up and shouted at the red-haired boy who was already running away.

"As sheriff of Mablethorpe, I command you to stop! I demand that you return my pouch to me at once," he said, starting after the boy, dodging others on the street, and almost twisting his ankle in a deep rut in the road.

The thief stopped at hearing his words and slowly turned around. He looked back at him. Zachariah thought that mayhap hearing he was a sheriff must have frightened the boy. When he moved a little closer he could see the boy's face. Zachariah stopped dead in his tracks. He knew this boy. And it was a face he hadn't seen in a very long time now.

"Adrian?" asked Zachariah in surprise, barely able to speak the boy's name aloud. Could this honestly be happening? He was sure this was Vivienne's missing brother from seven years ago. Sure, Adrian had only been nine when he disappeared, but this tall, lanky thief with no shoes and ragged clothing looked so much like the boy he'd known, that it was uncanny. This lad seemed to be about six-and-ten summers, and that would be about the right age of Vivienne's brother now. If he were truly still alive.

"Adrian? Is that you?" he asked again, slowly taking a step closer to the thief, causing the boy to take a step backward. Fear, along with what seemed like a scant amount of curiosity, filled the lad's eyes.

"I don't know who you're talking about," said the boy, in a voice that was deeper than Zachariah remembered but still sounded similar in a way to that of the missing boy. Adrian would nearly be a man now. Yes, things would have changed throughout the years, but he'd still be Vivienne's brother deep inside.

"Come here, lad. I won't hurt you." He reached out while taking another step closer. "I just want to bring you back to your sister, Lady Vivienne Harlowe."

The boy's eyelids fluttered and he seemed a bit startled at

first. But then he was back to his stoic expression again in no time flat. "I don't have a sister." The thief turned and took off at a sprint, disappearing down a dark alleyway before Zachariah could even follow.

"Did you just call that thief 'Adrian'?" asked Isaac, running to catch up with him. "As in Lady Vivienne's little brother, Adrian?"

"Aye. That's the one." Zachariah kept his gaze focused on the boy's back but unfortunately the thief quickly disappeared from sight.

"It couldn't be him," said Isaac, stretching his neck, trying to take a look. "You must be mistaken."

"Nay, I'm not. It was him, I'm sure of it. Didn't you recognize him, Isaac?"

"I don't know." Isaac shrugged. "I don't remember Lady Vivienne's little brother that well, and I didn't get a good look at that thief's face."

"It was him, I tell you." Excitement built up inside of Zachariah. If this were so, it would be a miracle. Another miracle to happen in Lady Vivienne's life.

"But he didn't seem to acknowledge you, Zachariah," said Isaac. "I mean, I heard everything between the two of you. That lad didn't even react to having a sister. There is no way that the Adrian we knew could be that cold and uncaring."

"You're right. It doesn't make sense," said Zachariah in thought. "I don't understand why he acted that way."

"Zachariah, mayhap you're just imagining it was him. I know how badly you still want to find him for Lady Vivienne, but this can't possibly be true. We're not even that close to Mablethorpe where the boy originally disappeared. I think it is someone else. There is no hope in finding Vivienne's brother after all these years. It has been too long."

"Why not?" asked the sheriff. "After all, Lady Vivienne

found her son after seven years and that was supposedly impossible too."

"If that thief were Lady Vivienne's brother, then why didn't Adrian come to you when he heard what you had to say?" Isaac waved away a fishmonger who was waving smelly mackerel in his face now. "Why would he be pretending that he doesn't know you or that he doesn't even remember his own sister?"

"I don't know. I don't quite understand it, myself," said Zachariah. "But I intend to find out the answers to all these questions. I'm going after him, Isaac."

"So you're really going to let Bear go into the tavern alone? Is that wise, Brother?" asked Isaac, perusing him. "After all, you did promise both Nairnie and Lady Vivienne that you'd bring Bear right back after he picked up his shipment of oysters."

"I know, but this is important. Don't you understand what it would mean to Lady Vivienne if I find her brother?"

"Don't you understand how devastated she'd be if you are mistaken and that wasn't really Adrian, after all?"

"Sadly, you're right." Zachariah started doubting himself after hearing what his brother had to say. What Isaac pointed out, had merit. Perhaps he had just imagined the thief was Adrian. After all, he hadn't seen the boy in years now. He could have been mistaken, he supposed. Especially since his guilt was still eating away at him for not being able to help Vivienne find any answers concerning what happened to her family.

"Are ye two coming into the Blue Mermaid or not?" Bear called out from across the road, standing at the door to the establishment, holding it wide open. It was dark inside and not where Zachariah wanted to go. Where he really wanted to be was in the bright sun with Vivienne and the children, cooling off his hot feet by walking in the water.

He looked over his shoulder again to the path the boy thief had taken. He'd run into the dark as well. Zachariah had enough dark in his life right now, and what he needed was to shed light on this situation quickly. Why couldn't things start to change for the better?

"The sheriff just had his pouch stolen by a lad that he thinks might be Lady Vivienne's missing brother," Isaac shouted, heading back toward the tavern. Zachariah cringed at his brother being so loud and basically telling everyone his business. Still, he reluctantly followed.

"What did you say?" asked Bear as they approached him.

"Do you personally know these thieves on Rook Row?" asked Zachariah, hoping Bear could give him some valuable information that might help him.

"Nay, not really." Bear shrugged. "All I know is that they work for Adder."

"Who?" asked Zachariah, thinking how odd that sounded.

"Adder," repeated Bear. "I don't know his real name, but everyone around here calls him Adder since he's such a snake," explained Bear. "He's a pickpocket and a cutpurse—the worst. He takes in orphans and then teaches them his rotten trade. In return for his help, food, and a place to stay, the boys hand over everything they steal, giving it all to Adder."

"This man takes in orphans?" asked Zachariah. "And they give him everything?" This was so horrific of a thought, that he had a hard time making sense of it.

"Aye to both," said Bear. "Or should I say that sometimes he even pays men to bring him boys to train. He's got quite a reputation, not to mention a huge operation that spreads out across the land. He's supposedly got others working for him up and down the coast, and his main spot is at the docks."

"God's teeth, this is awful. It's worse than I thought." Zachariah's head started to hurt just trying to believe what he was hearing.

"Yes, this is all pretty shocking," agreed Isaac.

"I've got to find out for certain if that pickpocket was indeed Adrian and not just someone who looks like him," continued Zachariah. "After hearing that sad story, I know I have to save the boy if it proves to really be him. I mean, if it is Adrian and I just leave, I'll never be able to forgive myself, or to be able to face Lady Vivienne ever again. I have to find out for sure. For Lady Vivienne's sake. It's the least I can do to help her." Zachariah felt reluctant to tell Vivienne that her brother was now a thief who wouldn't even acknowledge his friends and family. After all, how could she ever accept that? Family meant everything to her. Plus, to make matters worse, she already blamed herself for the disappearance of her little brother, thinking she should have been able to protect him.

"Where can we find this Adder so we can ask him some questions?" Isaac asked Bear.

Bear smiled. "If you want to find Adder, then take a step inside, my friends. After all, anyone who works on Rook Row ends up in the Blue Mermaid sooner or later. However, you might have to stick around a bit to wait for him to appear. Most no-goods don't venture out until at least sunset but preferably nightfall."

"Wait for him," repeated Zachariah. "In the tavern." He kept thinking about his promise to the women, knowing how angry both Vivienne and Nairnie would be with him for spending time at the tavern instead of returning to the beach to be with the others. They would think he was no better than Bear. Then again, sticking around here for a while might very well be his best chance to find out what really happened to Adrian. If he was right and the thief was Vivienne's brother, he might even be able to bring him back to her so she could take him home with her to Mablethorpe Castle. This far outweighed breaking a promise. He'd been working this case for seven years now, and up until today, he'd never found a single clue or even

43

been able to solve any part of it. It was time for that to change. A lost child was involved. A child who was now a young man. Reuniting Adrian with Vivienne was surely of utmost importance. He needed to do this. For Adrian. For Vivienne. And also for himself.

"Are you two coming in or not? Make up your mind," Bear growled, still holding the door open.

"What do you think, Brother? Shall we venture inside?" Isaac asked his opinion, but then gave his own thoughts before Zachariah could even answer. "I mean, we might as well have a drink while we're here. I see no harm in that. It'll help to pass the time while we're waiting for this Adder fellow."

"Of course," said Zachariah knowing Isaac and Bear both most likely wouldn't know when to stop drinking. "One drink only," Zachariah warned them, pushing past his brother and entering the Blue Mermaid. He said the words, but somehow he knew it was going to end up being so far from the truth, and he was the one who was going to have a lot of explaining to do to the women once they returned to the ship.

Sure enough, Zachariah was right. About Bear and Isaac, that is. They didn't stop at one drink, and kept on going. Actually, they were only there about an hour before a man walked over to them.

"Bear?" asked the man.

"Yes," said Bear, looking up at the man over the top of his tankard.

"Here's yer yearly standing order of oysters," said the man, plunking the bag down on the table. It was so big that it took up most of the top of the table and almost knocked over their tankards of ale.

"Do I know ye?" asked Bear.

"Ye do. I'm Scoop." The young man was probably in his late twenties, had dark hair and was dressed like a fisherman. He wore an open-chested tunic that showed off his strong chest, and a pair of tight breeches and thick boots. He had large, powerful-looking biceps and his tanned skin said he saw a lot of sun.

"Aye, I remember ye now. You're part of the fishing crew. But where is Roger?" asked Bear. "Roger usually delivers the oysters to me himself. We're good friends."

"Obviously not that good if you don't know that Roger died last year and I took his place as captain," said the man named Scoop. "I have his book of standing orders. Besides, I knew you'd be here like every year at this time. But I've been waiting for you since yesterday. You're late."

"There was a storm so we waited overnight and set sail this morning instead," Bear informed him.

"Who are they?" grunted Scoop, motioning to Zachariah and Isaac.

"I'm here with some friends," Bear answered, making Zachariah glad he didn't tell him who they really were. Since they were waiting for the head of a thieving ring, he didn't want everyone to know he and his brother were lawmen.

The man's palm shot out right under Bear's nose. "You've got your damned oysters, now pay up. You know no one gets oysters before they hand over the money."

Bear took another drink of ale, looking up at Scoop with his eyes narrowed. Slowly, he set down the tankard and reached for his coin pouch. "Grouchy today, aren't ye?" he mumbled, dropping a few coins into the man's hand.

Scoop quickly counted the coins, snorted, and shook his head. "Nay. This isn't right. The fee is eight pence for the bag of oysters. You owe me more."

"Eight?" gasped Bear. "That's not what I used to pay Roger. A standing order for a big bag of oysters is only four pence for me since we're friends."

"Well, Roger was a fool. Besides, this bag is bigger than

normal and we're not friends," said Scoop, his palm still stretched out. "You owe me four pence. I'm waiting."

"Nay, I don't think so. That bag looks the same size as always to me," said Bear, glancing down at the shipment.

"The price was written right in the book."

"Well, mayhap you misread Roger's writing, lad."

"And mayhap prices just went up. Now you owe me another four pence and I won't wait a minute longer. Pay me or I take the oysters back, simple as that."

"I think you're a crook, trying to bleed me dry."

"Bear, just give him the money," said Zachariah, not wanting a confrontation since they were strangers in this town. He was also eager to leave here as quickly as possible.

"I'll give ye two pence more but not another penny." Bear dug into his pouch and dropped two more coins in Scoop's hand.

"I said four, not two, you dimwit."

"What did ye call me, ye fool?" Bear slowly stood up, towering over Scoop even though he was tall as well. Bear's face darkened with anger. Zachariah saw a nerve twitch in his jaw and his fingers closed into fists. In another second, Bear was going to punch this man and they would have a fight on their hands. Dammit, he didn't want this to happen.

Scoop's eyes darted over to the other end of the tavern and then back again. "Never mind." He snapped his fist shut and quickly stuck the coins into his pouch.

"Arrrrgh," growled Bear, slowly sitting back down.

"However, to make up for the missing coins, I'll take your drink." Scoop plucked the tankard off the table and downed the ale in three gulps.

"That was my drink, not yers." Bear's anger was rising. "Ye need to pay for that."

"Scoop, I'd suggest you leave right now if you know what's

good for you," warned Zachariah, trying to make distance between the two men.

"Why? I'm not afraid of you," said Scoop. "I don't even know you."

"My brother is Sheriff of Mablethorpe," blurted out Isaac, making Zachariah cringe. "And I am his deputy, so you'd better listen to us."

"Deputy-in-training," said Zachariah under his breath, looking down to his tankard.

"Sheriff and a deputy, eh? Really. Well then, I don't want no trouble," said Scoop, raising his hands up over his head and backing away. He laughed, and Zachariah wasn't sure if he did it from fear or just in a mocking manner. "I'm going," said Scoop. Then he turned and quickly left the tavern.

Isaac chuckled. "That worked well, didn't it? Instead of having to draw my sword, I used my tongue and it was just as sharp and powerful. I think I'm going to enjoy being on the other end of the law from now on."

"Don't let that fool you, Brother," said Zachariah, picking up his tankard and taking a drink. "In my line of business, there are plenty of times when I have to use force."

"I don't like that man," said Bear. "There certainly seems to be no manners instilled in the younger people these days."

"Do you think he's telling the truth about Roger?" asked Zachariah.

"I suppose it could be true," Bear answered, flagging down the server for another drink by waving his empty tankard in the air. "But I still don't like him. Never did. Ye know, he got his name, Scoop, by scooping up more than his share no matter where he went. If I remember correctly, he had a problem with gambling." Bear paused as the serving wench stepped up and refilled his cup. "Known for his greed, that one," he added after knocking back a big gulp of fresh ale, then wiping his chin.

"Ah, he liked winning money," said Isaac with a nod.

"Nay. He never won. All he did was lose," said Bear. "I'm surprised the man can even run a business. Or keep it, I should say."

Zachariah could see this drinking was getting out of hand. "Bear, we really don't have time for this. The women are expecting us to come back to the beach to meet up with them right after picking up the shipment."

"Calm down, Sheriff." Bear lifted the tankard and drank again, this time releasing a satisfied moan. "We'll get back to the lassies, but not until we're good and ready to go. We can't let them think they control us. Sweetie, fill up their tankards as well," he told the serving girl, nodding to Zachariah and Isaac.

"No one is going to think that anyone is controlling us," said Zachariah as the server refilled his tankard next. "We really should be getting back. I also made a promise to spend time with my daughter."

"Brother, one more drink isn't going to hurt anyone. Besides, I'm surprised that since Lady Vivienne is a noble that she is spending time in the sun. Nobles don't do that. You know that. The more pale her skin is, the nobler she'll seem. That is what is expected of nobles." Isaac smiled at the girl server, holding up his tankard to be refilled as well.

"You know Lady Vivienne doesn't do anything that is expected of her, so why would it surprise you?" asked Zachariah. "She truly never follows a single rule."

"Ye want to find Adder don't ye?" asked Bear.

"Yes, of course I do."

"Then sit back and drink yer ale and wait. He'll show eventually," Bear told him.

"If I must," said Zachariah, drinking his ale but keeping a close eye on the door.

"If you're waiting for Adder, he usually arrives in here closer to the end of the day," said the server.

"See?" Bear raised his tankard in the air. "Patience, Sheriff. Patience."

After sitting in the tavern most of the day, Zachariah decided they needed to get back to the ship and that they couldn't wait for Adder any longer. He really wanted to be on the beach and playing in the water with his daughter, not sitting in a dark, dirty, dingy establishment such as this and waiting to talk to the leader of thieves.

"Adder is not going to show up," he told the others, getting out of his chair. "I'm leaving."

"He will show up. Give him a little more time," said Bear, reaching out and pulling Zachariah back down. "You heard what the serving girl said. He doesna come in until nightfall."

"That's true, but I did see him on Rook Row just a little while ago. Across from the whorehouse," said that same serving girl, overhearing their conversation.

"Then that is where I need to look, because I am not going to sit in here a minute longer." Zachariah got up and left the tavern, looking up and down Rook Row, not sure what Adder even looked like. He hoped to also mayhap see that thief again who resembled Adrian. Zachariah felt a slight tug on his tunic and with lightning-fast reactions, quickly reached down, grabbing the arm of another of those little thieves. This one was a boy with a dirty face and bare feet. His clothes were tattered and torn, just like the redheaded boy, but this one was much younger. He was mayhap only eight or nine years of age.

"Don't even think of stealing from me, you little vagabond," he hissed.

The boy cringed. "Don't hurt me. I'm sorry. I'm no good at this and never was." He closed his eyes and held his free hand up over his head, waiting to be struck.

Here was a child, a terrified child, and Zachariah was only frightening him even more. He noticed the bruises on the boy's arms and a big scratch across his right cheek.

"Do you work for Adder?" he asked, figuring he did.

"I can't say." The boy looked down, squirming and trying to get out of Zachariah's hold.

"You'll tell me or I swear I'll break your arm and then you'll really be no good at picking a damned pocket." He would never really hurt the child, but was desperate for answers. He thought he might be able to scare them out of the boy. Even if that was not an admirable thing for a lawman to do.

"Leave him alone," shouted someone from behind him. Zachariah looked over his shoulder to see a much older boy walk out from between two buildings. This one seemed to be about six-and-ten years of age, and was thin with dark hair and dark eyes. He seemed to be about the same age that Adrian would be right now. Or was, depending on if he truly were still alive.

"Who are you?" asked the sheriff. "Do you work for Adder too? I'm looking for him. Can you tell me where to find him?"

"Let Mouse go, and I'll tell you what you want to know."

"Mouse?" He looked down at the young boy who was staring up at him with big, brown mousey eyes. He swore he saw the boy wiggle his nose.

"Mouse is what everyone calls me," said the boy softly. "It's because I'm so quiet and good at hiding in the shadows. And since I wiggle my nose when I'm nervous."

"Interesting," said Zachariah, thinking of a few pet names he could call people he knew as well, but wouldn't.

"If Adder finds out that you caught me, he'll hit me again. Please don't let him know," begged Mouse.

"Nay. Of course not." Zachariah realized the poor child was really frightened, and now he regretted talking so harshly to him. He also didn't want Mouse to get in trouble with this horrible person named Adder. On the other hand, Zachariah also didn't want to let his only lead walk away. His main purpose was to find Adrian and mayhap these boys could help him. "What's your name?" he asked the older boy with a jerk of his head.

"His name is Fingers," said Mouse, before Fingers could speak. "Everyone calls him that because he is the best at picking pockets, and has the fastest fingers out of all of us. He never gets caught. Not like me. I'm slow." Mouse frowned and looked down at the ground.

"Shut up, Mouse! You're saying too much," warned Fingers. "Don't tell this stranger anything."

"I'll only release Mouse if you give me some information," Zachariah called out, trying to make a deal with adolescents. He felt silly about it, but would do whatever it took at this point.

"What kind of information?" asked Fingers, walking toward him.

"I want to know about a boy who picked my pocket earlier today, right here on Rook Row. He's about your age, Fingers, and has red hair," explained the sheriff.

"What do you want to know about him for?" Fingers seemed suddenly protective, perusing the sheriff in a trustless manner. "Are you going to turn him in or put him behind bars or something?"

"Nay, that's not what I want to do," Zachariah answered in surprise. "Why would you even say that?"

"You're a sheriff, aren't you?" Fingers crossed his arms over his chest and raised a brow.

"I am, but my jurisdiction is in Mablethorpe, not Whitstable. I'm not here to arrest anyone. I only ask about the red-haired thief because I believe I know him," explained Zachariah. "I think he is the lost brother of a good friend of mine. His name is Adrian Harlowe. Can you tell me about this boy and where I can find him right now?"

Fingers hesitated and looked around before he slowly uncrossed his arms and let them fall to his sides. "I can," he answered softly. Cautiously. Almost as if he didn't want someone to hear him. "But first, Mouse goes free."

Zachariah admired the way this older boy seemed to look after the younger one. It did his heart good to see even thieves helping out each other. He glanced down at the boy named Mouse who was staring up at him with curious, hopeful eyes. Zachariah's fingers still gripped his arm tightly. He could very well have all the answers he needed right at the tip of his own fingers right now. But not if he let the boy go. *Don't do it*, a little voice in his head warned him. Then his heart took over and he knew he had to have at least a little trust. He let out a deep sigh. Releasing Mouse was a big risk, but it could also be what led him back to Adrian. He had to do it. He needed information and this might be the only way to get it. Zachariah would do anything to help Adrian and Vivienne. Even if it was the last thing he ever did in his life.

"All right," he finally said, releasing the younger boy. Mouse took off at a run, hiding in the shadows of the buildings that were all connected or at least built very close together on Rook Row. He looked back at Fingers who had thankfully not run away as well. "I did what you asked. I set Mouse free. Now tell me. Do you know the boy with the red hair?"

"Yes, I do," said Fingers. "I knew him since the day he was brought to Adder."

"Brought? So you're saying someone kidnapped the boy?"

"Adder often pays men for young boys so he can train them to be thieves. If they don't have family, it's even better."

"So you saw the man who brought Adrian here?"

"I did."

"Would you remember him if you saw him again?"

"I would."

"Tell me everything you know. And leave nothing out." Zachariah figured this information might also help him get clues about the murders of Vivienne's parents. He hoped so.

"Pssst, Fingers," came Mouse's voice and then his head popped out from between two buildings that had a narrow alleyway going between them. "Adder is comin'. We have to go."

"Damn," said Fingers, turning to leave.

"Wait!" Zachariah reached out and grabbed him by the arm, spinning the young man back around. "You promised to give me information."

Fingers let his gaze travel down to the sheriff's hand on his arm and then his eyes went back to his face again. "I did."

"More information, I mean. Please. There were people murdered seven years ago, and some that went missing. There could very well be lives at stake right now. I need your help."

"I don't know," said the boy, seeming suddenly unsure of telling Zachariah anything else.

"My good friend, Vivienne, lost her brother, Adrian, seven years ago," Zachariah blurted out, trying to get the lad to spill what he knew. "Do you know how devastated she is? I see the way you care for Mouse. Wouldn't you do anything to help him if his life were in danger?" It was a gamble for Zachariah to say this, but his risk paid off.

"Yes. Yes, I would," Fingers responded, glancing back to the dark alley where Mouse hid. "All right, I will tell you whatever you want to know, Sheriff. I've spent a lot of time with Red and we've become good friends since he came to us."

"Red?"

"Yes, that's what we call him."

"Hurry, Fingers! Adder's coming," warned Mouse once more from the shadows.

"I can't talk now. Will you be here later?" asked the boy.

"Nay. We're only here for the day," Zachariah told him, releasing his hold on the boy.

"I'd like to help you. I truly do like Red, and I always felt as if he was too good to be cutting purse strings. But I have to leave now." Anxiety filled the lad's words and it was evident that he, too, feared this man called Adder.

"Meet me somewhere then. Later," said Zachariah as Fingers started to walk away.

"Where?"

"On the *Falcon*. That's the ship I came on. It's at the docks. Meet me in an hour?"

"The *Falcon*," said the boy with a nod, turning and dashing away.

No sooner did he leave than Zachariah saw a man look up at him from in front of the whorehouse. He was wearing a cloak and his hood was up so Zachariah couldn't see his face, but he seemed to be of average build and weight.

"Excuse me," Zachariah called out with a wave of his hand. "Are you Adder? I'd like to talk to you." Zachariah hurried across the street, slowing as he approached the stranger. He didn't know if the man was dangerous and if he needed to be careful.

"Who are you?" spat the man, keeping his head down and turning away a little. The sheriff still couldn't actually see him well.

"I'm...I'm just a visitor who is passing through." Zachariah decided if he admitted that he was a sheriff, the man might run. "I'd like to ask you a few questions about a boy with red hair who picked my pocket earlier. I think you refer to him as Red."

"Keep passing through and don't look back, lawman," came the man's deep and guttural warning.

This surprised Zachariah since he hadn't told the man his profession.

"Zachariah, are you coming back inside the tavern?" called out his brother, as Isaac crossed the street and headed toward him. Zachariah quickly turned his head to speak to him.

"Nay, not yet, Isaac. I'm busy talking to Adder right now." Zachariah turned back to the hooded man, but unfortunately, he was gone. "Dammit," he spat, feeling as if, once more, the information he craved had eluded him. But at least he still had Fingers to talk to. If the boy showed up on the ship like he promised, then mayhap all would not be lost.

Chapter Four

"Where is my father?" asked little Starah many hours later that day. "I thought you said he'd be here, Lady Vivienne." A look of sadness washed over her face.

Vivienne didn't know what to tell the child. The sheriff had promised to come right back and still he had yet to return with Bear and Isaac. His daughter was upset about it and so was Vivienne, for that matter. Zachariah had not kept his promise and she did not like that. He was starting to do this too much, and things needed to change.

Vivienne sat on the beach, watching as Martin and Grunt ran up and down the shore, playing. Maleine walked barefoot, hand-in-hand with Wymond in ankle-deep water. They let the waves wash over their toes. Nairnie was on the docks talking to some of the crew members. They'd all just had a meal at one of the inns, and Nairnie was being talkative and hadn't yet returned to the beach.

"I'm sorry, sweetheart. I'm not sure what's taking your father so long." Vivienne looked back at the dock and then over to the *Falcon*. Then something took her interest. She was surprised to see both Scythe and Tyne on the docks, talking with some of the workers. The two were laughing, and looked to be playing dice with the other sailors, throwing down the die atop a barrel. One of the men was big, but she couldn't see him well since he wore a cloak. "Now, what are they doing here?" she asked herself, thinking it was odd as they'd both been ordered to stay back and watch over the ship, yet here they were. This couldn't be good.

"I want to go back to the ship and be with Midnight," whined the little girl. It was getting late in the day and the clouds were already starting to cover the sun. It almost seemed as if there was a storm brewing on the horizon.

"I think mayhap that's what we'll do then." Vivienne watched Scythe and Tyne start up another game, but the tall man in the cloak hurried off and no longer joined them. She put on her shoes and threw a few of her things in her bag. "Martin!" she called to her son. "Bring Grunt."

"What? Why, Mother?" asked the boy, throwing another stick into the water. Grunt jumped into the waves, chasing after it.

"We're going back to the ship." She got up and slipped the strap of her bag over her shoulder. "Maleine! Wymond! Come along, we are leaving now." She called out to them, and they came running.

The group made their way up the wooden stairs and to the dock where Nairnie was talking with Stitch and Ramble. They were just outside one of the dock taverns.

"What's this?" asked Nairnie. "The wee ones canna go inside the tavern, my lady. There are too many drunken men in there."

"Nay, they're not going in there," Vivienne promised. "However, Starah is worried about Midnight and it is getting late so we're going back to the ship."

"Och, are ye still worryin' that Scythe will hurt that cat?" Nairnie reached down and smoothed back Starah's hair.

"Nay, that's not it, Nairnie," said Vivienne. "Scythe and Tyne are not even on the ship. They're on the docks playing dice with some of the other sailors."

"They are?" Nairnie pursed her mouth and seemed disgusted. "They can never seem to follow orders. Wait until Bear hears about this. Where the hell is that old buzzard?" She looked around. "They were supposed to be back hours ago."

"Yes, I know. I hope nothing happened to them," remarked Vivienne.

"Dinna fret. Bear and the sheriff and his brother can take care of themselves. Ah, here they come now."

"Father!" Starah saw the sheriff and broke away from Vivienne to run to greet him. Zachariah scooped her up in his arms and held her tightly to his body.

"Starah, I'm sorry I didn't make it back in time. And now it looks like it's going to rain," he told the little girl.

"Where were ye boys all this time?" asked Nairnie in a gruff voice.

"Yes, Sheriff. Where were you?" Vivienne didn't care that she sounded annoyed at the moment. She was so tired of Zachariah always putting his work or other things before family. Not to mention, he was always breaking his promises. "I thought you were going to come right back. What happened to that, Sheriff Fitch?"

"The day is nearly over now," added Nairnie. "Were ye boys in the tavern all that time?" Her gaze went to Zachariah and she scowled. The sheriff looked the other way.

"I got the oysters, old woman, so stop all yer hollerin'." Bear pushed the bag of shellfish into Nairnie's hands.

"Dinna think I'm goin' to cook these up now." She pushed the bag back to him.

"Ye said ye'd make a meal out of them for us." Bear scowled at his wife.

"And ye said ye'd be right back yet ye were gone all day."

"So does this mean you're not going to prepare the oysters for us?" asked Bear. He and Nairnie stared intensely at each other.

"Nay, I'm no' ye old fool. There's a storm approachin' and we need to get back to the ship and to Mablethorpe quickly. I canna be worried about yer stupid oysters at a time like this."

Their little argument was becoming quickly heated.

"A little rain never hurt anyone," said Isaac, his words almost sounding a bit slurred if Vivienne wasn't mistaken. It was obvious that he was well in his cups. Mayhap he was trying to help, but Vivienne realized his words defending Bear were only going to make Nairnie even madder.

"Hrmph!" Nairnie scoffed, putting her hands on her hips.

Bear looked up and sniffed the air. "Aye, it does smell like there's a storm approaching, and quickly."

"Yes, that's why we need to get to the ship and head back to Mablethorpe right away," said Vivienne, echoing Nairnie's words.

"Nay. We can't leave yet," Bear told her.

"Why no'?" asked Nairnie, her hands still perched on her hips and one of her eyes squinted now. "Have a few more taverns to visit, do ye?"

"Nay, that's not it. The sheriff's waiting to talk to someone first. His guest is supposed to meet us at the *Falcon*. Actually, he might already be there," said Bear.

"Yes, let's go see if he's arrived yet," suggested Isaac.

"Ye go on ahead. I'm goin' to gather up the crew," Bear told them, plopping the bag of oysters down at Nairnie's feet. Then he turned and headed down the docks in the opposite direction. Grunt hurried over to sniff the bag.

"Starah, why don't you walk with Martin and Maleine so I can speak to your father," suggested Vivienne.

"Uh oh. That sounds like trouble." The sheriff put his daughter down. "Go on, sweetheart. We'll be right behind you."

"I've got her, Sheriff," said Nairnie, taking the little girl by the hand. "Wymond, carry this bag of oysters to the ship because I refuse to do it. Besides, this way I can hold Starah's hand. I dinna like to let her get too far away with all these scurvy wharf rats all around us." Her gaze swept the dock and she continued to frown.

"Aye, Nairnie," said Wymond, putting his walking stick under his arm and picking up the bag with two hands.

Indeed, the wharf was not a safe place to be. Especially for women and children.

When they were alone, and far enough away from the others so they couldn't hear, Vivienne spoke to Zachariah. "I thought you were going with Bear to bring him back so he wouldn't sit in the tavern all day." She leaned over and sniffed him. "You were drinking too, weren't you?"

Zachariah jerked back and moved away from her a little, apparently not appreciating her sniffing him in front of everyone. "Yes, I was drinking, I admit it, my lady. But not much," he reported. "And for your information, I tried to come back earlier but we couldn't leave the tavern because we were waiting for someone."

"Who?" she asked. "Was the fisherman who delivered the oysters late?"

"Nay, not at all. Actually, he said he'd been waiting since yesterday for Bear."

"Then who could you have possibly been waiting for? You don't know anyone in Whitstable, do you?"

"Well...no. Not really." He seemed as if he wanted to say something else, but was holding back. They continued to walk, following the others past many docked ships. Sailors carried coiled ropes over their shoulders and some scrubbed out clothing in the water. The docks were a place bustling with activity. Sailors were loading and unloading fish and cargo. Merchants wandered back and forth either selling or buying goods.

They headed down the wharf and back toward the *Falcon* which was docked way down on the end and away from any of the other ships. Vivienne figured it was probably because someone might recognize it as having once been a pirate ship, which it was indeed used as in the past. People didn't take kindly to pirates anywhere. Even if these men did work for the King now.

Isaac hurried to catch up with them. "Lady Vivienne, did my brother tell you who he thought he saw on Rook Row? You will not believe it."

"Nay, he didn't say a word. Who did you see?" she asked the sheriff.

"Not now, Vivienne," Zachariah grunted under his breath. "I'll tell you later."

"Why are you keeping things from me? I don't like that." She frowned, reaching down to pet her hound on the head as they walked. "I thought we weren't going to keep secrets from each other anymore."

"I'll tell you all about it, I promise. But later. First, I need to talk to a boy I met in town."

"What boy?" They continued to talk as they reached the pier that led out to the shuttle boats that they'd use to take them to the ship.

"It doesn't matter."

"I don't agree. I think it does matter."

"Later, Vivienne."

She was about to object to his pushing her away, but decided this wasn't the place or time for that.

Their little group needed two shuttles to get them back to the ship, and some of the crew then took the shuttles back to collect the others. The wind started to pick up and Vivienne hoped everyone would be back on board before it started to rain. The rope ladder, thankfully, seemed to be getting easier, every time she used it. She and the sheriff had just gotten aboard when she heard a woman scream.

"That sounded like Maleine," gasped Vivienne. "Something is wrong." She hurried for Nairnie and the children with Grunt already there, barking, and leading the way. The sheriff was right on her heels.

"Maleine, what's wrong?" Vivienne shouted, coming to a halt when she met up with the group who were standing right under the main mast. Maleine clung to Wymond, her fingers digging into his arm. Wymond had dropped the bag of oysters at his feet. Grunt started barking furiously, making her realize now that this was more serious than she'd thought. Grunt didn't bark like that unless there was trouble.

"What's the matter?" asked Zachariah. "Maleine, why did you scream?"

"Uh...look up there, Brother." Isaac pointed up to the center mast of the ship.

Vivienne's gaze darted upward, following the path of Isaac's pointed finger. Then she saw what he meant and instantly, she felt as if she were about to retch. There, hanging from the yardarm, was a young man with a noose around his neck. His head lolled to the side and his eyes were wide open and bugged out. There was no doubt that the young man's neck was broken. "God's eyes!" screamed Vivienne. "Someone has been murdered aboard our ship!"

Chapter Five

"Nay. It can't be him!" Zachariah ran to the side of the ship to get a better look at the victim. The body of Fingers dangled above him, hanging from a noose around the lad's neck. The rope had been secured to the lowest yardarm of the center mast. "Damn it. Nay!" he shouted, smashing his fist into the bulkhead in anger.

"Zachariah!" Isaac rushed to his side, his gaze focused on the body swinging back and forth every time the ship listed in the waves hitting against the hull. "Isn't that...Fingers?"

"Aye," said Zachariah, feeling the anger rising within him. How could this have happened? Why? Could his luck get any worse?

"Who is Fingers?" Vivienne joined them now, staring up at the dead lad as well.

"Later, Vivienne," he said, looking around and seeing Ramble, Coop, and Goldtooth joining them on the ship now. Bear was with them. "Bear, can you get your crew to cut the boy down?"

Bear's eyes traveled upward. "What the hell?" He grimaced and shook his head. "Get him down, boys, quickly," he commanded as Nairnie walked up to him, still holding Starah's hand. The little girl's eyes fastened on the dead man and she screamed loudly.

"God's bones, get her out of here." Zachariah rushed over and scooped up his daughter. Starah cried, hiding her face against Zachariah's shoulder.

"Is that really a dead man hanging from a noose?" asked Martin, looking upward with wide eyes in amazement. He almost sounded a bit too fascinated about it. "I've never seen anyone hang before."

"Yes, Martin, it is a dead man," answered Zachariah.

Maleine and Wymond approached and Maleine was obviously shaken, still clinging tightly to Wymond.

"Maleine, I want you and Wymond to take Martin and Starah into the captain's quarters right away," instructed Vivienne. "Stay inside with them until we tell you it is all right to come back out."

"Yes, I think that's a good idea," agreed Zachariah. "The children shouldn't have to witness this." He put Starah down, but she still clung to his leg. "Go on, Starah. Maleine and Wymond will watch over you. I have work to do. I need to find out what happened here."

"I'll help protect her," offered Martin bravely, pulling his wooden sword from his belt. "If there's a murderer on board, I'll find and kill him, I swear I will."

Starah screamed again at hearing that.

"Damn, I'm not thinking. I'd better go check the cabin first," said Zachariah. "I suppose it is possible that whoever was responsible for this is still here." He was so upset by the death of the innocent boy that he found a hard time focusing on his job.

"Nay, Sheriff, it's all right. I'll check the cabin, and I'll make certain the young ones stay safe," Nairnie told him, taking the little girl's hand in hers.

"I'd better come with you, Nairnie," said Bear in a deep voice. "After all, this is my ship and I am responsible for all of ye."

"Buzzard, I dinna need ye to do anythin' that I can handle myself," answered Nairnie, with an edge to her voice. There was no doubt she was still upset with her husband for drinking in the tavern for such a long time today.

"Stop being that way, old woman." Bear reached out for Nairnie, but after one hit against his arm from her ladle, he pulled his hand back. Zachariah wondered if Nairnie ever went anywhere without her trusted ladle. "And dinna call me old!" She stormed away with Starah in tow.

"Then don't call me Buzzard," he yelled back to her.

"Wymond, bring the cat from the galley," commanded Nairnie over her shoulder. "And Coop, go to the hold and find the weasels and bring them to the captain's quarters as well."

"Me?" Coop thumped his hand against his chest. "They're not my weasels. Have the boy get them."

"Wymond's leg is still healin' and he canna be climbin' up and down those stairs," spat Nairnie. "It's bad enough he had to use a rope ladder."

"Do it, Coop," said Bear, when it seemed like Coop was about to complain again. "And Stitch, check the cabin and the rest of the ship for the killer in case he's still here."

"Yes," said Zachariah. "We can't let the children and women go into the cabin before we are sure the killer is not in there."

"Aye, Cap'n," said Stitch, hurrying to get to the cabin before Nairnie and the children.

"Goldtooth, Ramble, help me cut the boy down." With the lithe and grace of a much younger man, Bear grabbed on to the lines and started to climb with his dagger clenched between his teeth. If ever anyone looked like a pirate, it was Bear at this very moment.

"Who is he, Cap'n, and how did he get on the ship?" asked Goldtooth, following Bear and Ramble up the lines.

"I don't know, but Scythe and Tyne were supposed to be guardin' the ship and will have a lot to answer for as soon as I get my hands on them."

"I saw Scythe and Tyne on the docks playing dice," Vivienne called up to him.

"If they'd been here, this might not have happened," said Zachariah.

"What bad luck. Fingers isn't going to be able to tell us anything now." Isaac talked while shading his eyes with his hand, looking up at the body hanging from the mast. The sun had broken through the black clouds that were forming and the entire scene was ominous.

"I still don't understand," said Vivienne. "Who is Fingers, and how do you even know him?"

"Zachariah met him on Rook Row," said Isaac, before Zachariah could stop him. He continued to look up at Bear and the others.

"Isaac," Zachariah tried to warn his brother to stay quiet but to no avail. His brother wasn't paying attention to him and just kept on talking.

"Fingers worked for Adder," said Isaac.

"Adder?" asked Vivienne.

"Aye. He's a thief who trains young boys to be pickpockets," explained Isaac. "He runs a ring up and down the coast. He also knows the boy who stole Zachariah's money pouch today."

"A thief stole your money pouch? Why didn't you tell me?" Vivienne looked at him, frowning and shaking her head. "Thieves are no good. I hope you find whoever did it and punish him harshly."

"He was just a boy, Vivienne," said Zachariah.

"It doesn't matter. Boys grow up to be men. Men who are bandits. That is, bandits like the ones responsible for my parents' deaths. I hope the boy who stole from you hangs, just like this one. After all, they asked for it by becoming cut-purses in the first place." She had a fierce look on her face that Zachariah had never seen before. Ever since catching one of her parents' murderers at the joust, Vivienne seemed to have changed. She was angrier and more determined than ever to figure out who was behind the devious deed. Now she wanted any assassin, thief, or bandit to pay for their crimes even if it meant their deaths. She was becoming bitter, and he didn't like it. It wasn't at all in her nature to be unkind. He could tell that actually having come face-to-face with one of her parents' murderers at a recent joust, and having not known it at the time had shaken her to her very core. He hoped someday that she could stop feeling so vengeful.

Zachariah exchanged glances with his brother. There was no way he could keep the information he'd discovered today away from Vivienne any longer. He had wanted to ask Fingers questions to determine if the redheaded thief truly was Adrian before mentioning the matter to Vivienne. But now he had no choice. With the lad dead, Zachariah had to tell her the truth. Letting out a deep breath, he said something that he wasn't really ready to reveal, since he liked to have all the facts first before making an accusation. In his profession, it was really important to be thorough and to be sure.

"You might not want this thief punished when you hear who I think the lad might really be," he told her.

"What?" She made a face. "I don't understand. You know the boy who stole your pouch, too?"

"I think so," he said with a slight nod. "Yes, I am pretty certain. Vivienne, I believe that the boy who picked my pocket in town today was..." He stopped and once again exchanged glances with his brother. Damn, why was this so hard? If there was any way of keeping this from her until he knew more, he would. The last thing he wanted was to get her hopes up and then find out he was wrong and disappoint her. He wasn't sure she could handle that right now in her life. Then again, it was too late to keep anything from her.

"Who was he, Sheriff? Is the thief someone I know as well?" she asked, obviously having no idea what he was about to say.

"Yes, Lady Vivienne, I believe so," he told her. "You see, I am pretty sure that the boy who stole my pouch today was none other than Adrian."

VIVIENNE'S JAW dropped and she thought her ears were playing tricks on her when she heard what the sheriff had just told her.

"Say that again," she said. "Because to me, it almost sounded as if you were insinuating that my brother, Adrian, is the one who stole from you."

"Yes. That's what I meant." Zachariah cleared his throat and didn't explain further. Vivienne felt her stomach churn and the nerves in her entire body started shaking.

"Zachariah, please," she whispered under her breath. "If you know something about my brother and think he is still alive, then for God's sake tell me!"

"Watch out below!" shouted Goldtooth from the lines.

Zachariah looked up and then grabbed Vivienne's arm and yanked her to the side just as the body came crashing down upon the deck.

"God's feet, did they really just do that?" gasped Isaac, almost getting hit, but stepping to the side in time.

"Damn it, Goldtooth, I didn't mean for ye to just drop the

body," shouted Bear. "We were goin' to lower him down slowly, together."

"Sorry Cap'n, but you didn't specify that," came Goldtooth's excuse.

"Vivienne, mayhap you should go to the captain's cabin with the others while Isaac and I inspect the body," suggested Zachariah.

"Ah, I get to do my first job in training to be a deputy. Good," said Isaac with a satisfied nod.

"Nay! I won't go anywhere until you explain to me exactly what is going on here, and tell me more about my brother."

"Is that a dead body?" came a voice from behind them as the rest of the pirates made their way back onto the ship.

"It sure looks like one," said Peg Leg Pate, clomping over and staring down at the dead boy. The man was truly amazing to be able to climb a rope ladder with a wooden leg. He took the end of his wooden leg and poked at the corpse just to be sure the lad was dead. "Yep, he's dead all right. Doesn't even move."

"Was he strangled?" asked another crew member.

"He's got a goddamned noose around his neck," spat Zachariah. "What do you think?"

"Sheriff, I need to know about Adrian." Vivienne was persistent, feeling a sense of hope that her brother was truly alive. She hadn't felt this hope in years now.

"Where did that lad come from?" asked Birdman, leaning over to inspect the corpse. "And who is he?"

"I know that face," growled Jax. "He's the lad who picked my pocket earlier today. Let's go through his pockets and see if he still has my pouch."

In perfect pirate form, it seemed that the men didn't care about the dead boy, but only had concerns about their missing money. Or perhaps stealing whatever they could from the poor lad. Vivienne was about to say something regarding the matter, when she realized that she was being just as insensitive since she was asking about Adrian instead of paying attention to the dead boy. Suddenly, she felt no better than a pirate herself.

"Get back," instructed Zachariah, stepping in front of the men. "This is a crime scene and nothing is to be touched. The body will not be inspected by anyone but me and my brother, Isaac."

"And me," said Vivienne, stepping in front of the group of pirates to make her presence known. "If this is a murder investigation then I need to be present as well."

"Nay. You don't have to do that." Zachariah's caring manner showed in his big brown eyes. "I know this is hard for you, my lady. And I promise we will talk about things, but first, I need to pay attention to the fact that a young man has been murdered. He was killed right here in broad daylight and aboard the ship that we've sailed on. Someone must have seen something."

"You're right," she told him. "We will talk about Adrian later, but right now all that matters is that we catch the killer of this young man. Justice must be served."

"You...really mean that?" Zachariah raised a brow.

"Of course, I do," she told him. "And I am sorry if I sounded vengeful or insensitive. I realize I have a job to do as well, and I am here to help you as always."

Grunt sneaked in between the onlookers and started to sniff at the dead boy's body.

"What's going on here?" asked Tyne, walking up with Scythe. They were the last to make it back to the ship and both clutched flasks of what was probably whisky.

"Having a party and not inviting us again?" asked Scythe with a chuckle.

"Scythe, Tyne, I want to talk to you. You have a lot of explaining to do." Bear dropped down from the lines and stormed over to the men, grabbing each of them by the front of their tunics and shaking them hard. "Where the hell were you? You were supposed to be guarding the damned ship."

"We just wanted to have a little fun like the rest of the crew," whined Tyne.

"That's right," agreed Scythe. "We're always left behind and it's not fair. So we left the ship for a little while. What's the harm in that?"

"That's the harm!" Bear pushed his way through the crowd of pirates, still gripping the two, and pushing them forward to show them the dead lad on the floor.

"Oh," said Tyne.

"Did that happen here on the ship?" asked Scythe. Both the men just stared at the corpse.

"It did, but wouldn't have, if you two had manned your posts as required," Bear told them.

"So you're saying this is our fault?" asked Scythe, his eyes opening wide.

"Yes," answered Bear. "As far as I'm concerned, you two are responsible for this."

"But we don't even know the lad," said Tyne with a shrug. "Why would we want him dead? And why was he on the ship to begin with?"

"He was here because the sheriff asked him to join us here," said Isaac. "We were going to question him about—"

"It's personal business," broke in Zachariah. "Now, I am going to have to ask all of you not to leave the ship again until each of you is questioned by me first."

"We're getting questioned?" asked Coop who had rejoined them. "What for? We didn't do nothing."

"That's right. And why do we have to answer to you?" asked Peg Leg Pate. "It's not like we had anything to do with this. You should be looking at those two instead." He nodded toward Tyne and Scythe. "I agree with Bear that they're responsible."

"Move aside, let me through." Nairnie pushed her way to the front, followed by Stitch who was right behind her.

"Nairnie, I thought you were staying with the children in the cabin," said the sheriff.

"Stitch and Coop checked the ship and there is no killer aboard," reported the old woman.

"Stitch? Is this true?" Bear looked up to his quartermaster, or first mate.

"That's right, Cap'n," said Stitch. "We didn't find any intruders. The ship is secure."

"I'd still like you to stay with the children, Nairnie." Zachariah wasn't taking any chances.

"I canna," she informed him.

"Why not?"

"I'm goin' to need to whip up some food for everyone, since my guess is that we're no' goin' to be returnin' to Mablethorpe tonight as planned after all."

"We're staying here overnight?" called out one of the crew members.

"I never said that." Zachariah held up a hand over his head.

"But we're not leaving, right?" asked Isaac. "I mean, we can't. Not until we find out who killed Fingers."

"Isaac is right. We can't leave," said Vivienne, not wanting to go anywhere before she found out more about her brother possibly being here and hopefully still alive. "An investigation needs to be set in motion, and we need to keep everything the same as it was at the time of the crime."

"Lady Vivienne, I think it might be best if the children were taken back to Mablethorpe and for you to go with them. I will stay here with Isaac and continue with the investigation." Zachariah seemed to be trying to get rid of her, and Vivienne would not have that!

"I am not leaving Whitstable before I have answers!" she

retorted. "That is, more answers than just who killed this lad named Fingers. You know what I mean." She crossed her arms over her chest, looking the sheriff right in the eye. There was no doubt that he knew exactly what she meant. Vivienne wasn't going anywhere until she was able to find out if the sheriff had really seen her missing brother, Adrian.

Chapter Six

"Whitstable's sheriff and the coroner have both been summoned," said Bear a little while later. "They should be here soon."

"Good. That'll give us a little time to see if we can find out any information as to the killing." Zachariah knelt down next to the dead lad. In a way, he felt that this was partially his fault. If he had let the boy leave and had not talked him into meeting him on the ship, mayhap he'd still be alive right now.

"Who do you think did this?" Vivienne looked over his shoulder as Zachariah inspected the body, carefully removing the noose from around the boy's neck. Grunt watched, sniffing the dead boy's feet.

"Probably Adder, right Zachariah?" said Isaac, down on his knees as well. Some of the crew members watched from afar, all of them talking softly amongst themselves.

"We can't go pointing fingers before we have all the facts," Zachariah told his brother. "That is the first thing you need to learn in this line of work."

"I'm not used to waiting for facts before taking action," Isaac told him.

"I know," mumbled Zachariah, realizing Isaac's past profession of being a mercenary meant he killed on command without asking questions or waiting for answers.

"So this boy worked for a man named Adder that taught him and other boys how to be thieves?" Vivienne stretched her neck, inspecting the corpse as well.

"That's what I've been told," he answered.

"And the boy who pickpocketed you, the one you think was Adrian, works for this man named Adder as well?"

"That's right." Zachariah looked at her sideways, realizing she was sneakily trying to get information out of him about her brother, although he'd told her to wait.

"How do you think they got him up there?" asked Isaac, looking up to the high mast.

"It had to be more than one person to hoist him up there," said the sheriff. "And by the look of this bump on the back of his head, I'd say someone surprised him from behind."

"I think he was dead before they hoisted him up to the yardarm," said Vivienne. "I don't see any signs of struggle. No ripped clothing, or anything under his finger nails that would cause us to believe he fought back." She picked up the boy's hand to inspect it closer.

"I think you're right." Zachariah sighed and stood up. "But why take the time to hoist him up to the yardarm? I mean, that could risk exposure to the killer."

"Mayhap they did it as some kind of warning to you," suggested Isaac.

"Warning? What do you mean?" asked Vivienne.

"My days of being a mercenary taught me a lot," stated Isaac. "If one wanted to give a message to another, they did it in a way that said silently, don't interfere or this might happen to you too. Which is what this looks like to me."

"Isaac," said Zachariah, shaking his head, not wanting Vivienne to worry. But his brother didn't understand his silent warning in the least.

"Oh my!" gasped Vivienne. "That means we might all be in danger. Especially Adrian, if he really works for this man named Adder. This is not good at all. Sheriff, we need to go out and look for my brother before something like this happens to him as well."

"Vivienne, stop it," said Zachariah in a hoarse voice. "You are jumping to conclusions. And the fact of the matter is, we don't know for sure this is a message from anyone. Neither do we know if the boy who stole from me is truly your brother."

"But you said you were pretty certain that he is," said Vivienne, not seeming like she was going to give up.

Thankfully, just then the Sheriff of Whitstable boarded the ship with one of his deputies. A man whom Zachariah guessed to be the coroner was with them.

"I'm Sheriff Bertram Baldric, but you can call me Sheriff Whitstable. With me is Constable Hugh, and our town coroner, Gudmund. So I heard someone was killed on this ship?"

"I'm Sheriff Zachariah Fitch from Mablethorpe," he greeted the men. "This is my deputy-in-training, Isaac, and Lady Vivienne Harlowe, who partners with me on murder investigations. And yes, a boy died here and was found hanging from the yardarm today."

Grunt went over to sniff the visitors and then hurried back and plopped down at Vivienne's feet.

"This looks like one of those pickpockets from Rook Row," said Sheriff Whitstable, staring down at the corpse. Hmm. I guess he got what he deserved."

"Sheriff, how can you say that?" blurted out Vivienne.

"We've been having a hard time controlling the thievery in Whitstable," said the constable. "Believe me, we've been trying to catch and punish these boys for a long time now, but they always seem to get away."

"Mayhap they have no choice and are forced to steal," said Vivienne. Zachariah knew she was still thinking about her brother.

"Sheriff, we'd appreciate it if you let us assist you with the murder investigation since it did happen here on the ship we arrived on, and it is a lad from your town," said Zachariah.

"Since the murder happened on the water, I don't really feel as if it is my responsibility." The Sheriff of Whitstable didn't seem to want to help. Probably because it was a boy thief who was killed.

"I understand that the death took place on the water, but this ship is docked at your port."

"How do I know this thief didn't stow away on your ship and die on the high seas. I think that's what happened."

"What?" gasped Vivienne. "Sheriff Whitstable, I assure you that this lad did not die out at sea. It happened here."

"That's right," said Zachariah. "I saw this lad on Rook Row earlier today. His name was Fingers."

"Can you prove it?"

"Isn't my word good enough?" asked Zachariah.

"Who owns this ship?" asked the Sheriff of Whitstable.

"I do," said Bear, overhearing and stepping forward. "My crew and I work for the King. The *Falcon* is under the King's command."

"I see," said the sheriff.

"Sheriff, I recognize this man and his crew," whispered the constable. "They used to be pirates, I'm sure of it."

"You were pirates? Is this true?" The Sheriff of Whitstable raised a brow.

"Aye, but we've been pardoned by the King," said Bear.

"I don't want anything to do with pirates."

"So what are you saying?" asked Vivienne. "That you don't want anything to do with the murder investigation?"

"As far as I'm concerned, the murder happened on the high seas," said Sheriff Whitstable.

"It didn't," ground out Zachariah. "You can ask anyone on this ship. The murder happened today when we were all on shore."

"Ask anyone?" The Sheriff of Whitstable chuckled. "I'm sorry, Sheriff Fitch, but I won't take the word of a pirate."

"Ex-pirate," growled Bear.

"Sheriff, what should I do with the body?" asked the coroner.

"Mayhap the thief should be buried at sea where he belongs."

"I'll pay to give the boy a burial here in Whitstable," said Zachariah. "And we don't need your help to investigate, so don't bother. I will handle the murder investigation myself."

"Zachariah, what are you saying?" asked Vivienne.

"If Sheriff Whitstable wants to consider it a murder on the high seas, then so be it. I will investigate without his participation. Even a thief deserves to find justice. A life was lost here today, and I won't stop until I get to the bottom of it." Zachariah wasn't going to let this pitiful excuse of a sheriff stop him.

"Now wait a minute," said Bear. "I don't want a rumor like that attached to my ship. What will King Edward think? It won't bode well for me or my crew."

"Don't worry about King Edward, Bear," Vivienne told him. "If need be, I will vouch for you and the entire crew. He'll listen to me."

"You? Hah!" snapped the Sheriff of Whitstable. "Why would King Edward listen to a woman?"

"Because she is a noblewoman and also the daughter of the King, that's why," said Zachariah, finally shutting the man up.

"Constable, Coroner, we'll take the body to shore and there will be a burial soon," the sheriff finally agreed. "Sheriff Fitch, you are welcome to conduct the investigation, but I am a busy man and have better things to do than to hunt down the killer of a damned petty thief. However, if I am truly needed, then call for me. But I'd rather not get involved."

"Don't worry, Sheriff Whitstable. I am sure my brother and Lady Vivienne and I can handle this without you. Your participation is not needed."

"Good. We'll leave for now. Bring the body to the coroner's office when you are finished with it."

"We should do it?" asked Vivienne. "So you won't even take on that responsibility?"

"Like I said, the deceased was a troublesome thief. We're all better off without him. Come, Constable. Coroner. We have other things to concern ourselves with and have no time for murders on the high seas." He turned and left with his men.

"I can't believe that," said Isaac once they'd gone. "By the way Sheriff Whitstable acted, I'd say he was the murderer."

"I don't like him saying it was murder on the high seas. I don't want a story like that getting out. Being an ex-pirate, it won't be good for my reputation," said Bear.

"Dinna worry about it," said Nairnie, having watched in silence until now. "If Lady Vivienne said she'd smooth things out with the King, then she will. After all, she's his daughter."

"We really need to start the investigation," said Zachariah.

"What do we do first?" asked Isaac.

"We'll have to speak with all of the crew to begin with."

"Ye don't really think any of my crew did this, do you?" asked Bear.

"We were all on shore," called out Coop. "Don't blame us for it."

"No one is blaming anyone," said Zachariah. "It is part of the process that must be followed."

"What will happen to his body?" asked Vivienne, concern in her voice as she stared down at Fingers.

"Since he's an orphan and has no family, it won't be easy," said Zachariah. "Even though the Sheriff of Whitstable agreed to let the boy be buried here, he was still a thief and you can see how the sheriff feels about that."

"Thieves are usually just buried in a ditch behind a tavern," said Isaac.

"I feel so bad for him," said Vivienne, her caring, kind side showing forth again. "I am sure this poor boy didn't deserve to die."

"You can't say that," said Isaac. "We don't know the reason for his death yet."

"I think I have an idea why he might have died, and I have to say I agree with her," said the sheriff. "Lady Vivienne, why don't you go to the cabin and wait with the children. Isaac, can you escort her there?"

"Of course," said Isaac, holding out his arm.

"Go to the cabin?" she said, sounding insulted. "Nay. I am going to help you with the investigation like I usually do."

"The children are upset by what they saw and need you," he told her, meaning it partially. The other reason why he wanted her to leave was because he thought this was a little too close to home for her since now the information was made known to her about Adrian. He didn't want to answer questions about him yet, and was sure she was going to keep asking.

VIVIENNE DIDN'T LIKE BEING PUSHED AWAY, but started for the cabin with Isaac because she did want to check on the children to make sure they were all right. Seeing a dead boy hanging by the neck was nothing that any of them should have ever had to witness. Poor Starah and even Maleine seemed so scared and traumatized by it. She needed to be there for them, and for Martin as well.

"Come on, Grunt," she said, calling her dog who was sitting there looking up at the mast.

"Grunt, what are you doing? I said, come." Still the dog didn't move.

She walked back to get her hound, realizing that he was now howling and staring up in the air. She wasn't sure why he was acting this way. From the side of her vision she saw some of Bear's crew helping put Fingers on a stretcher. Zachariah was having a discussion with Isaac.

"Grunt, what is the matter with you?" she asked.

"He seems to be looking up at something. Mayhap it's the lookout basket that takes his interest." The youngest of the crew, Ramble, shaded his eyes and looked upward as well.

"Naw, the hound just sees a bird up there, that's all. It's sitting on the lookout basket. Don't you see it?" Birdman walked over with Jax. "It looks like a gull to me." Birdman whistled, imitating a gull, and the bird flew downward and swooped over his head before taking off again up in the air. "That should quiet the hound down now that the bird is gone."

Still, Grunt continued to look upward and howl.

"I don't know what's wrong with him. Mayhap he's been spooked by the hanging too." Vivienne looked up the mast, feeling that churning in her stomach continue. "He usually only howls like that when he's cornered a rabbit."

Jax laughed. "I hardly think there's a rabbit up there."

"Nay, but I just thought I saw something move in the lookout basket," said Ramble. "I'm going up to check on it."

"Be careful," Vivienne called out, not wanting the boy to fall. Just seeing the crew climb around in the lines made her really nervous. Especially since Fingers was just found dangling from the yardarm by his neck.

"What's going on?" asked Isaac, coming to join them.

"Grunt sees something in the lookout basket and Ramble is going up to investigate," Vivienne told him.

Ramble made it all the way up the mast quickly, and Vivienne was still trying to calm her dog.

"God's eyes, there is someone up here," Ramble called down to them from inside the basket.

"It's the killer!" Without hesitation, Isaac grabbed the lines and started climbing. "Get my brother," he shouted to her. "Tell him what we've found."

"Aye," said Vivienne, turning to go get Zachariah. But when she realized Grunt was no longer howling, but instead panting and wagging his tail as he watched Isaac climb, she knew there was no danger. That couldn't be the killer in the lookout basket. If so, Grunt would sense evil and be barking like crazy. The dog could always tell when something was wrong. She waited a minute, and then she saw a head pop up next to Ramble. She couldn't be certain but the intruder looked to be naught more than a boy. Struggling with if she should call to Zachariah or not, she decided on the latter since he had dismissed her so easily, not seeming to want her help. Besides, for all she knew, that could be her brother up there, and Zachariah was avoiding talking about Adrian. Nay, she decided, she wouldn't say anything to the sheriff. Or, at least not yet. She wanted to see who was up there first.

"Bring him down. Carefully," Vivienne called up to Ramble and Isaac. By the time they were halfway down, Zachariah was at her side.

"What are they doing up there?" he asked.

"Grunt brought to our awareness that there was someone

hiding in the lookout basket so Ramble and Isaac went to investigate."

"There is someone up there?" Zachariah's hand instantly went to the dagger attached to his waistbelt.

"There's no need for that, Sheriff. I assure you, it's not the killer," she said, gently resting her hand atop his.

"How do you know?"

"Look." She nodded, and when Zachariah looked up to see the three coming down the lines, he smiled. "You almost look like you know him. Do you?" she asked.

"I do. He's a thief from Rook Row," said Zachariah, hurrying over to help the little boy to the deck of the ship. "Mouse, what were you doing hiding up there?"

"Mouse?" she questioned, thinking these boy thieves all had some very strange names.

"Don't hurt me. Please. And don't tell Adder," cried the boy, seeming terrified.

"Don't worry. You're safe," Vivienne told him. "I am Lady Vivienne Harlowe."

"You're pretty," he said softly, seeming sad as well as shy, then quickly looking down at his feet.

"Why thank you," said Vivienne, liking the compliment, but wishing it had come from the sheriff instead of just a child.

"Did you come aboard the ship with Fingers today?" asked the sheriff. "Is that why you're here?"

The boy didn't even look up, but nodded slightly.

"So you know what happened then to your friend called Fingers?" Vivienne questioned him.

Now he looked like he was about to cry, but nodded once more.

"Did you see who killed him?" asked Zachariah. "I need to know."

Mouse's head snapped up and his eyes grew wide, but he didn't say a word.

"Was it Adder?" asked Isaac, adding his part to this investigation.

No answer. The boy was not talking.

"It's all right, Mouse, we'll protect you. You need to tell us everything you know." Zachariah put his hand on the boy's shoulder, but Mouse quickly pulled away.

"You're scaring the poor child," whispered Vivienne. "Remember, he just saw his friend murdered. Give him some time to catch his breath and calm down."

It was as if Mouse was fearful of saying anything at all to them. Almost as if he'd been warned to keep quiet.

"Mouse, can you tell us why you were up in the lookout basket?" asked Vivienne. "Were you hiding from someone up there?"

Still nothing.

"If you want us to catch the person who killed your friend, you need to help us," said Zachariah, finally breaking through the wall the boy held, but only slightly.

"Fingers told me to go up there. To see if you were coming," said Mouse.

"I see," said Zachariah. "So Fingers probably didn't want you two to stay too long so Adder wouldn't catch you, right?"

"Aye," the boy said. "We didn't want to be punished."

"So you went up to the lookout and that is when someone else came aboard the ship," said Vivienne, getting a nod from Mouse.

"Was there more than one person?" asked Isaac.

Mouse shrugged.

"Did you know who it was? Could you recognize the man if you saw him again?" Zachariah fired too many questions at once at the boy, making the child anxious. The sheriff's eagerness to know more only seemed to push him further away. Mouse clammed up and took a step backward. Vivienne wasn't sure he would not try to run. They needed him here, so it was crucial to be careful and not to overwhelm him with too many questions at once about the hanging.

"Perhaps the killer wore a cloak and a hood covering his head?" suggested Zachariah.

"I hardly think someone in a cloak could climb the rigging," scoffed Isaac. "I just had a hell of a time climbing up there. And if the killer had to drag Fingers's lifeless body, or hoist him up with a rope over the yardarm, that would take a lot of strength so he'd have to not only be really strong, but not have a cloak getting in his way."

"I agree. This job most likely required more than one person to pull it off," said Zachariah. "And it had to be someone who knew what they were doing."

"Like a pirate, you mean." Nairnie appeared at their sides, her hands on her hips. "It wasna Bear or any of his crew if that's what ye're thinkin', Sheriff."

Zachariah pinned her with a frown, Nairnie's sudden appearance annoying him. "Nairnie, it's not nice to sneak up on others." She'd been so quiet that he hadn't even realized she was there. For an overweight, old woman, she was light on her feet when she wanted to be. "And I never said that I thought any of the crew were guilty."

"Who's that?" She nodded at the boy from the basket.

"His name is Mouse," Vivienne supplied the information. "He came here with Fingers. You know...the dead lad."

"How old are ye, laddie?" Nairnie cocked her head.

The boy stayed silent but then slowly held up nine fingers.

"Nine? That's the same age as my son, Martin," Vivienne told him with a smile.

"Do you mean that blond-haired boy with the wooden

sword? I saw him from the lookout. He was very brave," said Mouse.

This was the most Mouse had said yet, and Vivienne hoped Zachariah would be impressed that she was the one to be able to get him to speak so freely. After all, she was much better with children than he was, and that included his own daughter.

"Yes. Yes, he was very brave," Vivienne said with a nod. "Would you like to meet Martin? He's in the cabin right now."

"Is that pretty girl with him too?" Mouse seemed looked down to the deck again as he spoke.

At first Vivienne thought he meant Maleine. But then she realized because of his age, he had to be talking about Starah. She smiled, since Mouse had called her pretty as well. He was at the age when he was obviously starting to notice females.

"The pretty girl with Martin is Starah. She's the sheriff's daughter," she explained.

"Aye. I'd like to meet them both," said the boy, grinning just slightly. "I don't have any friends my own age."

"Well, then, by all means, give me your hand and I'll take you to them right now." Vivienne held out her hand, hoping to gain the boy's trust.

"Vivienne, I'm not sure that's a good idea," the sheriff said with a shake of his head.

"Don't be silly. Of course it is."

"I need to question the boy and he should stay here for now."

"I'm sure ye're probably hungry and thirsty, Mouse," Nairnie broke in. "Would ye like some food and mayhap a little cider?"

"I'd love that!"

"Vivienne, Nairnie, please." Zachariah frowned. "He is a key witness in this murder investigation and I really need to question him."

"That can wait," said Vivienne, with a wave of her hand. "Some things are more important."

"When did ye eat last?" asked Nairnie, taking the boy by his other hand.

"I don't know. A few days ago mayhap."

"A few days ago?" Nairnie looked over at Zachariah, giving him the evil eye. "This boy willna answer any more questions until he has a full belly."

"God's toes, what is that look all about?" asked Isaac, taking a step backward and faking a shiver.

"I'll tell you exactly what it means," said Zachariah. "It means, I'm not going to even get close enough to the boy tonight to attempt to question him more. Not with the women on board making my job harder every chance they get."

"You'll have your chance. Just be patient and wait," said Vivienne, having overheard him and throwing his words back at him as they walked away. "Mouse, I'd like to hear all about your friends. Especially the boy named Red." She looked back over her shoulder and smiled at Zachariah. In her own way, she was letting him know that nothing or no one was going to slow her down from finding her brother, if he really was out there and still alive.

Chapter Seven

As the sun set, Zachariah and Vivienne sat on the deck of the ship together, having eaten a delicious meal that Nairnie cooked up that included the oysters Bear brought back from town, and some root vegetables with spices and garlic. It was amazing that she could even cook aboard a ship, much less make something this tasty. She truly was skilled. The crew all kept to themselves this evening and the mood was sullen. Instead of boisterous singing and drinking and jesting like Zachariah expected, there was very little talking amongst the ex-pirates. He supposed it was because no one felt much like being happy after finding the dead boy on the ship. It had taken him a long time to calm down his daughter and convince her that the same thing wasn't going to happen to any of them.

It was worrisome to him that someone managed to get aboard the *Falcon*, kill a strapping young lad, and then leave as they pleased. Some of the crew, including Bear, blamed Tyne and Scythe for the death of Fingers, since they were supposed to be the ones guarding the ship. Zachariah, however, couldn't help but blame himself.

"I never should have asked Fingers to meet me on the ship,"

he said, leaning over to speak softly to Vivienne without everyone overhearing. Martin and Starah were playing with Mouse now. The boys had proved to be a good distraction for his daughter. Especially Martin, since he didn't seem to let much bother him. He was a brave little boy, and like Vivienne said, would someday make a fine knight.

The children threw a ball around that Bear had constructed from old rags wrapped tightly with twine. Grunt kept running back and forth trying to catch the ball, his jaws snapping air once or twice before getting it and then hightailing it around the center mast with the young ones trying to catch him. Maleine and Wymond sat together, seemingly inseparable so far on this journey. They'd thankfully left the ferrets and the cat back in the cabin, so that, at least, was one less thing for Zachariah to have to worry about. Maleine had been so frightened by seeing Fingers swinging from the noose, that she didn't want to leave Wymond's side. Of course, Wymond rather liked that.

"Zachariah, why did you ask Fingers to come to the ship in the first place? What did you want to talk about with him?" Vivienne picked up a wooden cup and took a drink of ale. "You never explained anything to me, and I am still waiting to hear the details."

"You're right," he said, knowing that he couldn't wait any longer to tell her more about what he suspected about her brother. "Vivienne, I owe you an explanation."

"Go ahead," she said, sounding cautious, as if she thought he might change his mind again, since he'd been doing that a lot lately.

"I am sure Adrian is the thief who stole my pouch of coins today."

"So you said. However, Sheriff, I find it difficult to believe that my brother is a thief. He was always such a good and obedient boy." She put down the cup, not looking at him when she spoke.

"Whether he is or not, I don't really care," continued Zachariah. "What I am trying to tell you is that he didn't seem to remember me. I told him who I was, but he had no reaction at all."

She smiled. "Well, it has been seven long years, Zachariah. And he was just a boy when he disappeared. I'm sure a lot has happened to take his attention in that time."

"True. But your brother was nine when he disappeared, and he knew me well." Zachariah's attention was on little Mouse, who was the same age as Adrian when the event happened. His heart ached for Vivienne. For her entire family. No one should have to endure what they'd all been through.

"I'm sure he could have forgotten you, Sheriff. I mean, he went through a very traumatic time, so you must understand and not take it personally."

"All right." Zachariah nodded. "Mayhap that's true. But he didn't even seem to know you when I mentioned your name, Vivienne. Even after I called you his sister."

"What?" That seemed to shock her, and make her angry. She violently shook her head, not willing to accept the truth. "Nay. That could never be. My brother knows and loves me. If Adrian is alive, he'd remember me. We were very close. That couldn't have been him, after all. If so, he would have reacted to hearing my name. You made a mistake because that thief could not possibly be my brother."

"This is exactly why I didn't want to tell you yet that I saw him." Zachariah was already regretting not being able to hold back this information from her. "Without more evidence I cannot prove it truly was Adrian, though I am pretty convinced it was. My lady, I didn't want you to get your hopes up in case I was wrong. And if I am right, I swear, the last thing I wanted was to tell you that your brother doesn't remember who you are."

"Oh, this is awful," she said softly, brushing away a stray tear from her eye. "I suppose I can see your point now. But Zachariah, we need to find out for sure. If it is Adrian...and even if he truly doesn't remember me...I still need to know."

"That is exactly how I feel, Vivienne," he answered. "That is why I was meeting with Fingers. He said he was good friends with Red and would tell me whatever I wanted to know."

"Please, don't call him Red. His name is Adrian." Vivienne's eyes closed briefly and then reopened as she let out a deep breath. She was obviously quite shaken.

"I didn't mean to upset you."

"Nay, it's all right. I will call him Red for now. But only until I know his identity for certain," she finally agreed.

"Well, Brother, what will I be learning to do next, regarding my job of being your new deputy?" Isaac sat down on the deck in front of them, ready to work.

Zachariah needed to set his brother straight. "Slow down, Isaac. I never said you'd be my deputy. First you need to learn to be a simple constable. And remember, you are only in training."

"Simple constable?" Isaac made a face that showed he was disgusted. "Nothing about me is simple, Brother, and never will be."

"That's for sure," Zachariah mumbled under his breath. "Well, let's just start slowly and we'll see where it goes, shall we?" He was tired and perplexed by the situation at hand, and the last thing he needed tonight was an argument with his brother. He'd just recently made amends with him, and wanted to keep things under control.

"Fine," said Isaac. "Want me to question some of the crew then? How about the boy? He surely knows the most about

Fingers since he was his friend and also aboard when the murder happened."

"Nay." Zachariah didn't want to start questioning tonight. "Everyone is too upset and tired. Besides, nightfall has arrived. We'll all just get a good night's sleep and the questioning will begin in the morning."

"Good idea," said Isaac with yawn. He stretched his arms over his head. "I hear there is a pallet on the floor of the captain's quarters and also a couple hammocks hanging from the beams in there. I'll take one of the hammocks, I don't mind."

"Nay, you won't. The cabin is for the women and children only," Zachariah let him know.

"Why? What about us? Surely, we deserve a good place to sleep since we're the lawmen here and conducting a murder investigation." Isaac wasn't at all happy with the sleeping arrangements.

"I don't totally trust Bear's crew around Vivienne and Maleine." Zachariah stood up. "And the children need to be watched over by the women. As well as the animals, too. We'll let the females do that, and we'll sleep out here on the deck with the crew."

"I still think I should have a pallet," complained Isaac, not looking as if he were going to let this go.

"Ye can stay with me in the galley if ye want," offered Nairnie, walking up to join them. "But we'll have to share the pallet. It's really only big enough for one, but we can cuddle." She smiled wickedly, obviously jesting with Isaac. "Of course, Bear might no' take kindly to that idea. Then again, I'm still angry with him, so it doesna matter."

"Share a pallet? With you?" asked Isaac, almost sounding for a moment as if he were considering it. He rubbed his chin in thought. Then he turned to see the captain watching him from across the deck. Bear held a flask of whisky in one hand, raising it up to his mouth for a drink. His intense stare never wavered from Isaac.

Isaac cleared his throat and looked back at Nairnie. "Thank you, Nairnie, but actually, I think sleeping under the stars in this fresh air would be good for me, after all." He got up and hurried away, giving Bear a wide berth as he made his way up the stairs to the sterncastle, the raised section at the back of the ship.

"Children, time for bed," called out Vivienne, getting up and shaking out her gown. She seemed a little too chipper after the events of the day, and at this time of night. Zachariah got the feeling she was up to something, and he didn't like it in the least.

"Lady Vivienne," he said in a warning voice. "I don't want you questioning Mouse unless I'm there with you. We'll do it together. Tomorrow, first thing in the morning. Promise me you won't go behind my back."

"Would I do that?" She blinked several times.

Yes, she would, he realized. "Actually, I think mayhap I'll keep the boy out here on the deck tonight instead, where I can keep an eye on him."

"I believe it would be better if he were tucked safely away where this Adder fellow can't find him," said Vivienne. "After all, we have no assurance that Adder or Fingers's killer won't come here looking for Mouse tonight."

"If anyone does, he'll have a dozen pirates, a sheriff, and an ex-mercenary to deal with, so I wouldn't worry your head about that," he told her with a chuckle.

"Please, let me take Mouse to the cabin with the rest of us," she begged him. "He seems so frightened. When he's around Martin and Starah is the only time I've seen him actually smile."

Zachariah thought about it, and realized she made a good point. Perhaps it would be the best for the boy after having lost his friend.

"All right, go ahead," he told her. "But Wymond needs to sleep on deck."

"Wymond needs to stay inside the cabin to watch over the ferrets. Don't worry, I'll put Maleine in one of the hammocks and make him sleep on the floor."

"Just make sure to keep all those animals in the cabin because I don't want them wandering around the ship stirring up trouble."

"I'll take Midnight with me to the galley tonight," offered Nairnie.

"Oh, thank you," said Vivienne. "That would be good, since the cat gets along with the ferrets but not Grunt. Good night, Sheriff." Vivienne walked away smiling.

"I'm posting men to watch the water overnight," said Bear, coming to talk to Zachariah. "I don't want any more killers sneaking on board while we sleep. One murder aboard my ship is bad enough. I don't fancy telling King Edward about this at all."

"Don't worry about that. Remember, Lady Vivienne is the King's daughter. Like she said, she'll do what she can to smooth things out for you if need be."

"Sheriff, I don't like the women and children being here. It's too dangerous. If anything happens to them, I'll never forgive myself."

"I know what you mean," said Zachariah. "I feel the same way. But I have an idea that will ease both our minds if we can carry it out."

"What's that?" asked Bear.

"It's nothing that Vivienne is going to agree with or like in the least. Neither will Nairnie. But hopefully we can carry it out while they sleep and then they won't try to stop us. Listen closely, because I think this is in the best plan for all involved."

I<small>T DIDN'T TAKE LONG</small> for Vivienne to fall into a deep sleep. After the events of today, and trying to calm the children, she was exhausted. She fell asleep wondering about her brother. That, however, only triggered her recurring nightmare once again. It was the same nightmare she always had, reliving the events of that awful night seven years ago when bandits killed her parents, and her brother and son went missing...

Gripping the hilt of her father's sword with two hands, Vivienne slowly stepped around the front of the wagon, just in time to see a shadowy figure stab her mother with his sword and then throw her body to the ground. Too scared to even speak, she froze. Standing in the dark, fear consumed her, making her feel as if she were in hell.

"Someone's coming. Hurry, let's get out of here," came the voice of another shadowy form atop a horse. The man who stabbed her mother withdrew his sword and headed toward his waiting horse.

"Mother! Nay!" screamed her little brother. Vivienne's head snapped around to see Adrian standing in the hay in the back of the wagon, looking over the edge, terror on his face.

"Dammit. There's someone else," shouted the first bandit to the second.

"Kill him, too," commanded the ruffian's companion. "Leave no witnesses."

The first man rushed over, but Vivienne wasn't about to let him kill her brother too. Guilt already ate away at her that she wasn't able to save her parents. She stepped out in front of the attacker, wildly swinging her father's sword in the air. Mayhap it was her anger controlling her actions, but somehow she managed to stab the man on his right shoulder with her blade. The tip stuck into his flesh and she was sure she felt the blade meet his bone. Quickly, she pulled the blade back, seeing the blood oozing from the man's wound.

"Aaaaah!" the attacker screamed, one hand gripping at his bleeding shoulder from where Vivienne had struck him.

"Dammit, there's a girl here, too," shouted the other man from his horse.

The fighting frightened the horses, causing them to rear up and paw at the air, whinnying loudly. The wagon jerked and her brother fell back in the hay with his feet in the air. Then the horses took off down the road at a run, pulling the wagon along with them. The sound of Vivienne's crying baby from the bench seat inside the basket caused her to panic and become furious all at the same time. Even in her weakened state from just having given birth, Vivienne's motherly instincts kicked in and she fought like a lion. She started swinging the sword wildly at her attacker as she lunged forward, stabbing at him over and over again. All the while, she gritted her teeth. No one was going to kill any of her family and get away with it! She was so angry right now, that she wasn't even scared. She wanted both of these bandits to die.

"You bastard! I'll kill you for what you've done," she shouted, causing him to actually back away from her now. His sword dangled from his fingers as he gripped his bleeding sword arm which she had injured. God's eyes, she wished she had severed his arm altogether.

"Let's go," called out the man's friend from his steed. "Someone's coming."

The man she'd struck mumbled something under his breath that she couldn't decipher, but it sounded as if he'd said the words, 'too soon.' He then turned and ran, mounting his horse, taking off with his friend, leaving her stranded all alone.

"Vivienne," came her mother's soft cry from the ground. Vivienne spun on her heel and ran to her mother, dropping the sword and falling to her knees at her mother's side.

"Mother!" she cried, cradling the woman's head atop her lap. "They killed Father. And the horses ran off with Adrian and my baby." Tears gushed from her eyes as she looked down at her mother bathed in the scant light of the partial moon that broke through the clouds. "Mother, please don't die too! Do not leave me, I beg you. I need you!"

"Mother? Mother, wake up."

Vivienne's eyes slowly opened, and she suddenly remembered she was in the captain's quarters with the children aboard the *Falcon,* and thankfully what she'd just witnessed was naught but a dream. "Martin?" She bolted upright to a sitting position, almost falling out of the hammock which she occupied. Her seven-year-old son was below her, standing on the floor and reaching up to tap her. "What's wrong?"

"Grunt is acting funny. I think mayhap he's feeling sick from the ship rocking so much on the waves as we sail in the storm."

"Rocking? Waves? Sail?" She rubbed her head and yawned. "Nay, Martin, that's not possible. We're tied up at the dock, we're not sailing." She heard thunder rumbling outside the small portal window and could smell the falling rain, as well as hear it whipping against the hull of the ship. "You're right, though. It is storming." Her gaze flashed over to the small window in the cabin. Instead of seeing the other ships tied up in the harbor or even the wharf, she saw only water. "God's eyes! We really are moving."

Vivienne jumped out of the hammock, almost stepping on Wymond who was sleeping right below her. The hammock swung back and forth as she ran over to peer out the window. To her dismay she could see Mablethorpe Castle on the horizon as they got closer to shore. "He's taking us home! How dare he!"

Her temper grew, since Zachariah didn't discuss this with her first. Even though it was only meant to be a one-day trip, things were different now because of the death of Fingers. They couldn't leave before investigating the murder. And they certainly couldn't leave before discovering the true identity of Red. Her brother could be so close, but now the opportunity to find out for sure just slipped through her fingers.

"We're going home?" asked Martin. "Why?"

"Who's taking us where?" Wymond sat up and rubbed his sleepy eyes. Grunt gave a few barks, showing his dismay as well.

"Dammit, did they really think they could sneak this by me and get away with it? I won't let them do that." She slipped into her shoes, threw her cloak around her and yanked open the door.

"Ooomph," came Nairnie's voice as the boat tossed in the waves, and she stumbled, falling right into Vivienne's arms.

"Nairnie! Did you know they were taking us back to Mablethorpe?"

"Nay! I was awoken by all the yellin' and just figured it out and came to tell ye. That old buzzard is goin' to pay for this."

"We were supposed to stay longer," said Vivienne. "Sheriff Fitch agreed we'd investigate the murder."

Rain pelted down on the deck as the crew members ran to and fro.

"Prepare to dock," shouted out Bear from the helm.

"I'm going to find Zachariah and give him a piece of my mind," snapped Vivienne. "How could he do this behind my back? Nairnie, can you stay with the children?"

"Aye, my lady. And give the old buzzard a piece of my mind for me as well. He is really annoyin' me lately."

Vivienne ventured out into the rain, holding on to anything she possibly could in order not to slip. The sails flapped and whipped about in the wind above her head as the crew frantically tried to lower them to half-mast. The ship tossed about in the water, heading straight for Mablethorpe Castle.

"Shorten the sails before we're ripped apart in the storm. Shorten the sails, I say, before we capsize. Now!" yelled Bear.

"Aye, Cap'n," answered Goldtooth, seeing to the crew since he was the bosun and that was part of his job. "Ramble, there's a line tangled. Get up to the lookout basket and tend to it, quickly."

"Aye, Goldtooth." In bare feet and nothing but a short pair of breeches that just reached his knees, the young lad scurried up the line with the greatest of ease.

"What is going on?" yelled Vivienne, getting soaked from the blowing rain that pelted down.

"Vivienne, get back into the cabin. You can't be out here." Zachariah stopped helping the crew and hurried over to her. Isaac was helping as well.

"Why did we leave the dock? We should be in Whitstable, not going back to Mablethorpe," she shouted. "I never had a chance to find out if Red is my brother."

"It's for the best of the children. I won't have my daughter out here on turbulent waters or exposed to killers. Now go back into the cabin at once. This is an order, not a request."

Just then, a shout was heard from the lines and next came the sound of a man falling. One of the crew slammed down, landing on the deck right at her feet. She looked down to see Birdman lying there with his eyes closed. She was certain he was dead.

"I'm going," she said, her heart beating rapidly from fright. She made it back to the cabin and hurried inside, pushing against the wind but finally managing to close the door behind her.

"Where's my father?" asked a sleepy Starah. "I'm scared of storms."

Grunt looked at Vivienne and whined, knowing something was wrong.

"Ye'll be fine, lassie," said Nairnie, taking Starah into her arms and giving her a big hug.

"We all need to stay put," instructed Vivienne. "There is a raging storm out there, but we'll be safe if we stay in the cabin."

"I'm afraid for Father," cried Starah. "I don't want him to die too."

"He's not going to die. No one is," she told her firmly. However, Vivienne couldn't stop thinking about Birdman, who had just fallen to the deck from up in the lines. Hopefully, he wasn't dead, because then she'd prove to be a liar where Starah was concerned. "We'll all be fine. We're approaching the shores of Mablethorpe and we're almost home."

"Oh, praises be," said Maleine, cuddling up against Wymond. "I am glad we're going home. I've had enough of this."

"Home?" asked Martin. "I don't want to go back to Mablethorpe. I want to stay in Whitstable with my new friend Mouse."

"Mouse," she repeated, quickly scanning the small room. "Where is he, Martin?"

"I don't know," answered the boy with a shrug. "When I woke up, he was gone."

"Mouse left the cabin during the night," said Wymond. "He said he wanted to sleep in the galley. You were so tired that I didn't want to wake you, so I told him it would be all right."

"What?" she asked, wondering why this was the first she'd been told about the boy's disappearance. "Wymond, you should have woken me."

"I'm sorry," he said, sounding so forlorn.

"I didn't see the boy on deck, and Mouse never came to the galley," said Nairnie, shaking her head. "I would have heard him since that dang cat kept me awake all night with her constant meowing."

"Where is Midnight?" cried Starah. "I want my cat."

"She's fine, lassie. She's safe in the galley. I locked her inside with some fish to keep her quiet." Nairnie smoothed back Starah's hair and continued to hug her. "And dinna ye worry, lass. I gave her some prime bits of filet, the bones removed."

"Thank you, but—" Starah broke loose and ran to Vivienne, hugging her and burying her face in Vivienne's wet gown instead. "I'm scared, Lady Vivienne. I don't want anyone else to die."

Vivienne could see that the little girl was affected more than she thought, after seeing Fingers hanging by the neck. Plus, Starah was frightened of storms, and this one was a violent one. Or at least it seemed to be since they were on a ship on the water instead of locked away safely in her uncle's castle.

"I'm frightened too, my lady," said Maleine. "I know I said I wanted to be an investigator like you, but I really don't like being at sea. I'm also afraid Mouse might have gone up to the lookout basket."

"If he did, he's certainly been swept away by the storm by now," said Wymond as the ship rocked violently back and forth. That only made Starah and Maleine cry more.

"I don't want to lose my new friend. Mother, we have to find Mouse." Martin sat on the floor hugging Grunt for comfort. The dog whimpered, lying down and putting his nose between his paws.

Vivienne was almost knocked off her feet when the ship jerked and then listed to the side again. The hammocks swung as if they were being used by ghosts. Cups and an ewer that had held water slid by her feet, and then when the ship listed again, they slid back the other way. She held on tightly to the table, glad it and also the trunks in the room were bolted down.

"Nairnie, I understand now why the sheriff decided to take us back to Mablethorpe," she said softly to the old woman. "It isn't safe for the young ones on the water, or in Whitstable right now either. As much as I hate to admit it, I think Sheriff Fitch made the right decision. It will be good to know the children are all safely back home."

"What about your brother?" asked Nairnie, standing next to the wooden table, but not needing to hold on. Her sea legs and impeccable balance were amazing for such an old woman. The rocking of the ship and the sliding of items back and forth didn't even seem to bother her. Vivienne figured Nairnie had gotten used to this from living with Bear and her grandsons on the high seas when they were still pirates.

There was so much rocking in the storm that Vivienne started feeling like she was about to retch. Especially with the thought of her brother possibly still being alive and the *Falcon* having left before they could find out for sure. The last thing she wanted was to abandon her brother.

"If Adrian is still alive, the sheriff and I will find him, I promise you that," said Vivienne. "I will never give up the search."

"Then ye'd better start thinkin' of a way to convince the sheriff to let ye return to Whitstable with him, because I dinna think he plans on taking ye along."

"We'll see about that," she said, determined to go back to Whitstable, no matter what it took. "We'll just see."

Chapter Eight

"What do you mean they can't find the boy called Mouse?" Zachariah asked his brother several hours after they'd made it back to Mablethorpe, thankfully all still alive. "Why wasn't I informed about this immediately upon our return?" The children and women were safe at the castle, and the storm had let up. Zachariah was back on the ship now with the rest of the crew. The storm had been fierce but Bear and his men had done an incredible job keeping them all safe. Unfortunately, Birdman had taken a hard fall from the lines in the storm and was hurt badly, but the healer at Mablethorpe was tending to him and his wounds, and said he would recover in time but just needed to rest.

"Just like I said, Mouse is not on the ship," reported Isaac with a shrug. "The crew members checked everywhere, including the lookout basket and even in barrels in the hold, but the boy seems to be missing. Do you think he fell overboard in the storm?"

"I hope not," spat Zachariah. "He was a fine, wee lad, and our best hope in finding out who killed Fingers. Not to mention,

I was hoping to get information from him regarding if the redheaded thief might really be Adrian, after all."

"Sheriff," said Bear, coming down the stairs from the stern-castle to join them under the main mast. "If we're going back to Whitstable, we need to leave now. I have to report to King Edward in a few days, so if ye want our help, we mustn't tarry."

"All the repairs are done," said Goldtooth, approaching on Bear's heels. "The men are ready to sail, Cap'n."

"Then let's go." Bear looked over to Jax standing at the side rail. "Bring up the shuttle boat and reel in the rope ladder. Weigh anchor, and prepare to sail," he shouted.

"Aye aye, Cap'n," answered several of his men, including Jax.

"Nay, wait!" came the shout of a female. Zachariah groaned, knowing that voice only too well. "Don't leave without us."

Zachariah looked over to the side of the ship, seeing Vivienne's head pop up as she emerged above the side wall, having climbed up the rope ladder. She carried a large canvas bag over her shoulder. Grunt was sitting inside the bag, looking out and panting. She also wore her father's sword at her side.

"Nay, Vivienne," he groaned, running over to help her, taking the dog first, then putting him down on the deck. "What are you thinking, carrying Grunt in a bag over your shoulder? Do you know how dangerous that is for both of you?"

"Well, I didn't want to leave him behind," she answered, taking his hand as he helped her over the side wall and to the deck.

"I thought I told you to stay behind and watch the children. Starah is still pretty shaken after seeing a man hanging from a noose by his neck. I'm not sure she'll ever be able to get that image out of her mind."

"Don't worry. She's being watched," said Vivienne with a smile, shaking out her gown.

"Thank goodness, that at least Nairnie had sense enough not to return to the ship."

"Someone give me a hand," came Nairnie's voice, as her head popped up next after she, too, had climbed the ladder and approached the top of the sidewall.

"Oh hell, no." Zachariah turned around to see Jax helping Nairnie aboard. She waddled over to him carrying a frying pan. Her ladle swung from her belt.

"Ye boys, take the shuttle back to shore and collect the rest of the bags and boxes we left there," she commanded, and instantly Jax and Coop started climbing down the rope ladder to do as told.

"Nairnie, you can't be here," said Zachariah.

"Sheriff, I need to cook for ye and the men. I brought some fresh rations from the castle's kitchen."

"Old woman, ye need to go back," said Bear, crossing his arms over his chest.

"Dinna even try to send me off this ship, Buzzard," snapped Nairnie. "I willna hear of it, and I refuse to go."

"Ye don't belong at sea," said Bear.

"I've spent a lot of time on the water, and ken just as much about sailin' as ye, so dinna cause me any problems." She reached out and yanked on Bear's long beard. That only seemed to make him angrier.

"Don't do that! How many times do I have to tell ye that I don't like it when you pull my beard."

"Please, stop the fighting," said Vivienne. "We must work hard to get along since we have a murder to investigate. Everyone's participation is important in one way or another."

"Nay. I don't agree with this," said the sheriff. "I want you and Nairnie to go back to shore."

"Sheriff Fitch, we always investigate murders together. Since this one might lead us to my brother, there is nothing you can do or say to stop me from going back to Whitstable with you."

"The same goes for me," added Nairnie.

Isaac held a hand up to his mouth and leaned over to talk to Zachariah. "They're a couple of headstrong, feisty, stubborn wenches, aren't they?"

"You're telling me," he answered. "Fine, Lady Vivienne can stay, but Nairnie you need to watch over the children. That is what I pay you to do."

"Hrmph," she scoffed. "Lady Mablethorpe said she'd care for them. And Maleine and Wymond are doin' so as well. They're stayin' at the castle until we return, instead of goin' back to yer house in town. So, ye see, there is no need for me to be there too. I can help much more by returnin' to Whitstable with ye."

"Nay. I don't like it," said Bear.

"I dinna care what ye like," she answered. "My place is on the *Falcon* and in the galley. Right now, that is where I belong."

"I agree with Nairnie. She needs to be here too," said Vivienne.

"You would," mumbled Zachariah. Grunt barked, almost as if he expected Zachariah to tell him to leave next, and was already objecting.

"I rather like when Nairnie cooks for us," Stitch called down from the helm.

"So do I," agreed Goldtooth. "Her cooking is much better than what Peg Leg makes. His grub tastes like saw dust."

"I do my best," snorted Peg Leg Pate, stomping his wooden leg over the deck as he rushed over to defend himself. "I'm a bloody carpenter, not a cook."

"Bear, I'm surprised ye dinna cook for the crew," said Nairnie. "After all, ye are always braggin' how yer cookin' is better than mine."

"I'm a bloody captain now, not a cook," snapped Bear. "I have important things to do. More important than making up a pot of slumgully."

"I like Nairnie's garlic butter buns better than Bear's," said Ramble, hanging from the lines, holding on with only one hand. "Let her stay, Cap'n. Please?"

"Enough!" Zachariah's hand shot up in the air. "Just let the women stay, because all this squabbling is only going to slow down my investigation. Bear, can we set sail now?"

"Aye," grunted Bear, still giving his wife a nasty stare. "Goldtooth, is the shuttle raised?"

"Not yet, Cap'n," answered Goldtooth, "We have to wait for Jax and Coop to get back with the supplies that Nairnie brought."

"We don't need them," said Zachariah.

"She brought food. And lots of it," said Vivienne. "As well as wine and ale."

"I think we should wait," said Isaac. "I'll head over to the sidewall and then help them unload."

After all the bags and boxes were on deck and the shuttle boat had been hoisted out of the water, they were finally ready to leave.

"Coop, weigh anchor," shouted Bear. "Men, raise the sails. Stitch, take us out of here as fast as ye can before any more mouthy women decide to climb aboard."

"I heard that and dinna appreciate it," snapped Nairnie.

"I want this investigation over with quickly and the old woman out of my hair as soon as possible," said Bear, making the announcement to the entire crew and getting another disgruntled snort from Nairnie.

"Aye aye, Cap'n," answered the crew, all rushing back and forth, going about their chores.

· · ·

VIVIENNE STOOD at the sideboard of the ship, watching as they sailed away from shore. The storm was over now and the sun had actually peeked out from behind the clouds. It was proving to be a pleasant day, after all.

Grunt wandered the ship sniffing around, while Zacharia and Vivienne stood at the rail, side by side, neither of them saying a word. Finally Zachariah spoke.

"I tried my best to make Starah understand that she'd be safer on shore, but she really didn't want to leave me."

"I know. Martin was not happy with me either," Vivienne answered. "But they'll be fine. They're together, and have Maleine and Wymond with them, their animals, too. Plus, my aunt will keep them occupied until we return."

"I'm hoping this won't take more than a few days," he told her. "Of course, the investigation would go a lot faster if Mouse was still here. I should have just questioned him right away like I wanted to do before you talked me out of it."

"The boy was frightened, Sheriff." She looked directly at him. "I was trying to gain his trust."

"Oh. I see."

"Where do you think he is? Would he have left the ship and gone back to Adder?" She certainly hoped not, since that man sounded as if he were a monster, even hitting the little boy and making him bruised.

"Well, not unless he swam ashore, since none of the shuttle boats were missing last night."

"So you think he swam ashore then? Would he dare? During the night?"

Zachariah nodded. "I hope so. Because the only other thing I can think of is that he climbed back up to the lookout basket and was tossed overboard in the storm."

"What?" Her heart jumped. "Please don't say that. Oh, Zachariah, do you really think Mouse drowned?"

"Nay," said Zachariah, staring out at the sea as he spoke. "I'm sure the boy is fine and that we'll find him again once we return to Whitstable."

"Do you really mean that?"

"Vivienne," he said, looking over at her. "Your guess is as good as mine, but it would be better for both of us if we kept faith that Mouse is still alive."

"You're right. I'm sure Mouse is fine. He swam back to the shore."

There was silence for a few minutes until Grunt came over and started to lick Vivienne's hand. She bent over to pet him. "Do you think he went back to get Adrian?" she asked, still thinking about Mouse. "After all, Fingers told you he was friends with Adrian, so mayhap so was Mouse."

"You mean Red." Zachariah looked over at her. "Vivienne, I don't want you getting your hopes up about the boy really being Adrian."

"But you said you were sure about it."

"I said I was pretty sure. Remember what I already told you, he didn't seem to know me or even react to hearing your name. I'm starting to think that mayhap I could have been mistaken. He might just be another boy who looks similar to your brother. I mean...it's been seven years, so I can't remember every detail about him."

"That's why I want to see this boy named Red." Vivienne stood up straight. "I'll know for sure if it is Adrian or not. There is no way I would not recognize my own brother."

"Nay. I'm not going to allow you to go to Rook Row. It's too dangerous."

"I went to Rotten Row with you and even confronted that monster, the Pied Piper. I can handle it, Zachariah. You need my help for this investigation. A young lad is dead. Since the Sheriff of Whitstable doesn't seem to have any interest in finding the killer, it is up to us to bring about justice for Fingers, finding and punishing his murderer ourselves."

"I have to say, you're right about Sheriff Whitstable not seeming to care about finding the killer. He seems to think the more thieves from Rook Row that die, the better."

"There is an urgency to find answers, Sheriff," she told him. "Because the next thief to get murdered might end up being Red. Or Adrian, as I believe him to be. And if he really is my brother and he dies now after having survived for the past seven years...I will never be able to live with myself. I need to find him and save him from that awful Adder and bring him home where he belongs."

"I know, Vivienne. And I agree. Together, we will find out who murdered Fingers. And if the redheaded thief truly is Adrian, I promise you that we will not be leaving Whitstable without him."

Vivienne's emotions soared to hear Zachariah say this. It was all she wanted. In her heart she knew this boy thief truly was Adrian, even if he had forgotten about his family. Even if he no longer remembered her. She was going to find him and bring him home. It was going to be another miracle like when she found her son, Martin. It had been so long, but finally they were going to discover answers. She felt it in her bones that it was true. Before long, she'd be hugging her brother in her arms and reuniting him with part of the family that he lost the day all hell broke loose and all of their lives were changed forever.

They were nearly to Whitstable when Vivienne noticed Grunt acting oddly. The hound kept putting his front paws up atop a large wooden crate that the men had unloaded from the shuttle. It was being kept under the storage area at the bow of the ship for now, since Nairnie said she needed to reorganize the galley before bringing in the rest of the things. Grunt barked occasionally but the weirdest part was that he was wagging his tail.

"Bear, what's in that crate under the forecastle?" she asked, walking over to speak with the ship's captain.

"I don't know, probably food and drink. It's whatever Nairnie packed. But I'll tell ye whatever is in there is heavy. Me and the boys had a hell of a time hauling it up the rope ladder. Why do ye ask?"

"No reason," she said, walking over to her dog. "Grunt? Did you corner a rat?" she asked, knowing Grunt didn't wag his tail when he saw a rat.

"We're approaching Whitstable. Lower the sails to half-mast and prepare to dock," Bear called out to his crew.

"Lady Vivienne, you'll need to get out of the way," said the sheriff, coming to her side. "The crew needs to start with the docking procedure. You might want to wait in the captain's quarters until the anchor is dropped."

"Nay. Not yet." She reached out and flipped open the top of the wooden crate. Grunt put his front paws on the edge of the crate, panting, almost smiling as he looked inside the box. His tail wagged uncontrollably now.

Vivienne slowly peered over the edge of the box, her jaw dropping when she saw what was inside. "Martin!" she gasped, seeing her son curled up atop what looked like smashed loaves of fresh bread and a bushel of apples. He had his wooden sword at his side. His bright blue eyes looked up at her, and a smile spread across his face as he sat up and petted the hound's head with one hand, and a half-eaten apple in the other. "Hello, Mother. And Grunt." He leaned over and kissed Grunt on the snout. "I knew he'd find me. He's a bloodhound and good at his job."

"What the hell is he doing here?" Zachariah walked up behind her, looking over her shoulder.

"Sheriff Fitch, I'm going to help you find murderers, just like my mother does." Martin sprang up, dropping the apple and using both hands to hold on to the crate as he climbed out.

Vivienne grabbed her son and helped him get to the deck.

"Martin, you were supposed to stay back in Mablethorpe. Aunt Ellen is going to be frantic, thinking she lost you," Vivienne scolded her son.

"Nay, she won't. I told Starah I was going to sneak onto the ship so she'll know."

"Please don't tell me my daughter is hiding somewhere here as well." Zachariah frantically looked around.

"Nay, Starah was scared and wanted to stay back at the castle with Midnight," said Martin. "She doesn't like looking at dead people. But it doesn't bother me in the least." He seemed proud of his bravery. Actually, Vivienne admired it too. Such courage let her know that her son was resilient and would someday grow up to be a brave warrior, just like his late grandfather. And his real grandfather—King Edward III. The boy had the makings of someday being a fine knight. That made her smile.

"You shouldn't be here," grumbled Zachariah, as the crew went about preparing to dock the ship.

"You're not going to make me go back to Mablethorpe, are you?" Martin's bottom lip stuck out in a pout.

Vivienne watched Zachariah run a weary hand through his long brown hair. She waited for his answer, but knew he wouldn't take the time to head the ship back to Mablethorpe now. Especially if Bear was in a hurry to embark on his next job from the King.

"We've already wasted enough time," said Zachariah. "We can't afford to return to Mablethorpe again until we've found our killer."

"Our answers," Vivienne added, meaning the matter of Adrian.

"Good. Then I can help you," said Martin.

"Nay. You're a child and will just get in the way." The frustration creasing Zachariah's brow made the worry lines of his face even deeper.

"Sheriff, he can stay. I'll be personally responsible for my son," said Vivienne, pulling Martin to her with his back to her front. She wrapped her arms around him. Grunt reached up to lick the boy's face, making Martin giggle and push the dog away.

"This isn't going to be easy," remarked Zachariah, making Vivienne realize that what he said was exactly true, now that her son was back on board. She needed to watch over him at the same time she searched for her brother. And she was not going to lose either of them, ever again.

Chapter Nine

"So what's our first move?" asked Isaac after the *Falcon* had docked once again on the shores of Whitstable. Isaac and Zachariah stood with Vivienne, overlooking the docks from the ship, while Martin and Grunt stayed by Nairnie who was cooking something up for the men in the galley.

"Aye, what do ye want us to do?" asked Bear, joining them.

"No one leaves the ship until I've questioned them," said Zachariah. "I'm still not convinced the killer wasn't one of the crew."

Bear didn't agree. "Sheriff, I assure you, my men would never commit a murder. Not on the ship. They all have respect for the *Falcon*, as do I. Nay, it was someone from shore. It had to be."

"You could be right, but I need to make certain," said Zachariah. "We'll start the questioning at once."

"What about going to shore?" asked Vivienne. "I want to go look for Mouse and the boy who looks like Adrian."

"In time, Vivienne. First things first. Bear, bring your crew to us one at a time for questioning."

"Aye, Sheriff. But I still say, ye are wasting yer time. It is none of them. Ye should be goin' after that Adder. He's most likely the one who did it."

"Please, Captain. Start bringing them to me."

Vivienne tried to be patient, but the questioning of the crew was painstakingly slow and she longed to go to town and look for Mouse and the boy who looked like Adrian. However, she realized the sheriff was methodical and did things in a certain order. That was something about him that she didn't like at all. She was more prone to jump right in, acting on instinct and by spur of the moment. That was what made her feel comfortable.

"And where were you and Birdman when this hanging happened?" the sheriff asked Jax, since Birdman was injured and back in Mablethorpe, and he'd never had a chance to question him.

"Well, let's see." Jax scratched the stubble on his face. "If I remember correctly, Birdman was feeding the gulls on the pier and I was watching him," said Jax.

"The entire time?" asked Isaac. "You were gone for hours."

Jax shrugged. "You can't rush the exploration of birds, is what Birdman always says. Sometimes, it takes a long time to get them to land on his arm or shoulder. He's been training them to even land on my shoulder now."

"Can anyone vouch for this?" asked the sheriff.

Jax looked confused.

"Did anyone see you two on the piers feeding the birds?" asked Vivienne. "That would be proof that your story is true."

"Well, I suppose so," said Jax. "I don't know."

"We need proof, or your story means nothing," Isaac informed him.

"I ain't got no proof, and neither does Birdman," said Jax. "Unless ye want to ask the birds. They'll tell you that the story is true."

"Now, that is just ridiculous," growled Zachariah. "I am

talking about eyewitnesses who are people, or some kind of physical proof."

"Wait! What about the bird droppings on my shoulder?" asked Jax, reaching around to look, pulling his tunic forward. "Look right there. It's still fresh since it just happened yesterday." He ripped off his tunic, standing there with his hairy, bare chest exposed, and brought the tunic to his nose and took a big sniff. "Take a smell, Sheriff." His waved his tunic under Zachariah's nose. "Pure guano—bird poop, sure as I'm standing here."

"Nay, stop it." Zachariah pushed Jax's hand away. "Now put your tunic back on. You're in the presence of a lady. "Bring us the next two," he called out to Bear.

"Why did you let Jax leave when he had no one to vouch for their whereabouts?" asked Isaac, trying to learn what to do.

"Neither he nor Birdman did it," said Zachariah.

"How do you know?"

"They're too stupid to concoct a plan that they'd have to carry out silently and quickly," said Zachariah, surprised that either of the men could even function on a sailing ship.

"Sheriff, that's not a very kind thing to say," remarked Vivienne.

"All right then, let me say I can't see them killing a strong young lad, let alone hoist him up to the yardarm."

"Birdman is kind of skinny," said Vivienne. "And Jax is pretty short to even reach the lines."

"Those two don't usually go up in the rigging," said Bear, overhearing them. "That's probably why Birdman fell during the storm. They're not really used to it."

"Then bring me two crew members who do go up there," said the sheriff.

"Ramble! Goldtooth! Get down here," shouted Bear. The boy and the man came quickly.

"What is it, Cap'n?" asked Goldtooth, his big body already sweaty even though it was early in the day yet.

"The sheriff wants to question ye," Bear explained.

"Where did both of you go yesterday when you left the ship?" asked Zachariah.

"I spent time in the water," said Ramble. "Then walked some on the beach and sat a while in the sand."

"I took a nap," said Goldtooth, looking the other way.

"Goldtooth is lying," said Vivienne, usually pretty accurate at reading the body actions of people to know if they are telling the truth or not.

"Nay, I'm not." He rubbed his nose.

"He touched his nose. It's a lie," said Vivienne, wishing this questioning would go faster. "Where were you? Really," she asked. "We don't have time for lies."

"Tell them, Goldtooth," commanded Bear. "The truth."

"I'm not lying. I was in bed."

"He was in bed, that's true," said Nairnie, walking up with a basket under her arm. "In bed with a whore, that is. Goldtooth, dinna lie. I saw ye comin' from the hen house along with Coop, and ye both had big smiles on yer faces."

"Is that true?" asked the sheriff.

"Aye, I suppose it is." Goldtooth looked embarrassed, but at the same time happy and sated. "I just didna want to say it in front of a lady, Sheriff. Ye understand."

"And Coop was there too, and you can vouch for each other?" asked Isaac.

"Aye, but Coop wasn't with me and the whore in bed. I don't get into that kind of stuff," said Goldtooth with a fake shiver.

"And Stitch and Peg Leg were drinkin' in the tavern," said Nairnie.

"How do ye know that?" asked Bear. "Old woman, don't tell me you were in the tavern drinking as well."

"It's none of yer business if I was," said Nairnie. "Besides, ye were drinkin' in a tavern all day when ye were supposed to get the oysters and come right back to the ship, so dinna point accusin' fingers at me."

"Nairnie, don't you have something to do in the galley?" asked Zachariah. Vivienne could tell that all the arguing between Bear and Nairnie was making Zachariah irritable and uncomfortable. She didn't like it either.

"Sheriff, it's getting late," said Vivienne. "If we're going to go to town before it gets dark, shouldn't we get moving?"

"How many more of the crew need to be questioned yet?" asked the sheriff. "Besides Coop, Stitch, and Peg Leg, since Nairnie vouched for them?"

"Just Scythe and Tyne," Bear told him.

"I saw the two of them on the docks playing dice with some of the sailors," Vivienne told him.

"But I'm sure they weren't there all day," said Zachariah. "I'd like to question them anyway."

Bear brought the men forward.

"I hear you two were playing dice after you left the ship," said the sheriff.

"Ye mean when they sneaked off the ship against my orders," spat Bear.

"We weren't gone that long," said Scythe.

"But it was long enough to win enough for a few beers from the tavern," said Tyne.

"Who did you play dice with?" asked Isaac.

"Just some of the sailors from the other ships," said Scythe. "But they all left when we started winning so much."

"Not all of them," said Tyne. "Remember, there was that

one man in the hooded cloak who stopped to play dice, but he wouldn't talk when we tried to start up a conversation."

"That's right," said Scythe. "I almost forgot about him. He was in such a hurry until he saw us gambling. He played a few rounds, but was horrible at it and left as soon as we had all his money." Scythe chuckled and picked up the pouch of coins at his side and jingled it.

"Have you ever seen that man before?" This question came from Vivienne.

"Nay," they both said.

"Then again, we never really saw his face," said Tyne. "I just remember he smelled really fishy."

"I'm sure all the sailors on the dock smell like fish. Thank you," said Zachariah, even though the men weren't much help at all.

"I have food ready for the crew and I dinna want it gettin' cold," shouted Nairnie from the galley.

"Nairnie, yer food is not as important as the sheriff's work," complained Bear.

When it looked like the two of them were going to start arguing again, the sheriff stood up and raised his hand in the air. "I am finished with the questioning."

"Yay," said Martin. "That means we can eat. Did you hear that, Grunt?"

"Lady Vivienne, Isaac, let's go to town."

"Now?" asked Isaac, seeming upset. "But Nairnie has food for us."

"We can get a bite to eat while we're out," said the sheriff. "I don't want to waste any more time."

"I'd better come with ye, Sheriff," said Bear. "After all, I know the proprietors and some of the townsfolk since I come here every year, sometimes more than once."

"Ye'd better not ken the whores," scolded Nairnie.

Bear looked up and a muscle ticked in his jaw.

"I think that is a great idea," Vivienne quickly added. "Nairnie, can I ask you to watch over Martin until we return?"

"I suppose next ye'll want me to watch the hound, too," said the old woman, still glaring at her husband.

"Nay, Grunt will come with us. Come on, Grunt," she called out, bringing the dog as well as Martin running. "Martin, you stay here and be good for Nairnie." She bent over and hugged her son. "And don't leave the ship."

"Where are you going?" asked Martin.

"We're going to town," Isaac answered for her.

"I want to go too. I want to see if I can find Mouse." The boy's bright blue eyes lit up in excitement. He was always up for a new adventure.

"Nay, sweetheart. It's too dangerous." Vivienne smoothed back Martin's long blond bangs. "But I promise you we'll do our best to find Mouse, so don't worry."

"I don't want to stay here." The boy pouted, crossing his arms over his chest. "Even Grunt gets to go, but I'm always left behind."

"It's important that you stay here," said Zachariah.

"Why?" asked the boy.

"Because...because..." Zachariah looked over to Vivienne for help.

"Because if Mouse sees the ship, he might come back looking for you," she told her son. "He is frightened of the crew, and so shy that you're the only one he'll talk to."

"Oh, all right. I'll wait here and watch for him." Martin smiled, the explanation seeming to satisfy him for now.

"We won't be gone long," called out Vivienne as the four of them headed to the ladder to disembark. "Martin, you be sure to mind Nairnie."

"And save some food for us," called out Isaac, always thinking about his stomach.

"Thanks for the help with Martin," said Zachariah, once they'd left the ship and headed down the docks. "That was quick thinking back there."

"It wasn't a lie, if that's what you mean," she told him. "If Mouse sees the ship, he might come back looking for Martin, if he is still here in town. Especially if he's scared of that awful man named Adder."

"Martin and Mouse did seem to get along quite well," agreed Isaac. "Mayhap your son will be an asset to us in this investigation after all."

"Let's hope so," said Vivienne, glancing back to the ship where Martin stood sadly at the rail, waving his hand over his head. Grunt looked back at the ship and gave a playful bark. Vivienne feared for Martin's safety. Even though she'd told him to stay on the ship and mind Nairnie, she wasn't certain the boy would really listen to her. After all, he was her son. And if Vivienne were in his position, the last thing she'd do is to stay behind and just wait.

THEY'D SPENT a few hours in town, questioning people, but no one seemed to be of any use. The people of the town of Whitstable didn't want to help outsiders. And now that they were about to go to Rook Row, the Sheriff of Whitstable suddenly decided he'd go along with them. That was not at all what Zachariah wanted. If they did find Mouse or Red, the sheriff would want to immediately arrest them. If that happened, Zachariah would never get the chance to question either of them. Or find to out if Red was really Vivienne's brother. Even if they didn't solve the killing of Fingers, the most important part was to find out if Red was really Adrian.

"Sheriff Fitch, if we see any of those pesky thieves, I'm going to arrest them immediately, no questions asked," said Whitstable's sheriff. "I need to clean up this town once and for all."

Vivienne looked over to Zachariah in horror. He knew what she was thinking. If he was going to have any chance of talking to the boy thieves, he had to distance himself from Sheriff Whitstable.

"Sheriff, I think it might help in the search for the killer if we split up," said Zachariah. "Lady Vivienne and I will check out the area near the tavern. Bear, why don't you go with Sheriff Whitstable to the other side of the street, down by the whorehouse."

"Whorehouse. Nay. Not me," said Bear, shaking his head. "If Nairnie even thinks I went near the whorehouse, she'll be hitting me with her ladle until I leave on my next mission for the King. I'll never hear the end of it."

"I'll go with him," offered Isaac. "I wouldn't mind looking at a few pretty women."

"Good. Then, I'll check out the establishment back at the dock," said Bear. "I know a lot of the sailors, and they might talk to me without the threat of a sheriff looking over my shoulder."

"Good idea," said Zachariah. "We'll all meet back at the ship two hours after sunset."

"Nay, not me. I don't roam the streets after dark unless there's a problem," said the Sheriff of Whitstable. "I'll be headed back to town as soon as the sun hits the horizon."

They all started heading away, but Zachariah grabbed his brother and pulled him to the side. "Keep the sheriff away from any of the boy thieves," he whispered. "I can't take the chance that he'll lock up Mouse or Red."

"Sure thing, Brother." Isaac nodded and headed after Whitstable's sheriff, while Bear ambled down Rook Row, nodding to the questionable crowd as he made his way back to the docks.

"Finally," said Vivienne, releasing a puff of air from her mouth. "I thought Sheriff Whitstable would never leave. Now, can we please look for Mouse and Adrian?"

"Red," he corrected her. "And yes, we can. I suggest we head over to the area where I saw both of them the last time I was here. They must be working from close by. Mayhap, if we're lucky, we'll even run across Adder while we're here."

"Oooo, I don't even want to think about him." Vivienne wrapped her arms around her. "He sounds like a horrible man. I mean, what kind of a person would force young boys to steal for him?"

They started to walk with Grunt leading the way.

"Vivienne, there is something I don't believe I told you regarding Red."

"What is that?"

"Fingers told me that the boy was brought to Adder seven years ago, and the man who brought him here was paid a fee to hand him over."

Zachariah saw tears in her eyes, even though he could tell she was trying her best not to become emotional.

"I don't believe Adrian would have gone willingly and without a fight. Something just doesn't seem right. If he was brought here, it wasn't by his own free will."

"I agree with you," said Zachariah, seeing a quick flash of someone hiding in between the tavern and the row of neighboring shopfronts. He swore it was a child. "Vivienne, I think I just saw one of the boy thieves watching us."

"Where?" She started to look, so he grabbed her arm to keep her from turning.

"Nay. Don't turn around. You might alarm him. I'm going to

double back and see if I can catch him. You stay with Grunt and keep on walking."

"Nay, I want to come with you."

"I need you as a distraction. Work with me."

"But there are a lot of scary-looking men around here," she said, turning her head slightly one way and then the other. "Not to mention, the whores are giving me dirty looks. Now, I wish I would have brought my cloak along."

"I won't let you get out of my sight. Plus, I have my blade with me, if there is trouble," he said, tapping the hilt of his sword.

"That scarce matters. You won't be at my side." Vivienne frowned at him. "I wish I would have brought my sword from the ship now. But you were in too much of a hurry to let me get it."

"You have your dagger, don't you?"

"I do."

"Good," he said, holding her by her elbow. "Keep your hand on the hilt of it, but don't draw the blade unless you feel threatened. Otherwise, you might bring about an attack that could be avoided."

"You're not making me feel very comfortable. Are you sure I can't just stay with you?"

"You've got the hound. He'll protect you. And like I said, I won't go far. I'll constantly have you in my sight."

"All right," she said, letting out a deep breath. "But please, hurry. I really don't like being alone here."

"I promise. Now go. I've got a thief to catch."

Vivienne continued to walk down the middle of the street, reaching down to put her hand on Grunt, not wanting him to get too far away from her. "Keep your nose to the ground and bark if you expect trouble," she mumbled, not sure Grunt understood any of that, but feeling like she had to tell him. She hadn't gone far before she sensed someone watching her. Her stomach churned, the same way it did the night her family had been attacked by bandits on the road. She stopped in her tracks, noticing Grunt stopped too. The dog looked behind her and whimpered slightly.

"Adrian? Is that you?" Vivienne spun on her heel to see a boy with red hair reaching out for the pouch of coins attached to her side. He jerked back when he realized he'd been caught. "God's eyes, it's really you!" she whispered, recognizing her brother's slight smearing of freckles across his nose and face. He was much taller than seven years ago, almost as tall as her. He wore ragged and torn clothes and pretty much all of him was smeared with dirt. His hands were so filthy that they almost looked black. He wore a cap on his head, pulled down low, but she could still see his long, flaming-red hair. "Adrian, it's me. Your sister, Vivienne," she said, not wanting to move quickly for fear she'd scare him away. "Don't you remember me?"

He slowly shook his head, his green eyes perusing her from head to foot. When he looked like he was about to run, she knew she needed to do something to stop him. "Wait," she said, hurriedly releasing the ties holding her money pouch to her belt. "Here, take this." She held it out, the pouch dangling from her fingers. "I just want to take you home. To Mablethorpe. Where you belong."

The boy seemed frightened of her, but then he quickly snatched the pouch of coins and held it reverently in two hands. His gaze dropped to the dog.

"That's Grunt. My hound," she told him. Grunt started barking and looked as if he was going to chase the boy.

"Stay, Grunt," she commanded, at the same time seeing the fear in the lad's eyes. "Don't worry, Grunt won't hurt you. Adrian, you have a young nephew named Martin, and I want you to meet him. Oh, Adrian, don't you know me?"

"My name is Red," he spat, shoving the pouch of coins in the bag he wore over his shoulder. "And, nay, I don't know you, so leave me alone." He turned to go.

"Nay! Please don't leave, Adrian." She reached out for him, but it was too late. In a flash, he'd disappeared down a dark alleyway and the ruffians on Rook Row started closing in around her. "Stay away," she shouted. Grunt barked and showed his teeth as a couple of sweaty, dirty men got nearer to her.

"Back off! Leave her alone. Vivienne, are you all right? I heard you shouting." Zachariah ran to her, his sword drawn as his gaze flashed back and forth. "I am the Sheriff of Mablethorpe and will arrest anyone who takes another step toward the lady."

Slowly, the group of men moved away from her, and then took off, the lot of them disappearing into doorways where whores welcomed them with open arms.

"Get yer own street, ye hussy," shouted a whore. "We don't share with the likes of ye."

"Come on, Vivienne. It's time to go." Zachariah still held his sword in one hand and clutched her wrist with his other hand, so escorting her down the street. Grunt trotted alongside them, still growling lowly. The sun had started to set and darkness would cover the land soon.

"Nay, we can't go." She fought against the sheriff's hold, pulling out of his grip. "Zachariah, you were right. I saw Adrian. I saw him and gave him my money pouch."

"You did what? Why?"

"I wanted him to trust me," she told him. "He's alive! He didn't die seven years ago, after all."

"Vivienne, mayhap you're mistaken."

"Nay, I'm not," she ground out, becoming angry with Zachariah. "You were right. It is Adrian, and for some reason he

131

doesn't remember me at all. Zachariah, he went down a dark alley. Let me show you the one. We need to go after him and bring him back to the ship." She started to retreat, but this time he grabbed her by the arm and would not let go.

"I said *no*. Now stop it, Vivienne. It's getting dark and you are a comely lady in the worst part of town. I don't like the looks of what I'm seeing. I'm taking you back to the ship right now."

"But I need to find Adrian."

"He's never going to go with you if he doesn't know you. Leave this to me and Isaac. We'll come back at first light and search for him. But I don't want you back on Rook Row again."

Vivienne looked over her shoulder as the sheriff pulled her down the street against her will. She hoped to see her brother again, but instead she just saw drunkards and whores and people who looked like they wanted to hurt her. She supposed Zachariah was right. This wasn't a safe place for a lady. But now that she'd seen Adrian and knew that he hadn't died after all, her heart soared with joy. She might go back to the ship, but she would never agree to leave Whitstable unless her brother was with her.

Chapter Ten

"I still can't believe I saw Adrian, Nairnie." Vivienne sat with the others on the deck of the *Falcon* later that day, finishing off a meal of pottage that included roasted pork, cooked carrots, and oats that she'd brought directly from the castle. They also had boiled eggs and chunks of hard cheese, accompanied by crusty brown bread, cider, and ale. The woman had even talked Cook from Mablethorpe Castle into throwing in some candied ginger for a sweet treat. Of course, Nairnie probably gave Cook the evil eye and threatened to hit him with her ladle if he didn't cooperate. Either way, if it weren't for Nairnie being there, they'd most likely be dining on naught but salted herring and oatcakes and some half-rotten apples right now. "My little brother isn't dead after all. I am so happy that I could just spit."

"Go ahead and spit, lassie," said Peg Leg Pate, turning his head and spitting onto the deck. "It'll make you feel more like one of the crew."

"Bid the devil, I don't allow spitting on board. Stop that, Pate," Bear reprimanded the one-legged man. Bear leaned back on the railing of the *Falcon*, with whisky in his grip. Ever since they'd all returned from town, Nairnie and Bear continued to quarrel. Nairnie accused Bear of stopping at the whorehouse and drinking in the taverns, and Bear accused her of being an old busybody who couldn't cook a good meal if her life depended on it. After the sheriff warned them both that he wouldn't put up with their arguing anymore, and that they were distracting him from doing his job, they both ended up going to opposite ends of the ship to avoid each other. They hadn't spoken to one another since then. It was sad to see. Bear and Nairnie had seemed to be so much in love when Bear first showed up at the sheriff's house with his crew. He'd even hugged and kissed Nairnie and picked her up and spun her around. Vivienne wanted to see them act like that again. She wasn't sure what was happening between them.

"How did yer brother look, lassie?" asked Nairnie, starting to collect the dirty plates, which were wooden and square. The square dishes insured that the plates wouldn't roll away if the seas got rough.

"Adrian looked...grown up," said Vivienne with a smile. "I remember him as a child, but now he looked so much more like a man. A man who was dirty and smelly, that is. However, a young man just the same." She sighed deeply, still smiling. She noticed Martin coming back for seconds, and putting a lot of food on his wooden plate. More than he usually ate. It was odd but she figured it was because he was a hungry, growing boy. "Martin, you're quiet tonight. Aren't you excited to know that your uncle is still alive, after all?"

"Aye, Mother. That's nice." He got up with the plate of food and started walking, going slow as if he didn't want to spill it. Grunt's nose was right next to his arm in case he did. The dog followed Martin wherever he went.

"Where are ye goin' lad? Ye havena even finished eatin' yet," said Nairnie.

"I know. I'm going back to the cabin to eat," said Martin, still walking slowly and keeping his eyes on the mountain of food. A hunk of cheese teetered and fell off but never had the chance to hit the deck. Grunt's jaws opened wide and were there waiting. The hound downed the cheese in one bite and licked his lips, looking for more.

"Martin, why are you going to the cabin to eat?" asked Vivienne. "You should stay with the rest of us. And why in heaven's name do you have so much food on your plate? You can't possibly eat it all."

"I got some food for Grunt too," said the boy, still walking toward the cabin. Grunt got in front of him and he stumbled slightly, almost dropping the plate, but managing to balance the food. However, a hunk of bread fell off, and the dog hurriedly gobbled that up too.

"Wait, let me help you carry that so you don't spill it all before you even get to the cabin." Vivienne got up to help him, but before she could make her way over to him, he stopped her.

"Nay, Mother! I can do it myself," he called out over his shoulder.

"All right," she said with a smile, knowing how independent Martin was and that he liked to prove he could do anything. "Then, I'll just come and keep you company while you are eating." She had been so distracted today and gone on shore for a long time, while Martin had stayed back on the ship. She hadn't spent much time with her son, but wanted to do so now to make up for it.

"I said no, Mother! I just want to be alone." Martin's words shocked Vivienne, and it hurt her heart that he didn't want to be with her.

"Well, all right," she said, wondering if Martin was just a little jealous, since all she'd been talking about since she returned to the ship was Adrian. She figured that must be it. After all, Martin had been missing for seven years too, and when she discovered he was her son, she talked all the time about him. Now, he wasn't the main subject of her conversations anymore. Since Martin liked to be the center of attention, this must truly be bothering him, she realized. "Go ahead then, Son," she told him. "I'll be there soon and we can talk if you want." She was giving him an opportunity to tell her how he felt and hoped that he would take it.

"I don't feel like talking. I'll probably just go right to sleep when I'm done eating." He stopped and turned around to face her and yawned, but for some reason it seemed a little fake to her.

"Tired, are you?" she asked.

"Really tired." He yawned again. "I think it's from all this sea air. Come on, Grunt."

"Stay in the cabin and if you leave it, be sure to tell me," she called to her son.

"All right, Mother."

"Good night," she called out, as he disappeared into the cabin with the dog and closed the door behind him. She didn't really worry about him since she knew he was safe if Grunt was with him. The dog looked after the boy and would let her know if anything was wrong. Still, Martin was a child on a ship filled with hardened ex-pirates, and she wanted to be aware of his whereabouts every minute of the day.

"What's wrong with him?" asked Isaac, using a splinter of wood to pick the food from his teeth. He leaned up against the bulkhead, making himself comfortable.

"I think Martin is just a little jealous since I've found Adrian," she whispered. "I can't blame him. After all, I haven't been paying much attention to him since he sneaked onto the ship."

"Martin does seem to be acting odd," agreed the sheriff, joining them. "Lady Vivienne, mayhap you should go back to the cabin and get some shut-eye too."

"Nay, I couldn't sleep now if I tried. I'm too excited."

"Get to your evening chores, boys," said Bear. "I'm going up to rest my eyes on the sterncastle. Stitch, you take first watch."

"Aye, Cap'n," said the older man, picking up his plate and handing it to Nairnie.

"Dinna give me yer plate. Ye lazy fools can at least put the dirty dishes in the barrel of water. Do I need to do everything around here?"

"I'll take that, Stitch." Vivienne jumped to her feet and collected the dirty plate from the man, and then started picking up the other crew members' plates as well.

"Ramble, help the old lady with the dishes," came Bear's command, as he disappeared up the stairs in the darkness, not even using a lantern to light his way.

"Me? I was going to go up to the lookout basket to watch for another storm. And to gaze at the stars while I'm there. I think it's going to be a clear night, actually."

"Don't worry about it, Ramble. Isaac will be happy to help Nairnie instead," said the sheriff.

"I will?" Isaac looked like he didn't like the sound of that. "But I'm a deputy. Deputies don't do dishes."

"You're still in training and will do anything I tell you to do. Now take the dirty plates from Lady Vivienne because I need to talk to her."

"Fine," said Isaac, taking the dishes from Vivienne. "But don't think I'm going to be doing this back home, even if I am staying with you." Isaac collected up dirty plates and headed to the galley, talking softly with Nairnie as they went.

"Come up to the bow of the ship with me," said Zachariah, holding out his hand to escort her.

"All right," she said, wondering why he was acting so gallant aboard a pirate ship. It certainly didn't seem the place to do so.

They climbed the steps to the forecastle and stopped at the railing to stare up at the stars.

"It is proving to be a beautiful night, Ramble is right," said Zachariah. "But not quite as beautiful as you."

"What?" she gasped, since that took her by surprise. Surely he hadn't forgotten that they'd agreed to keep their relationship professional only. "That almost sounded to me like something a man would say when he was trying to woo a woman. It doesn't sound like something a sheriff should be telling his partner in crime solving."

"I'm not saying it as a sheriff, Vivienne. I'm saying it as...a man."

"Really." She wondered what he was up to. Yes, they were attracted to each other, but this was so unnatural of him to speak to her like this with so many others around. "You're just trying to get my mind off of Adrian, aren't you? Well, it's not going to work, Sheriff. I saw my brother, and now I am more than determined to bring him home. I will not let him—"

Her words were cut off when Zachariah's mouth pressed down upon hers in a full-blown kiss. His lips were soft and warm and very appealing. His manly essence filled her senses, suddenly making her feel heady. Without thinking what she was doing, she raised her hands and rested them on his shoulders as she returned his kiss, right there under the stars in the vast evening sky.

"What's this? A little tryst?" came Scythe's voice from the dark, causing Vivienne to quickly pull away from Zachariah. She turned and gently touched her mouth with the tips of her fingers.

"Mayhap the sheriff is going to roger the lady at the rail," said Tyne, laughing. Both of the men were standing in the dark watching them, and they'd been so quiet, that Vivienne didn't even know they were there. And when they moved closer, she could smell the whisky on their breath.

"That's enough with that kind of talk," growled Zachariah.

"Why didn't you make your presence known?" asked Vivienne. "You're being intruders."

"It's our ship. Our home," said Tyne.

"That's right. You two are the intruders, not us," added Scythe. In the moonlight, the two men looked even more eerie than they did in the light of the day.

"If you don't mind, I'd like a little privacy talking to Lady Vivienne about the murder," said Zachariah.

Tyne raised the side of his mouth in a half-cocked smile. "So that's what you're calling what just happened? Talking about a murder?"

"That's my business, not yours," said Zachariah. "Now please leave. We'd like a little privacy."

"Sure, we'll go," said Scythe. "But when you're done, we'd like a turn to have some *privacy* with her too."

Zachariah's hand went to the hilt of his dagger, but before he could draw it, a hand shot out in the dark and gripped Scythe tightly around the throat. Scythe gagged and struggled to get free.

"If I hear talk like that on my ship again, ye're getting keelhauled. Savvy?" growled Bear with eyes of fire. "Show some respect to the lady, ye wretched cur. Don't ye know how to act around a woman?"

Scythe wiggled out of his grip, rubbing his throat. "Me? You don't seem to show that wife of yours respect at all. So, I'm not acting any different than you."

"What I do is my business," snapped Bear. "Now both of ye go sleep in the hold tonight, because I want ye out of my sight. If I see you on deck again before the sun rises, it's only going to anger me more." He pushed his face up against Scythe. "And believe me," he said in a deep, snarly voice. "Ye don't want to see me mad."

"We're going," said Tyne, pulling his friend along with him. "Come on, Scythe. You can fight off the rats in the hold while I hold the lantern to find them." They hurried away down to the dank bowels of the ship where no one ever slept by choice.

As soon as they left, Bear apologized. "My lady. Sheriff. Sorry about the rudeness of my men. I hope ye can both forgive them and forget what ye heard just now, even though I know it won't be easy."

"It's fine, Bear. I'm not offended," said Vivienne.

"Well, I am. I don't like those two and don't want them near Lady Vivienne or her son again."

"I'll see to it, Sheriff," answered Bear. "Now, I'll leave you two to yourselves then." He turned to go.

"Wait, Bear. I'd like to talk to you," said Vivienne to stop him.

"Me? About what?" he asked, seeming surprised and perplexed all at the same time.

"I hope you don't mind me asking, but I was curious. Why are you and Nairnie arguing so much? I mean, I know you love each other. I saw how you two acted when you showed up at the sheriff's home the other night. Things seem so...different now."

"My lady, Nairnie is a hot-headed wench who won't let me get a word in to defend myself," he told her. "And even if I do, she doesn't believe me. It seems as if she just doesn't trust me anymore and I don't need that kind of treatment from anyone. Especially not my wife."

"Oh, I see. I'm sorry," said Vivienne. "Did you want me to talk to her for you?"

"Nay," said Bear, sadly shaking his head. "It's too late for talking. It's as plain as the nose on my face to see that we are no longer compatible. I'm afraid that things have soured and it's over between us. Well, good night, Sheriff Fitch and Lady Vivienne. If Scythe and Tyne give ye any more trouble, just let me know and I'll take care of them." He left, disappearing into the dark like the others.

"I wonder why they can't get along?" asked Vivienne.

"I wonder why no one has told Bear that he can't see his own nose," added Zachariah, making them both smile as he referred to Bear's analogy.

"Sheriff, I think he meant it was plain for others to see, just like the nose on his face. He wasn't talking about himself." She said the words and then wasn't really sure. "I mean...I think. Or should I say, I hope." They both chuckled this time. With Bear, one never knew what he really meant. Bear and his crew were quite unusual, and Vivienne realized they couldn't really compare them to anyone else they knew.

"Every couple has their problems, Vivienne. Just let them work it out on their own, and please don't get involved."

"I was only trying to help."

"Don't," he told her firmly. "I have a feeling it might only make things worse."

"Mayhap you're right. I'll mind my own business. It's just that I guess I feel sorry for them." They both were silent for a few minutes, continuing to stare up at the stars. Then they both started to talk at once.

"Zachariah, we need to talk," said Vivienne, at the same time he said, "Vivienne, we need to talk."

"Go ahead," she said with a nod. "You first."

"All right." He wet his lips with his tongue and then cleared his throat. "I'm sorry for overstepping my bounds. I know we had an agreement to keep our distance except in a professional manner, and I broke that promise. I wasn't keeping my word, was I?"

"Nay, I suppose not," she said, wetting her lips too, savoring

the taste of his manly essence, wanting to experience the pleasure again. But this wasn't the time or place. They had a murder
to solve, and her son, as well as an entire crew of ex-pirates, were
on board. Plus, she had to keep her head free of anything not
tied to Adrian or their murder investigation. What she needed
was a plan to find and bring back her brother in a timely
manner. "I'm sorry too, Zachariah. I guess it was just such a
beautiful night that I got a little carried away. I won't let it
happen again."

"Nay. Neither will I." He looked down into the water over
the side of the ship. "We won't ruin things between us. We'll
just remain friends and partners in solving murders only from
now on. I mean, that's what we both want, right?"

"Yes, Sheriff. Of course it is." She told him what she felt he
wanted to hear, but deep down she was no longer sure she still
felt this way. His kiss had awakened something inside her that
had more or less been dead since the death of her husband. But
mayhap he was right. They shouldn't tempt fate. They had a
good friendship and she enjoyed solving murders at his side.
Why ruin things when they were going so well? From now on,
she had to force herself to be naught but his friend and partner
when she was with him.

They were both quiet again for a few minutes until she
finally broke the silence.

"I never even had a chance to ask you. Did you, Bear, or
Isaac happen to find out any information that might help us
solve the murder of Fingers and to find his killer?"

"Nay, I'm sorry to say today was naught but a waste of time.
We discovered nothing new. We still don't have anything at all
to go on."

Her head snapped up and she looked directly at him. "Nay,
that's not true. We found Adrian, so that is something. Sheriff,

my brother is not dead after all! And who knows. That alone might somehow help us in solving the murder."

"Vivienne, I don't want you to think that things are going to be the same between you and Adrian if you happen to convince him to come back to Mablethorpe with you. I mean, he doesn't even seem to know who you are. And don't be surprised if he doesn't want to return with you, or for that matter, even talk to you or have anything to do with you at all."

"I understand. It'll take some time. But I plan on finding him again and convincing him to come back here to the ship, where we can talk about what happened seven years ago. I also want to find out why he doesn't seem to remember me."

"He might never get his memories back. That is something you are going to have to accept, my lady."

"I know. And if I have to accept that, I will. But mark my words, I will never stop trying to help him remember his life before he was a thief. And to remember Mother and Father, and even me."

"Don't forget, we've only got a few days before Bear has to return and report in to the King for his next mission."

"Then we'll have to search quickly for Adrian. Because I refuse to leave Whitstable without him."

"My lady, unless I must remind you, we are in the middle of a murder investigation. A young lad was hanged on this ship. The ship we sailed here on. If the Sheriff of Whitstable wanted to, he could arrest Bear for the murder."

"What?" She blinked several times, trying to comprehend this. "But Bear didn't do it. He was in town with you and Isaac the entire time. Didn't you tell him that?"

"He didn't ask," said Zachariah. "But thankfully for us, Sheriff Whitstable doesn't seem interested in going after the thief's murderer. In fact, he doesn't seem to care about the poor lad's hanging at all. But if he changes his mind, and it ends up that we can't find the real killer, one of us aboard this ship might end up getting blamed for the murder. And be assured, if that happens, it is going to be a very bad thing."

"We can't have that," said Vivienne. "That would be awful."

"Nay, we can't have that," he agreed. "So I need you to promise me that you're going to focus on helping me find the murderer, instead of being obsessed with bringing your brother back to the ship against his will."

"It's not against his will."

"Isn't it? You told him who you were and asked him not to leave, yet he did. He didn't want to go anywhere with you, Vivienne. You have to accept that he doesn't know you, so why would he listen to you at all?"

"I still can't believe that. I am sure that, deep down, he wants to know the truth about what I told him."

"Nay. All he wanted was the money you gave him. Listen to me, Vivienne, Adrian is no longer the brother you knew and loved. Evil men like Adder have changed him and it has scarred him deeply. Now he is naught but a common street rat. A thief. He doesn't care about you, or Mablethorpe or his past life at all, since he doesn't remember it. And you can't bring those memories back or make him change back into the boy he used to be. It's too late. Seven years is a long time. He is now an entirely different person."

She reached out and slapped him hard across his cheek. His head turned to the side from the force, and his hand went to his face to cover the sharp sting. When he turned back to her, he looked shocked that she'd hit him.

"I don't ever want you to talk to me like that again," she warned him. "I have held on to a thread of hope for the last seven years, and now that I find out my brother is still alive, you are telling me to let him go? How can you be so heartless? I thought you supported me with this quest?"

"I'm sorry, Vivienne. I didn't mean it like that. It's just that, I don't want to see you hurt."

"It's too late for that, Sheriff. You have just cut me to the bone, and that pains me deeply." She tried to storm off, but he reached out and grabbed her arm to stop her from going.

"Vivienne, wait. We need to discuss this."

"I have nothing more to say to you tonight," she spat, feeling her heart breaking. "I thought you were on my side. I believed you when you said you never stopped trying to find Adrian or my parents' murderers."

"It's true. I never stopped searching."

"Well, it seems like you have now, or you wouldn't be telling me to let Adrian go."

"I never said to let him go. You are twisting my words."

"Nay, I'm not! Even if you didn't say that directly, I know it is what you meant."

"You are letting your pain keep you from thinking clearly."

"You're not here to support me," she kept on going, letting her feelings flow out of her, not trying to stop them. "Admit, it Sheriff. You are here to dash my dreams, that's all."

"Adrian doesn't know us anymore, Vivienne." He sounded as if he were starting to lose his patience. "How are you possibly going to deal with that? I know you. You'll be devastated when he refuses to return to Mablethorpe with you because he has a new life now. I don't want to see what that will do to you."

"Well, you won't have to, because that is not going to happen. Before I leave Whitstable, Adrian will remember me as well as everything about his old life. It'll all come back to him, you'll see."

"You can't know that."

"He'll come to me with open arms and be that same boy I knew and loved." She couldn't hold back the tears from falling now. Zachariah boldly reached up and brushed a tear from her

145

cheek with his hand, but she pushed it away. "And please don't touch me so intimately, or ever kiss me again," she snapped. "Our relationship is not the same as when we grew up together, either. Now we're professionals, and only working with each other to solve murders and bring about justice. And there will be nothing else between us. Did you hear me? There will be...nothing more." She turned and ran back to the cabin, almost stumbling in the dark, when she realized the crew members were lying belly-up on the deck and she hadn't seen them through her tears.

At last, she pushed open the cabin door, and saw Martin look up to her with wide eyes. He was on the pallet on the floor and the dog was lying next to him. He yanked at the blanket, pulling it over him and dog, creating a large lump beneath it. "What's wrong, Mother?" he asked.

"I'm just a bit sad, that's all," she told him, trying to regain her composure and not worry her son with her problems. "Martin, I want to hug you." She went to him, holding out her arms, needing to feel love from someone right now. Sadly, instead of falling into her arms like she hoped he would do, he turned onto his side, putting his back to her, and hunkering down under the covers.

"Not tonight. I'm tired," he said, closing his eyes tightly and doing another of his fake yawns.

Vivienne looked down at him, her heart hurting. She didn't understand why Martin was treating her this way. It only added to her confusion as well as her irritation with the sheriff. She needed love and compassion right now more than anything else. She needed understanding. A hug. A kiss.

But she got none.

Vivienne blew out the candle and crawled up into the hammock at the other side of the room, not bothering to undress. She felt like wailing her lament, but didn't want

Martin to know she was crying. So she bit the inside of her mouth so hard that she tasted the irony tang of blood on her tongue. Her world was crashing down hard around her and she didn't understand why. She'd just found her brother after seven years of thinking the boy was dead. This should be the happiest time in her life, but yet she felt so filled with grief and sorrow right now instead of happiness and joy.

And then, just as she thought she'd die from holding in her unhappy feelings, a little voice spoke to her in the darkness. It was a light shining through in the bleak fog of all that had made her so sad and confused. It was exactly what her heart needed at this trying moment.

"Good night. I love you, Mother," said Martin, bringing back just a spark of hope and light inside her once more.

"Good night, sweetheart. I love you too, Martin. My son." She turned onto her side in the hammock and hugged the pillow to her chest, feeling that mayhap things weren't so bleak after all. And hopefully, tomorrow would be a much better day for them all.

Chapter Eleven

"You did...what?" Isaac asked Zachariah the next morning as the two of them leaned on the ship's railing atop the sterncastle, staring back at the shore. It had been a restless, sleepless night for Zachariah, and he couldn't still his mind after what had happened with Vivienne yesterday.

"You heard me," mumbled Zachariah. "I did something stupid. I kissed Vivienne. Damn it, what the hell was I thinking? Now I went and ruined everything between us." He ran his hand over the back of his neck, feeling the tension residing there, twisting into a tight knot.

"My guess is that you were thinking you're attracted to her," said his brother, pulling an apple out of his pouch.

"Obviously. And where did you get that apple?"

"I snitched it from the barrels in the hold," said Isaac looking at the apple and shining it on his sleeve.

"Don't be taking food without asking."

"I can't help it. I'm hungry!" He took a big bite and talked as he chewed. "I was going to smooth-talk Nairnie into giving me some bread or mayhap some salted herring from the galley. But when I heard the shouting between her and Bear coming from inside, I just kept on walking and ended up in the hold instead. Did you know I found Scythe and Tyne down there? I guess Bear made them sleep in the hold for some reason."

"I know," Zachariah answered, not wanting to repeat the rude things that Scythe and Tyne had said regarding Vivienne. "It seems I'm not the only one who has a female angry with them right now. Bear said that it is over between him and Nairnie."

"Aye, that's how it sounded." Isaac crunched the apple, taking another bite. Then he made a face, looked at the apple, picked out a worm, and threw it over the railing into the water.

"Things might be over between me and Vivienne now too, Isaac."

"What do you mean? Didn't Vivienne like the kiss?" He held out the apple, offering a bite to Zachariah.

Zachariah, shook his head, refusing the wormy apple. "Nay."

"Nay? She rejected your advances? Wow, you must be an awful kisser, Brother." Isaac's eyes opened wide in surprise.

"Nay to the apple, you fool! And for your information, there is nothing bad about the way I kiss."

"Then did she like the kiss or not? I'm confused."

"Yes, she liked it. Of course, she did. Or at least I think she did." He ran a hand over his head, smoothing back his hair. "Oh, hell, I don't even know anymore. I mean, I thought there was something special between us, so I made an advance, thinking it was all right. But unfortunately, I believe I crossed a line that mayhap I shouldn't have stepped over."

"Hell, I'd take intimacy any day over maintaining a professional relationship." Isaac finished off the apple and tossed the core overboard, wiping his hand on his trews to dry them.

"You'd better change your mind about what you just said, if you're really planning on someday being my deputy. After all, in this profession, it is important to keep a clear head or you might miss an important clue."

"Is that why we have nothing to go on yet regarding the murder of Fingers? You didn't have a clear head?"

"Mayhap." Zachariah let out a deep sigh. "Probably. I need to avoid distractions and focus on the case. Vivienne said she only wanted a professional relationship between us, so that is what she'll get from now on. Isaac, if I even *seem* like I'm about to stray again where she's concerned, I need you to promise you'll put me back on the path."

"I'll do my best, Brother. But I really don't like to get involved where love is concerned." He stared out at the shore with a huge grin on his face.

"Love? Who said anything about love? I don't love Vivienne. Not in the way you mean."

"Mmm hmm," he said, one corner of his mouth turning up in a silly grin.

"Keep your mind on the case, will you? A deputy-in-training should not be talking to the sheriff in this manner."

"I was talking brother to brother, but all right, if that's what you really want."

"It is what I want."

"So...I'm a deputy-in-training now, and not just training to be a common constable? I mean, that is what you just called me, after all."

"You know what I meant, Isaac, now let it go."

"Ah. It's what you mean but not what you actually say. Got it." He turned and looked directly at Zachariah. "Does that go for the part about stopping you from being intimate with Vivienne too?"

"Just forget about it, will you?" Zachariah threw his hands in the air in frustration. "Now, Bear needs to leave in the next few days, so our time in Whitstable is limited."

"Then we need to find this man named Adder quickly."

"I agree. We'll take Bear along and go back to town today. We need to make some progress."

"Dammit, old woman, I like it better when you're not talkin' to me," came the shouting of Bear and then the sound of things crashing about inside the galley.

"Ye stinkin' old buzzard! I told ye no' to call me *old woman*, so dinna do it again."

"Ow! Stop pulling my beard."

"Och, if ye dinna like that, then how about this?" The slap of something hitting what sounded like flesh came next.

"Dammit, use that ladle for cooking, not as a weapon," shouted Bear.

"Are you sure you want to take Bear with us?" asked Isaac, as they both stared at the galley. "It doesn't really sound like he's in a good mood this morning."

"Keep clear of the galley, everyone," said Goldtooth, passing by. "It sounds like a war zone down there."

"I'm going to the hold to hide out until things calm down," said Coop, hurrying across the deck to the small door that led to the storage area below.

"I'll be up in the lookout basket." Ramble scurried up the lines, quickly disappearing. Then the door to the galley burst open, hitting against the wall with a loud bang. Bear stumbled out, looking like he was drunk since he couldn't seem to walk straight. Zachariah could see Nairnie's arm sticking out of the galley and she was holding her iron pan now. He was sure she must have just hit Bear in the chest with it, replacing the infamous ladle with the heavy pan now.

"Mayhap ye'd rather feel that instead of my ladle!" screamed Nairnie, followed by the slamming of the galley door as she closed her husband out. All the men of Bear's crew scattered in different directions, trying to get as far away from Bear and Nairnie as they could.

"No good ever comes from having a wench on board!" snapped Bear, righting himself and pulling the wrinkles out of his tunic. "Wenches are nothing but bad luck."

The door to the galley banged back open and Nairnie stepped out with her hands on her hips this time. Even from where he stood, Zachariah could tell she was giving Bear the evil eye. He shuddered, just seeing it in motion.

"What did ye say?" asked Nairnie, staring at Bear.

"Never mind, sweetheart." Bear turned and all but ran in the opposite direction, making Isaac laugh.

"Don't laugh," Zachariah told his brother. "That could be us next."

"Oh." Isaac's smile quickly faded.

"I hope Nairnie doesn't teach Vivienne how to do that evil-eye thing. After all, Vivienne was just as angry with me last night as Nairnie is with Bear right now."

"Why was she angry?" asked his brother.

"I can't say I really know." Zachariah shrugged. "Can any man really figure out the moods of a woman?"

"Mayhap we'd better get Bear off the ship before it's demolished," suggested Isaac.

"I think that's a good idea. Let's head off to town as quickly as possible. Since Bear is probably in need of a drink right now, I'm sure he will agree to join us." Zachariah started for the stairs.

"Should I wake Lady Vivienne and tell her our plans?" asked Isaac.

"Nay," he answered.

"Isn't she coming with us? I mean, I'm sure she's anxious to look for Adrian again."

"And that is the exact reason we're going to leave her

behind. We've got work to do, Isaac. This murder investigation is not going to solve itself. I'm afraid with Vivienne's obsession to not only find Adrian but to make him remember her, she's only going to prove to be a huge distraction."

"You're probably right," said Isaac, following him down the stairs. "Bear makes sense saying women on board are bad luck. Mayhap we'll have better luck finding clues regarding the murder without a woman tagging along with us."

"Point taken," said Zachariah, not really sure about anything anymore. At least, not anything that had to do with Lady Vivienne Harlowe.

VIVIENNE AWOKE to the sound of whispering inside the captain's cabin. It sounded like Martin was talking to someone and she had a feeling it wasn't Grunt.

Slowly opening one eye, she laid still in the hammock, not wanting him to know she was watching and listening. Martin had been acting odd since yesterday and she needed to find out exactly what was going on.

Her son sat on the pallet on the floor with his back facing her. Grunt was lying next to him, but Martin wasn't looking at the dog when he spoke.

"I'll get us something to eat, but you'd better stay here. We don't want anyone to find you."

It sounded as if he was about to leave the cabin without telling her and she didn't like that. He was her son and she was responsible for his safety. He needed to tell her when he was going somewhere, even if it was just from the cabin to the galley. "Martin?" Vivienne sat up in the hammock that was across the room. "Who are you talking to?"

He flipped the blanket over something and quickly turned and petted the dog. "Just Grunt, Mother."

"Oh really?" She lowered herself out of the hammock and walked toward him. Martin faked another yawn and laid back on a bump under the blanket. "Stand up," she told him.

"Why?" he asked.

"Because I think you are lying to me, and I don't like it."

"Why would you say that?"

"Martin, move." She reached around him and yanked back the blanket, exposing a small person hiding there. "Mouse?" she said, recognizing the boy thief.

"Please, don't hurt me," said the boy, hurriedly sitting up and backing away from her.

"I won't hurt you, but tell me why you're here?"

"He's hiding from Adder," said Martin, before Mouse could even answer.

"Ah, now I understand," she said, thinking about all the food Martin had piled on his plate last night, and why he said he wanted to eat alone. It also made her feel better because she realized that Martin only said he didn't want her to hug him because he was trying to keep Mouse's presence a secret. "You've been here since yesterday, haven't you, Mouse?"

"Yes, my lady," said the little boy, looking so forlorn.

"He sneaked on board when you were in town and when no one was looking," said Martin. "Actually, I saw him from the lookout basket and helped him get onto the ship."

"Martin, you know it isn't right to keep Mouse's presence here a secret. The sheriff wants to question him about the murder of Fingers and what or whom he might have seen."

"I don't want to talk about the death of my brother," said Mouse. "It hurts too much."

"Your brother?" she asked in surprise. "I didn't know Fingers was your brother."

"Mouse was only two when he and Fingers were sold to Adder to be trained as thieves," Martin gave her the information.

"You poor thing," said Vivienne, sitting down and putting her arm around Mouse. He was hesitant at first, but then relaxed enough to let her hug him. His little body felt so thin, and she could feel it shaking in fear. "Don't you worry because I'm going to protect you. I promise, nothing is going to happen to you, like it did to your brother."

"Mother, we can't tell anyone he's here," said Martin. "If Adder finds him, he'll be beaten and punished."

"But that's not right," she told the boys. "You can't ask me to be a part of this secret. After all, I'm helping the sheriff find your brother's murderer," she told the young boy. "Don't you want his killer found and punished?"

Mouse didn't answer, just nodded.

"Then, you're going to have to help us by giving us information that will aid us in tracking down the killer. Plus, I'd like to know if you can help me find my brother, Adrian."

"She means Red," explained Martin, in terms that the little boy would understand.

"Do you know where I can find Adrian? I mean, Red?" she asked, keeping her voice calm, trying to get the boy to give her information.

He nodded, and when he did her heart jumped. Luck was on her side this morning and that made her happy.

"Can you tell me where he is right now? I'd like to talk to him."

He shook his head. She could see she was going to have to offer him something he wanted in exchange if she was going to get him to tell her about Adrian. She didn't want to make this deal, but she had no other choice than to do it, if she was going to find Adrian again.

"I promise I won't tell anyone you're here, if you tell me what I want to know about Adrian. Red," Vivienne quickly corrected herself. "So what do you think? Do we have a deal?" She held out her hand to shake on it, waiting for Mouse to accept.

"You can't even tell the sheriff," Martin told her. "This has to be our little secret. You have to promise."

"I understand," she said, still holding out her hand.

"Go on, Mouse. Shake her hand and accept the deal," instructed Martin. "My mother will keep her word. She doesn't lie."

"All right," said Mouse, slowly holding out his hand, interlocking it with hers in a quick shake.

The door to the cabin burst open just then, surprising them all and causing them to jump.

"Missy, if ye're goin' to be sleepin' all day, ye'll miss out on everything." Nairnie entered the room, stopping in her tracks when she laid her eyes on Mouse. "What is he doin' here?"

"Nairnie, shut the door. Quickly." Vivienne jumped up and ran over to shut the door to the cabin for her.

"It's a secret that Mouse is here," explained Martin. Grunt barked, as if saying he agreed. "No one can know."

"Lady Vivienne, what is going on here?" asked Nairnie.

"Oh, Nairnie, I'm sorry you accidentally got involved, but now you know. Mouse is here, but we cannot tell anyone. I made a promise to keep his presence a secret."

"Hrmph," she scoffed. "Well, I didna make a promise. The sheriff should know about this."

"Nairnie, please don't tell," begged Martin. "Mouse is scared. No one can find out that he is here."

"Nairnie, just this once?" asked Vivienne.

"Well, I dinna ken." She put her hand to her chin in thought. "Then again, I'm no' talkin' to Bear, so he willna hear

157

about this from me. But dinna ye think ye should tell Sheriff Fitch? I mean, he is tryin' to solve a boy's murder."

"I promised Mouse that I wouldn't say a word if he told me where to find Adrian," answered Vivienne.

"Oh, I see," said Nairnie with a nod of her head. "Ye made a deal."

"Aye, she did," said Martin excitedly.

"Besides, I'm not talking to Sheriff Fitch right now either," continued Vivienne. "The men don't need to know about this. Yet. Do they, really?"

"Bear said wenches on board were bad luck, but it seems to me they're the unlucky ones, since they canna find a clue to save their lives," remarked Nairnie.

"Mouse's brother was Fingers," Vivienne told the old woman.

"Och, nay. I'm sorry, laddie."

"Mouse was only two when a man sold him and Fingers to Adder to be trained as thieves," said Martin, petting Grunt behind the ears as he spoke. The hound's eyes closed halfway and his mouth opened in what looked like a smile.

"That is a sad and horrible story," said Nairnie.

"And that is why he can't go back to Adder, and why he doesn't want to be found," said Vivienne.

"Adder beats him," Martin added. "Nairnie, you have to help him. Help us keep his secret."

Nairnie looked at each of them, cocking her head. Then she wrinkled her nose and finally nodded. "Bear will kill me for no' tellin' him, but right now, I dinna care about what Bear thinks. If I can help ye, Vivienne, and also Mouse, then I will. Aye, yer secret is safe with me."

"Yay!" said Martin, jumping up and pulling Mouse up to a standing position as well. Grunt ran around the boys in a circle.

"You two need to stay quiet," Vivienne warned them.

"There are men on this boat who hear and see everything. It's not going to be easy to keep a secret aboard the *Falcon*."

"Mouse can stay in the cabin," said Martin. "Then no one will see him."

"Nay," said Nairnie. "Today is the day that Scythe and Tyne clean the cap'n's cabin."

"I'll tell them not to bother," said Vivienne.

"Ye do that, and Bear will have their heads for no' followin' orders. They're already on bad terms with him since they left the ship when they were supposed to be guardin' it."

"Oh. I don't want them to get into trouble because of us." Vivienne wondered where she could hide the boy and for how long.

"We'll take him to the galley for now, but it might be better if we got him off the ship for the day," said Nairnie. "The crew will be swabbin' the decks later. It's cleanin' day around here."

"Mouse, if I promise to protect you, will you go back to town with me and bring me to Adrian?"

"Missy, is that a good idea?" asked Nairnie. "Ye really want to go back to Rook Row?"

"If that is where I'll find my brother, then, yes, I do."

"I'm coming too," said Martin. The dog barked. "Me and Grunt will protect you." Her son ran over and picked up his wooden sword.

"That's somethin' to think about," said Nairnie. "We'll need protection since the men willna be with us."

"We?" Vivienne looked over at Nairnie and smiled. "Does that mean you'll be joining me?"

"Dinna think I'm goin' to let ye and the children go alone. I'll bring along my ladle, and even my iron pan if need be. If anyone even looks at ye or the wee ones cross-eyed, I'll wallop them until their eyes spin in their head."

"Thank you, Nairnie. And I'll bring my father's sword along

for protection." She walked over to the table and picked it up in two hands.

"You know how to use a sword?" asked Mouse in a soft but curious voice.

"I do," admitted Vivienne.

"But you're just a girl."

"Dinna ever underestimate the power of a female," Nairnie told the boy.

"It is heavy?" asked Mouse.

"Did you want to try to hold it?"

Mouse nodded, his eyes as big as dinner plates.

"Here, hold out your hands," she said, holding her sword horizontally. "I'll let you feel how heavy it is, but I won't let go of it."

She placed it in Mouse's hands and a smile lit up his face.

"Let go, Mother," Martin urged her. "Let Mouse feel how heavy a knight's sword really is."

"This sword isn't as heavy as one for a knight, but I will let go if you really want me to."

"I do," said Mouse.

She let go and the weight of the sword was too much for Mouse. He started to drop it, but she caught it and put it back in the sheath. "I think you might have to wait a few years to be able to be strong enough to hold it."

"He can hold my sword. It's light." Martin handed over his wooden sword to Mouse. It was what pages used to learn to fight as part of their training.

"I like this sword better," said Mouse with a huge grin, holding up the wooden weapon proudly. "Could I actually kill Adder with this?"

"That's enough," said Vivienne, not wanting to hear a child talk about wanting to kill anyone. Even if the man named Adder probably deserved it. She took the wooden sword away from the boy and handed it back to her son.

"I think we'd better prepare to go to shore now, before the crew starts their cleanin'," said Nairnie. "I'll give the men somethin' to eat and we'll sneak away while they're bein' distracted."

"Thank you. Nairnie, you are proving to be a good friend and I cherish that." Vivienne really meant what she said. She didn't know many people who would be as loyal to her as Nairnie.

"Thank ye for sayin' that, but I dinna think Bear would agree with ye, my lady."

"You two seem to be having a lot of fights lately," said Vivienne. "Is there anything I can do to help?" Even if the sheriff told her not to get involved, it went against her true nature to help those in need. Nairnie was helping her, so she wanted nothing more than to do the same for her in return.

"Nay, lassie, but thank ye." The old woman's face changed, and she looked so sad and disappointed now. "I think mayhap my time with Bear is sadly comin' to an end."

"Don't say that, Nairnie. You and Bear seemed to be such a happy couple. Until all the arguing started, that is."

"We *were* happy. At first," she told her. "But he's away on this blasted ship for such long periods at a time that I swear I dinna even ken who he is anymore. And when he does come home, he doesna even ask how I've been. Our squabblin' used to be a way of flirtin', but now it's turnin' into somethin' different."

"Oh, Nairnie, I am so sorry to hear this."

"I miss the man Bear used to be, Lady Vivienne."

"You miss him being a pirate?"

"Nay. I miss him bein' my husband."

"But he is your husband."

"No' the kind I want."

"What do you mean, Nairnie?" Vivienne wanted to help,

but she needed to understand first exactly what the problem was between Nairnie and Bear.

"I want a husband who stays at my side instead of runnin' off on one adventure after another and who is never with me. I want to make a home. We've been together for years, and still I dinna have that. I'm gettin' older, lassie, and I canna keep up with his pace."

"Did you ever tell him that?"

"It wouldna matter. Bear's blood runs wild. He is a man who finds his happiness on the sea, no' in a hovel in front of a warm fire. I'm afraid our marriage is comin' to an end."

"Oh, Nairnie. I won't accept that. It can't be true," said Vivienne.

"Dinna let a man's job ever come between two people. Like ye and the sheriff," said Nairnie. "It's no' worth it."

That surprised Vivienne, because she didn't realize that Nairnie knew about her feelings for the sheriff. Yet, this woman did seem very wise. Nothing much seemed to go unnoticed when Nairnie was around.

"Nairnie, I don't know what you mean." Vivienne felt her cheeks blush. She glanced over at Martin, not wanting him to hear this. Fortunately, he was talking with Mouse. Grunt was keeping them both occupied by licking their faces.

"I think ye ken exactly what I mean, my lady. I heard ye two arguin' last night."

"Oh, I'm sorry. I guess we were louder than I thought."

"Sound carries on this ship."

"I must admit that I'm not really on talking terms with the sheriff right now either. Just like what's happening between you and Bear."

"And that is why we arena goin' to tell either the sheriff or that old buzzard what we're about to do. Now get the boys ready. As soon as the meal is in progress, we'll sneak off the ship on the shuttle boat and go to town to find that missin' brother of yers. I swear we'll no' only find him, but also bring him back to Mablethorpe where he belongs."

"Thank you, Nairnie," said Vivienne, feeling excited and thankful and blessed all at once. "I would like that." Finally, someone was giving her the support she needed and wanted regarding her brother. Mayhap going to another woman for help is what she should have done from the start. Vivienne had a renewed sense of hope that mayhap they could really find Adrian again and bring him home, even if all the sheriff seemed to care about was finding Fingers's killer.

Chapter Twelve

"Do you really think it's a good idea for you two to be drinking in a tavern right now?" asked Isaac, taking the tankard of ale from a comely serving wench and flashing her his best smile as they occupied a table at the Blue Mermaid. "I mean, the women in your lives seem so angry with you both, and I don't believe being here is going to smooth things over any."

"Since when did you get to be such a sage?" Zachariah couldn't believe his brother was coming up with such words of wisdom. Isaac had never been the one to make good choices before, and neither did he ever care about his decisions, one way or the other. That was until now. He was correct in saying this wasn't the answer of how to get back in the good graces of Nairnie and Vivienne. But on the other hand, he had to do whatever it took to get information that would lead them to a murderer.

"No wench is going to tell me what to do." Bear cradled his tankard in two hands, looking forlorn, but trying not to show it.

"We're only in here looking for Adder," Zachariah explained, taking a swig of his drink. Right now he needed something to take his mind off of Vivienne and the way she'd exploded with anger at him after he'd told her that her brother was no longer the boy she once knew and loved. In hindsight, perhaps he could have been a little more understanding and sensitive.

But honestly, he always figured Vivienne was someone who wanted to hear and know the truth, no matter what the circumstances. She was a strong woman who had lived through a lot of heartbreak, but she'd endured. So why did she seem so unwilling to accept the truth now where her brother was concerned? The fact of the matter was that Adrian had a new life now. He'd moved on and wasn't the same boy Vivienne remembered. But Vivienne wasn't about to stop trying to bring him back to the boy he once was, even if he warned her that it might not be the best thing to do.

"The sheriff is right. We're only doing our job," agreed Bear.

"Did I hear you're looking for Adder?" That same comely wench that Isaac had flirted with a moment ago walked back to their table.

"Aye, and so much more," Isaac told her, slipping an arm around her waist from his sitting position. "What are you doing later?" Now this was the brother Zachariah knew. But if Isaac was going to have a job in law enforcement, he needed to control his wandering eye and keep his mind on the matter at hand.

Zachariah cleared his throat. "Isaac, please. You're supposed to be working."

"Oh, sorry," said his brother, hurriedly removing his arm from around the wench and putting both of his hands on the table. "Yes. Yes, we are looking for Adder," he told the girl. "Do you know where we can find him?"

"I'd hope so," she said with a flighty giggle. "He's sitting right there at the next table. If he were a snake, you'd be bitten by now." She hurried away when another patron called out to her.

"See you later?" asked Isaac, raising his hand in the air as his voice trailed off, getting lost amongst all the noise of the boisterous drinking men, even this early in the day.

"So, that's the infamous Adder," said Zachariah softly, eying up the man at the next table. He was of medium build with deep-set black eyes and ebony hair. The stubble on his jaw was thick, but looked like he tried to shave on occasion.

"Should I go get him, Sheriff?" asked Bear, followed by a belch. He wiped the ale from his upper lip with a swipe of his sleeve. "I can hold him in a neck lock if ye want, or I'd be happy to rough him up a bit just for effect."

"Aye, that might help us get him to spill some information," agreed Isaac. "I say we do it."

"Nay. That's not how I work." Zachariah shook his head. These two sitting with him were used to using force, but being so aggressive was not necessarily the answer.

"Well, then tell us. What's your plan, Zachariah?" asked his brother. "Because, it sounds good to me. I have my sword and I'm not afraid to use it."

Zachariah had his sword strapped to his belt too. But yanking out that weapon in a tavern of drunkards was most likely only going to cause more problems.

"I'll go over to his table first," said Zachariah. "Alone. We don't want to scare him off." Zachariah got up out of his chair, stopping when he saw Bear's friend, the oyster seller, approaching Adder's table. The two men said a few words and then Adder slid a pouch across the table. The oyster fisherman picked up the pouch, quickly looked inside, and then turned to go.

"Bear, isn't that your friend?" asked the sheriff.

"Who?" Bear turned in his chair. "Ah, Scoop. Over here,"

called out Bear, waving his hand in the air. The man looked both ways and then slowly walked over to greet them.

"Good morning, Bear. How were those oysters I sold you? Did you need more?" Scoop pulled an oyster out of his pouch, using his black-handled knife to pry open the shell. "Here. Taste the fresh catch of the day." He held out the oyster to Bear who took it and held the shell up to his mouth, letting the oyster slide down his throat. Bear didn't even chew, just swallowed.

"Delicious," said Bear, smacking his lips. "Nairnie cooked up the ones I brought her into a fish stew and they were the best I ever tasted. But then again, the one you just gave me was fresher. I could eat a dozen or two of those without cooking them at all."

"So do you want one or two dozen?" asked Scoop. "I have them right outside in my cart and can be back in a minute."

"Thank you, but we're working," said Zachariah. "Besides, something tells me they might not all be that fresh." Zachariah had known men like Scoop. They lured you in with one thing and then replaced it with another before you could discover you'd been swindled.

"The sheriff's right," said Bear. "I don't want more yet. Besides, I'm not sure I'd be able to convince Nairnie to cook them right now, since she's not even talking to me."

"Well, good to hear you liked them. Nice seeing you again, but I've got to go." Scoop wiped his knife off on his tunic and stuck it back into his belt.

"What brings you here to the Blue Mermaid so early in the day?" asked Zachariah, keeping his eye on Scoop as well as Adder at the same time. He didn't want Scoop to leave yet, hoping he could give them some information about Adder. "I figured you'd be out fishing in the mornings."

"Usually I am," said Scoop. "However, I was just picking up payment from a client. For the oysters I sold him."

"I don't see any oysters," said Isaac, stretching his neck to look over at Adder's table.

"That's because I gave them to him yesterday. But he didn't have enough money to pay me at the time. So I collected the fee from him today instead." Scoop turned to leave.

"Is that man's name Adder?" asked the sheriff, with a nod to the man at the next table, where Scoop had been a minute ago.

"Aye, I think that's what they call him. Well, I really need to go. Excuse me." Scoop hurried away, leaving the tavern.

"Such a surprise to see your friend Scoop here again," said Zachariah. "Especially since he already told us he'd been wasting time waiting for you for an extra day. Plus, this is the best time of the day to fish. I figured he'd be out on the water and not in the tavern."

"Aye. Me too. And I can't believe he let someone pay for oysters the next day, yet he let them take them ahead of time," said Bear. "Roger never let me do that, even after all the years I've been getting oysters from him. And Scoop was so adamant about me paying him more than was proper." Bear shook his head.

"Wait, who's Roger? I thought his name was Scoop," said Isaac.

"Roger was Scoop's employer. Scoop told me he died last year," Bear explained.

"Uh oh. Adder's on the move," said Zachariah, seeing the man abruptly stand and head for the door. "I'm going after him." Zachariah hurried out the door, calling to the man. "Adder? Can I have a word with you, please?"

The man looked over his shoulder and then started to run. Zachariah took chase. He followed Adder around the corner of the tavern, but quickly halted when he saw Bear standing there holding the man by the back of his tunic.

"I got him, Sheriff, don't worry," said Bear.

"Wait for me," shouted Isaac, running up behind Zachariah to join them. "How did Bear get here already?"

"I know a back way and took a short cut," Bear bragged.

"You can't detain me. I didn't do nothing wrong," complained the man named Adder.

"Calm down. We just want to ask you some questions about a boy named Fingers, that's all," said Zachariah.

"Do you know Fingers?" asked Isaac.

"What's it to you if I did know him? I don't have to answer. You're not the town sheriff. Leave me alone. I didn't kill him."

Zachariah was surprised to hear Adder talking about Fingers in a past tense. Plus, he sounded as if he knew the boy had been murdered, but yet they hadn't mentioned the fact to him.

"Nay, I'm not the Sheriff of Whitstable, but I am the Sheriff of Mablethorpe," Zachariah explained. "And the hanging of Fingers happened aboard a ship that I sailed on, coming here to Whitstable with friends and family."

"Then why don't you look at them instead of me?"

"We never said you did it," said Isaac. "However, you are acting pretty suspicious right now."

"We know you have a thieving ring," grunted Bear, still holding on tightly to the man.

"So what? Everyone has to make a living somehow. Are you here to put all of us in jail?"

"Nay, I'm not here to put anyone in jail," said Zachariah. "We just want to know what you were doing yesterday and where you were during the time of the murder."

"I wasn't here."

"But I saw you here earlier that day," said Zachariah. "You were outside the whorehouse."

"I didn't kill anyone and you can't prove that I did."

Zachariah knew this wasn't working. The man wasn't telling

him anything that would help him solve the murder. So, he decided to take a different approach.

"My friend is looking for her brother who disappeared seven years ago."

"I don't know what you're talking about."

"We know you buy orphan boys," said Isaac, getting a strange look from Adder.

"The boy we need information on is Adrian Harlowe, and we've seen him here on Rook Row. He actually stole my pouch of coins. You and your boys call him Red," said Zachariah.

The man stopped struggling. "Red?" he asked. "You know him?"

"Aye," answered Zachariah. "Can you tell us where to find him? My friend would like to take him home."

"Red is a loner and a simpleton," spat Adder. "He stinks at picking pockets, and is nothing but a pain in my arse. He disappeared a while ago, and I don't know where he went. If you see him and want him, then take him. I don't care. I don't want him working for me anymore."

"Well, where can we find him?"

"How the hell should I know? He comes and goes as he pleases and didn't have any friends except for Fingers."

"I think someone killed Fingers because he was going to give me information about Adrian," said the sheriff.

"Well, that's what he gets for being a snitch."

"Let him go, Bear," said Zachariah. "He's of no help to us."

When Bear released him, he pushed the man hard. Adder fell to the ground and his glove fell off. When he went to pick it up, Zachariah noticed he was missing his thumb and part of his index finger on his right hand. He also had a difficult time getting up off the ground.

"Did you buy Red from someone who brought him to you seven years ago?" asked Zachariah.

The man brushed himself off but didn't seem as if he were going to answer.

"Please. I need to know." Zachariah needed at least a scrap of a clue to go on.

"Are you going to arrest me if I say yes?"

"The town of Whitstable is not my jurisdiction. I can't make arrests on my own."

"Then, yes. I did buy the boy. But he ended up not being worth a penny. I had a feeling the boy was too simple since he didn't even know his own name. That's why I cheated the man out of the price we agreed upon." He chuckled, as if he thought himself so clever for this.

"Who sold him to you?"

"I don't bother to ask names. It's better for both of us that way."

"What did he look like?" asked Isaac. "Would you be able to identify the man if you saw him again?"

Before Adder could answer, there was a shout that took their attention from down the alley passageway.

"What's going on down there?" It was the Sheriff of Whitstable along with his constable. "Sheriff Fitch, what are you doing here on Rook Row?"

Adder took advantage of the distraction to turn and run, disappearing before they could even chase after him.

"Do ye want me to bring him back?" asked Bear.

"Nay," said Zachariah with a deep sigh. "Now we have the town sheriff to deal with, and by rights we shouldn't have apprehended anyone the way we did."

"Sheriff Fitch, I need a word with you," growled Whitstable's sheriff, as he and his constable trudged toward them. "I want you out of my town. You are asking a lot of questions and stirring up loads of trouble. You have upset just about everyone I've spoken to about you."

"Sheriff Whitstable, I am looking for a murderer whom you don't seem to be in a hurry to catch," said Zachariah.

"I told you, it was a thief who died. Nobody cares. Whoever killed him, did me a huge favor. That's one less piece of trash on my town streets that I have to do something about now."

"Did you know that man named Adder pays men to bring him orphans so he can train them as thieves?" asked Isaac.

"Yes, I'm aware of the rumors surrounding Adder, but you can't believe half of what you hear. People like to gossip, and every time a story is told, it seems to grow."

"Well, this one is true. And now, thanks to you, Adder has just gotten away," Isaac continued. "Don't you think you should be the one to go after him? I mean, after all, it is your town."

"What goes on in Whitstable is no concern to any of you," snapped the constable.

"We can help you clean up your town," offered Zachariah. "We should work together."

"When I want your help, I'll ask for it," said Sheriff Whitstable. "But don't hold your breath. As of right now, I don't want it or need it. And you're not welcome. So leave before I have to run you out of my town myself."

"Come on," Zachariah told Bear and Isaac. "This is proving to be a lot more challenging than I thought it would be. Mayhap we should go back to the *Falcon* because I feel like I should make amends with Vivienne."

"I could go for some of Nairnie's cooking right now. I'm hungry," said Isaac, leading the way.

"Well, not me. I don't want any of that old woman's cooking. But I could go for some whisky," said Bear. "I'll need it if I'm going to be listening to Nairnie's squawking for the rest of the day."

"We can question some of the men on the dock," said

Zachariah. "Perhaps someone saw something there that could help us. Let's go."

～

"Are ye sure you want to do this without the sheriff along?" asked Nairnie, as they headed toward town in a horse-drawn wagon. Vivienne had given all her money to Adrian yesterday, and couldn't afford to actually pay to use someone's horse and wagon. She had decided to try to make a deal with the baker to borrow his horse and wagon, when luck was on her side. The baker saw the ring on a chain that Vivienne wore around her neck. It was the ring of King Edward. Her mother had given it to her when she was dying, telling Vivienne that her true father was the King. Vivienne had met the King...her father...at the castle tournament at Mablethorpe not too long ago, and so had found out that she was not only his bastard daughter, but that her parents who'd raised her had secretly been spies for the King.

When the baker noticed her ring, he told her that he'd heard the story about her being the King's bastard. He also said that he'd be happy to lend her his horse and wagon, since she was related to their country's ruler. Vivienne said that in return for the baker's kindness, she promised to speak highly about him to the King the next time she saw him. That made the man's day. After all, the King was known to look with favor on anyone who, at such times, gave aid to those dear to him.

"I will find Adrian with or without the sheriff, and I will bring him home where he belongs if it is the last thing I ever do," Vivienne told Nairnie, feeling excited, determined, and a little bit frightened all at the same time.

"Stop here," said Mouse from the back of the wagon, where he rode with Martin and Grunt.

"Here?" she questioned, looking around. They were on the outskirts of town, but right at the beginning of Rook Row. They'd stopped in front of the tannery, and it stunk terribly. "Are you sure?" She coughed and held her sleeve to her nose, barely able to breathe because of the rancid stench.

"Go to the tanning pits at the far end, but up near the street," said Mouse. "That is where Adrian lives."

"He sleeps in a dying pit?" asked Vivienne thinking this had to be the most horrible thing she'd ever heard. It was right up there with the rats she'd encountered back in Mablethorpe on Rotten Row.

"Aye," said Mouse. "It's one of the old pits that aren't used anymore."

"He really lives there?" Vivienne stopped the horse and looked up at a partially dilapidated building that had a large outdoor yard where tanners preserved animal hides to convert them into leather. It was a smelly, long process. No one purposely came here of their own will. "Well, all right," she said, climbing out of the wagon, not happy about it, but willing to do anything to find and save her brother.

"Did ye want me to follow ye, lassie?" asked Nairnie.

"Nay, Nairnie. Stay in the wagon with the children," Vivienne told her, not wanting to have to expose the rest of them to this filthy, stinky place. "If trouble arises, get the boys back to safety right away."

"But what about ye, missy?" asked Nairnie. "I'd never leave ye stranded here on Rook Row without a way to get back to the ship. And with no one to protect ye either."

"I'll be fine. I have Grunt. Come on, boy," she called to her dog, and he jumped out of the wagon, eager to go anywhere with her. "I will take my father's sword with me for extra protection." She reached over the side of the wagon and picked up the sword, fastening the scabbard to her waist belt.

"Mother, I'm coming with you." Martin jumped up and put one leg over the side of the wagon, preparing to follow.

"Nay, Martin. You stay here and protect Mouse," she told him. "And watch over Nairnie too," she added, wanting Martin to think he had an important job.

"Sit down, lad," said Nairnie from the front of the wagon. She reached out and put the reins of the horse in one hand. "If I start up suddenly, ye're goin' to fall right out on yer face."

"But I want to go with Mother to help find my Uncle Adrian."

"Yer mother kens what she's doin', lad. Or at least, I hope she does," Nairnie mumbled the latter part. "Now sit down, be quiet, and keep yer eyes open for trouble. Lord kens we dinna need any of that, even though we're sittin' right in the middle of it."

"I'll be fast," Vivienne promised, trying to calculate her steps carefully, so as not to step in the puddles and piles, not sure what was actually in them. She didn't fancy ruining a good pair of shoes by stepping in dung or smelly animal entrails.

She pushed open the gate and slipped inside, trying her best not to breathe. Still, the foul air filled her nostrils and turned her stomach sour. She couldn't wait to get out of here. It made her wonder how her brother could stay in such an awful place such as this.

"Adrian? Adrian, are you in here?" she called out softly, seeing the tanners across the yard, working. They were bare-chested, dirty men wearing leather aprons. Some of them were cleaning and removing the hair from animal flesh, throwing the fat, organs and scraps into a vat or directly onto the ground. They used a long sharp instrument to scrape the hides. Others were laying the hides in the tanning pits that were layered with bark and filled with some kind of solution. Here is where they'd soak for long periods of time to continue the tanning process.

And still other workers were stretching out and oiling more hides in order to dry them properly in the sun.

She knew they often used urine to soak the hides, and sometimes even used animal dung in preparing the hides. The smell in the place alone was worse than the gong pits of the castle on a hot day in summer. She wanted nothing more than to find her brother and take him away from here as quickly as possible. He was noble and this place wasn't fit for even the lowest of thieves or bandits.

After looking for a while and not finding him, she felt sure that if she didn't leave now, she was going to vomit on her own feet. She turned to go and spied something bright red down in one of the old tanning pits that was empty and no longer being used. Walking over to the pit, she leaned over the side and saw Adrian. Sure enough, Mouse was right. Her brother was really here. He'd stretched out on a blanket in the pit, and actually looked to be sleeping. Her heart about broke to see her brother in his manner. It just wasn't right. And to make matters worse, in his hand, he clutched the velvet pouch with coins that she had given him, as if it were his last lifeline.

"Adrian," she said under her breath, seeing the young man stir. She didn't want to frighten him, so moved slowly. "Red," she called out, even though it pained her to do so. "It's me. Your...it's Vivienne." She was going to say she was his sister, but that hadn't worked last time and only managed to frighten him. She needed to be careful and choose her words carefully this time. It might be the last chance she had to bring him back home. "Come here. I have something for you," she lied, only wanting her brother to come to her.

He sat up and looked at her curiously, and then glanced down to the pouch of coins in his hand. "Do you have more money for me?" he asked.

"Well, nay."

"Then I'm not interested." He climbed out of the pit and looked as if he were going to run until he saw Grunt. "You brought your dog again."

"I did. Maybe you forgot his name? It's Grunt, and though he barked at you last time, he was only trying to protect me. He's very friendly. He won't hurt you. You can pet him if you want to." Grunt trotted over to him and started to sniff him up and down. Adrian didn't touch the dog, but he did smile.

"I also have this." She reached down and held up the ring she wore on a chain around her neck. The sun hit the ruby stone, making it light up and gaining his interest.

"Wow. That ring looks expensive." He took a few steps toward her, squinting and craning his neck to see it better.

"It's King Edward's ring," she told him. "It has a ruby and is worth a lot of money."

"Is the band...made of gold?"

"Yes. Pure gold. Come closer and you can see for yourself if you don't believe me."

She never planned on giving him the ring, but she needed to use it as a lure. As bait to get him close enough to her to grab him.

"Did you steal it from the King?"

"Nay. It was given to me."

"I don't believe you. You're just trying to trick me because you think I'm someone called Adrian, but I'm not. My name is Red." He started to back away. Damn, this wasn't good. He didn't trust her and was going to run again. She had no idea why he couldn't remember her, or even remember his own name, but she had to find out the answers. However, it was going to take a while to do so at this rate.

"Come. Take it," she said, removing the chain from around her neck and dangling it in front of her like a carrot in front of the nose of a horse. He looked curious, but cautious at the same time.

"I don't trust you."

And neither should he, but she wasn't about to tell him that. "Please. Just at least come take a look. And you don't have to tell Adder you have it. This is just for you."

He seemed to like the sound of that. Adrian slowly crept forward, all the while keeping a good eye on her every move. He was just about up to her, his hand reaching out to take it, when a little voice came from the gate near the street and ruined everything.

"Red?" It was Mouse. He stood there looking frightened, helpless, and so tiny.

"Mouse? Where is Fingers?" asked Adrian. "I haven't seen either of you in days now. I thought you abandoned me."

"Fingers is dead," said the boy.

"What?"

"Someone killed him."

Adrian whirled around, his green eyes glaring now at Vivienne. "It was you who killed my friend, wasn't it?"

"Me?" she asked in shock. "Nay. I would never hurt anyone. But I am looking for his murderer, and hopefully you can help me find him."

"Mother, Nairnie said to hurry," came Martin's voice next, as he joined them. Grunt ran over to Martin and stayed at his side. "She said the sheriff is down the street and headed this way."

"You brought the sheriff to arrest me? How could you?" spat Adrian.

"Nay, Adrian, I didn't. And the sheriff isn't from this town. He's a friend of mine from Mablethorpe. We will both help you."

"Come on, Mouse. Let's go." Adrian grabbed the little boy

and was about to leave with him. Vivienne couldn't allow that to happen. She needed to move quickly and did the only thing she knew that would keep Adrian, and also Mouse, with her.

"I'm sorry to have to do this, Adrian," she said pulling her father's sword from the scabbard. "But I don't have a lot of time and I have no other way to keep you with me."

"What?" the boy looked over his shoulder just as Vivienne brought the hilt of the sword smashing down over Adrian's head. His eyes rolled back in their sockets, his knees buckled beneath him, and he fell to the ground right at her feet.

Chapter Thirteen

"**I**s that Nairnie?" Isaac stopped walking and peered down to the end of the street.

"Where?" asked Bear, who had decided to go with them back to the ship instead of staying in town to drink after all.

"In that wagon." Isaac pointed.

"On Rook Row? It better not be or she's going to be in trouble with me," warned Bear.

"Nay, I think he's right," said Zachariah, surprised to see the old woman in town. "It certainly looks like her."

"She's probably here checking up on me," spat Bear. "Such a busybody. She doesn't trust me after all this time. Well, I'm going to give her something to see and talk about for days to come."

"Wait a minute," said Zachariah as Bear took a step toward the whorehouse. "That looks like Vivienne too. Yes, it is. I also see Grunt."

"Vivienne is here too? What is she doing?" asked Isaac, shading his eyes from the sun, trying to see.

"It looks like she's pulling something behind her," said Bear.

"Not something...someone. Oh, hell, no." Zachariah took off

down the street at a run with Bear and Isaac right on his heels. He made it to them just in time to see Vivienne pulling the body of Adrian by his feet. She was taking the lad toward a wagon. Mouse and Martin were trying to help her by each taking one of Adrian's arms, but they were not strong enough to pick up his body off the ground. Instead, he was dragged through the mud and filth of the street. Nairnie was getting off the bench seat to come to Vivienne's aid. Grunt saw Zachariah and started barking, causing Vivienne to look up in surprise.

"Zachariah," she said, dropping the feet of the prone lad she was dragging toward the wagon.

"What in God's name did you do?" he shouted, approaching and hunkering down to check on her brother.

"I hit him over the head with the hilt of my sword. But don't worry, he's fine. I didn't hit him that hard and he's not bleeding at all. He just passed out."

"Why? What would possess you to do such a thing?" he asked, checking to make sure Adrian had a pulse and was still breathing.

"She wanted him to come with us, but he didn't want to go," said Martin. "He was pretending not to know us and he was about to take Mouse away from us too."

"Mouse is here?" asked Isaac, first noticing the boy.

"He was on the ship since yesterday. He slept in our cabin," Martin provided the information, causing Vivienne to cringe.

"He was, was he?" Zachariah looked up at Vivienne and she shrugged. "And you couldn't bother to tell me? What about our promise not to have secrets between us anymore?"

"This is no time for a squabble," scolded Nairnie. "The boy is startin' to wake up, and I see the Sheriff of Whitstable coming out of the whorehouse."

"Zachariah, please. Help me." Vivienne looked at him with

such desperation in her eyes that he couldn't say no. "I can't lose Adrian again. Please, I beg you."

Zachariah glanced down the street to see that what Nairnie said was true. Sure enough, the Sheriff of Whitstable was coming out of the whorehouse and it would be only minutes before he noticed them and what they were doing.

"Boys, take Grunt and get in the back of the wagon. Quickly," instructed Zachariah. "And keep your heads down. Isaac, help me get the lad into the cart."

"I'll do it, Sheriff," said Bear, not waiting for the others to help. He was a big, strong man with large muscles. He picked up Adrian, tossing him over one shoulder and in seconds had deposited the lad into the back of the wagon next to Mouse, Martin, and Grunt.

"All right, then," said Zachariah, amazed at what this ex-pirate could do. He brushed his hands together to remove the remnants of dirt. "Everyone else, get in quickly. I'll drive."

"Nay, I'm no' gettin' into the wagon with that old buzzard," complained Nairnie, putting her hands on her hips.

"Nairnie, you were the one who just said we don't have time for squabbling," Zachariah pointed out.

"That's right. We don't have time for yer incessant chatter, old woman." Bear picked up Nairnie next, bringing her to the back of the wagon, kicking and screaming. "If ye don't shut up then I'll kiss ye so hard that ye won't be able to breathe," warned Bear, tossing her into the wagon, right in the hay, and then climbing in after her.

"Come on, Vivienne," said Zachariah, helping her up to the bench seat and climbing aboard after her. She once again had her father's sword strapped to her side. "We need to get the hell out of here before the lot of us are strung up from the yardarm next."

"What do you mean?" she asked, as he turned the horse and hightailed it out of town.

"I mean, we're not high on the sheriff's list of favorite people to begin with. Once he discovers we've kidnapped not one but two of the boy thieves that he thinks are nothing but boils on his neck, he'll be more than ready to arrest all of us."

"Just one boy was kidnapped," she corrected him. "Mouse came to us of his own free will. And if the sheriff hates the boy thieves so much, he should be grateful to us, so what does it matter?"

"I assure you, he won't be thanking us any time soon. Oh, Vivienne, why didn't you just come to me instead of keeping all these secrets and attempting something so dangerous on your own?"

"Because you seemed to dismiss the fact that I wanted my brother home...even if he doesn't remember me for some reason."

"I know, and I'm sorry. I was just trying to protect you."

"Well, stop it. I am not a child," she retorted. "I don't need your protection or you making decisions for me. I'll do what I want."

"Aye, that you will," he said, not even bothering to point out that if he hadn't shown up, she would have been at the mercy of Whitstable's sheriff and probably imprisoned by now.

"Where am I? What happened?" asked Adrian from the back of the wagon, sitting up and rubbing his head.

"Stay down, Red," warned Mouse. "We're trying to hide from Adder and the sheriff."

"What's going on?" Adrian looked over at Nairnie and Bear who were both sitting there in a huff with their arms crossed over their chests, not saying a word to each other. "Who are they?"

"They're our friends," Mouse told him. "And they're going to help us find out who murdered Fingers."

"They are?"

"Sure, we are. I'm Martin," said Vivienne's son. "And you're my Uncle Adrian."

"I don't understand. Why are you calling me your uncle, and why does everyone keep referring to me as Adrian?" The lad rubbed the bump on his head that he'd gotten from Vivienne's sword.

"Because that's who you are," said Martin. "And this is Grunt," he said, petting the dog. "As soon as my mother and Sheriff Fitch find the killer, we're all going back to live at Mablethorpe Castle."

"Me too?" asked Mouse with a squeak.

"Sure. You too," said Martin. "Right, Mother? They're all coming back to Mablethorpe to live with us?"

"Vivienne," said Zachariah under his breath, looking at her from the corner of his eye. "You can't keep taking in every orphan you meet. Your uncle isn't going to like it."

"Well, I can't very well leave my brother behind, can I?" she answered. "And Mouse has no family. I certainly won't leave him in the hands of that awful man named Adder." She looked over the side of the wagon and smiled. "Yes, Martin, that's right. Adrian and Mouse are both going to come live with us at Mablethorpe Castle."

"Did you say *castle*?" asked Mouse. "Did you hear that, Red? We're going to live like kings in a real castle. Will we have lots of food?"

"More food than you can possibly eat," said Martin. "And lots of meat like venison and boar, and even peacocks that are cooked and then their feathers are put back on. They're this big." He held out his arms as far as he could, showing off to his new friends.

"This is so exciting, isn't it, Zachariah?" Vivienne's entire face lit up with happiness as she watched Martin and the others. "I thought I'd lost my entire family and now by the grace of God, I'm being reunited with them, and having people join my family, making it even bigger than before."

"Yes. Grace of God," he repeated, shaking his head, knowing that before this was all over, they'd probably all have the devil to pay.

~

"JUST FOLLOW ME," Vivienne told her brother, when they'd finally made it back to the ship. She put her cloak over him with the hood up, not wanting the crew to see that she was bringing another boy thief on board. Mouse followed along closely beside Adrian, his head and eyes down, not looking at anyone. Martin and Nairnie were with them, and so was Grunt. The sheriff stopped to talk with Isaac, Bear, and the crew.

Vivienne opened the door to the cabin, surprised to see Scythe and Tyne inside cleaning.

"Oh! I forgot about this," she said. "Can you two please leave?"

"We can't go until we've cleaned everything or the captain will have our heads," Tyne answered.

"Who do you have with you?" asked Scythe, reaching out and yanking the hood from Adrian's head. Adrian quickly stepped back and turned around, trying to keep his face hidden. "Don't I know you? Aye, I do."

"Ye boys need to leave. Now go!" spat Nairnie, walking in and raising her ladle in the air.

"All right, we're going. Don't hit us," said Tyne, rushing for the door.

"He's one of those boy thieves, just like that little one there, ain't he?" asked Scythe, nodding at Mouse as he made his way to the door. "They're no good and will only cause us trouble."

"It's none of your bloody business who they are—now shut up and move," screamed Nairnie, starting after him as she waved her heavy ladle over her head.

"Bear won't be happy about this, and you're the one to blame," said Scythe leaving the room.

"Hrmph!" Nairnie slammed the door after him. "I dinna like that one. No' at all."

"Have a seat, Adrian," said Vivienne. "I'll pour us some wine." She headed over to a side table and picked up a goblet and decanter of wine.

"My name's Red!" snapped her brother, pulling up his hood again over his head. "Why are you keeping me and Mouse here? What's going on?"

"I told you," said Mouse softly. "They're going to protect us from Adder."

"I'm not afraid of Adder. I'm not afraid of any of you either."

"Dinna talk like a fool," said Nairnie in frustration. "Now Lady Vivienne said to sit down, so do it!"

"Fine," he said, with an edge to his voice as he took a seat on the wooden bench that was pulled up to the small table. "But don't think Mouse and I are staying here, cause we're not."

"Red, I'm going to Mablethorpe with them. To live at the castle," said Mouse. "I want you to come too."

"Why should I?" he asked, taking the goblet of wine that Vivienne handed him. "I don't like stuffy nobles and don't want nothing to do with them or their silly castles."

"But...you're noble, too," Vivienne told him. "Our mother was a lady and our father was a soldier for the King. Don't you remember?"

"Now I know you're lying," he said, gulping down some

wine and wiping his mouth with his sleeve. "I heard the talk in town. You're the bastard daughter of King Edward. Is that why you wear his ring on a chain around your neck?"

"Well, yes. That's true." Vivienne's hand went to the ring and she caressed it with her fingers. "Our mother gave this to me and told me the secret just before she died. When she was killed by bandits on the road. You remember. You were there and saw it too."

"I was there, too," said Martin, plopping down on the pallet and lying on his back. "But I was a baby, so I don't remember anything about it."

"Nay. You're making it all up," scoffed the young man. "I've been an orphan my whole life. The only father I ever had was Adder."

"Stop it!" said Vivienne, banging down the decanter, spilling wine on the table. "Enough of this kind of talk, Adrian. Adder is not your father. He's naught but a conniving criminal who trains boys to be thieves."

"It's our profession and there's nothing wrong with it." Adrian ran the tip of his finger over the rim of the goblet.

"You were stolen as a child and sold by some man to Adder," Vivienne told him. "Don't you think there is something wrong with that?"

"Huh?" Adrian looked up, seeming disturbed and confused.

"It's the truth," she told him. "Sheriff Fitch got Adder to admit it just today. Adrian, you don't belong here in Whitstable any more than you deserve to be a thief."

"What do you know about what people deserve?" he growled. "You're just a bloody, stuffy noble who has everything you've ever wanted."

Hearing her brother say this to her, cut Vivienne to the bone. "You have no idea what I went through the night bandits attacked us on the road, do you?" She started to believe that

188

mayhap what the sheriff said was true. Perhaps Adrian had a new life now and wanted nothing to do with her. Mayhap he really didn't remember his parents, his nephew, or even her. How could someone who had been such a big part of her life and so close to her at one time act like he didn't even know her or even care anymore? She wanted the Adrian back that she once knew and loved. This Adrian was almost like an imposter.

"Ye are bein' a selfish fool," Nairnie said to the boy. "Ye may no' realize it, but all yer sister ever wanted was to find ye and her baby after that horrible night. She didna deserve to have her parents murdered right in front of her. She also didna deserve to lose her newborn and the brother that she cared for more than her own life. All she ever wanted was to find ye alive. Even though I dinna ken ye, I'd say that the brother she longed for really did die that night seven long years ago."

"Nay, Nairnie. It's all right," said Vivienne, heading to the door with her heart breaking in two. "I'm going to fetch the sheriff. He has questions for you...Red." With her head down and her hope diminished, Vivienne pulled open the door and stepped out on the deck, feeling once again as if life just wasn't fair.

Chapter Fourteen

"Hold on," Zachariah told Bear and Isaac, as he spotted Vivienne walking out of the captain's cabin looking like she'd just lost her best friend. Actually, he hoped she truly didn't feel that way, since he considered himself her best friend. Her gaze was on the ground, and he couldn't help noticing the frown on her face. She walked with no spring in her step and her shoulders were slumped over. "Something is wrong," he told the others.

"Aye," agreed his brother, Isaac. "Vivienne should be elated that she's finally found her brother, yet she looks like she's sad and about to cry."

"Don't try to figure out a woman," said Bear.

"I think I know what's bothering her. Excuse me," he told the men, hurrying to her side. "Vivienne. How are things going?"

"It's, just...fine," she said, releasing a deep breath.

Her reached up and used two fingers to lift her chin, so he could stare into her watery blue eyes. "I thought we said we were always going to tell each other the truth from now on."

"Oh, Zachariah, I'm afraid you were right about Adrian."

"In what way?" he asked, quickly wiping a stray tear from her cheek and then dropping his hand before any of the crew noticed. Or before she pushed him away again or slapped him. He didn't want her to think that he was trying to be romantic. Not after what he'd been through last night with her.

"He's still my brother, but he certainly doesn't act like it," she told him. "Adrian doesn't remember anything that happened the night we were attacked, and neither does he know me. I hoped it was just an act, but now I can see that it's not. He really has lost all his memories of me and his family. Oh, Zachariah, I don't know what to do."

"You can't do anything to change the circumstances," he told her. "Adrian went through a very traumatic time at a young age. It could be that his mind has blocked out the things that he just couldn't accept."

"Do you think that is what it is?" She sniffled and wiped her eyes with her long tippet sleeve.

"Yes, I do. I've seen it many times in my line of business."

"Really?" Her brows arched in surprise.

"Well, mayhap not that many, but once. It was a situation similar to this."

"Did the person ever regain their memories?" she asked, hope clinging to each word.

He felt so bad for Vivienne right now that all he wanted to do was lie and say yes. He didn't want to take away her last spark of hope. But how could he lie to her when he'd just made a comment that they promised to tell the truth to each other, no matter what?

"Nay, Vivienne, I'm sorry to have to tell you that in that instance it didn't happen."

"Oh." Her head was down again, and helplessness and despair seemed to wash through her.

"However, it doesn't mean that Adrian won't regain his memories. Mayhap now that he's with you and Martin, his memories will start to return. Perhaps he just needed something to give him a jolt and the memories will come back little by little. I'm sure it might even start happening by morning. He just needed a small thing to trigger him, and now the dam will break that he's put up, and all his memories will flood his mind, mayhap even all of them at once. Then he'll be the brother again that you remember."

"Zachariah, I appreciate what you are trying to do, but stop it."

"I don't know what you mean."

"I know you are trying to give me hope and want to show me that you support me, and I appreciate it, I really do. However, I've come to accept that Adrian is never going to remember me or our parents or even who he really is, either. It's too late, just like you said. Seven years of blocking his thoughts has turned him into someone else entirely. He even referred to Adder as being the only father he ever knew."

"Oh, nay. That's awful. I'm so sorry."

"I might be better off leaving him here in Whitstable after all."

"Vivienne, I know you and how much your brother means to you. You don't really mean what you say about leaving him behind."

"Nay, I don't. You're right. But since he said he doesn't want to go back with me to Mablethorpe, I am not sure I should force him to do so. It'll only push him further away, and might end up making him despise me in the end. Zachariah, I cannot go through the rest of my life knowing that my little brother hates me."

"Now don't say that, Vivienne. Adrian doesn't hate you and never will. Just stop that kind of talk right now. You are a strong woman who sticks to her beliefs, so don't throw it all away. I have never known you to give up like this before."

"I'm not as strong as you might believe." Her bottom lip quivered, and he wasn't sure that she wouldn't start crying. He hoped not. A crying woman was his weakness. That always made him feel so helpless and he didn't like feeling that way.

"Nay, I refuse to believe that. You are even stronger than you think. After all, for seven years now you never gave up hope of finding your son or brother. Because of it, you've been reunited with both of them once again. Don't you see? This is a sign. Everything is going to be all right after all. And it is because you never stopped trying, so don't stop now."

"I suppose you're right. I can't give up now."

"That's my girl," he said under his breath, wanting to hug her. But he wouldn't. That would only complicate things between them more.

Vivienne sighed again. "Even if things didn't turn out the way I'd hope they would regarding Adrian, at least he is alive and I found him. That is all that really matters."

"That's right, it is," he said, glad to see her snapping back to her feisty self again. "You also haven't given up finding justice for your parents' deaths by continuing to try to hunt down their killers. And for your information, I haven't stopped looking either."

"Thank you, Sheriff." The bright smile returned to her face. "I appreciate that and all you do."

He took a big risk and reached out and cradled her hands in his. He no longer cared who saw him do it, and only hoped that she wouldn't reject him at a time when they were both so vulnerable. "Vivienne, look at me. Look me in the eye," he told her. When she raised her weary face to do so, he said the words that he hoped would snap her out of her depression. "I promise you, we *will* find your parents' murderers and bring about justice someday soon. I also promise that Adrian will remember you again, even if it does take some time. But it will happen."

"You can't make promises you can't keep."

"I have every intention of keeping them."

"Honestly?"

"Didn't we agree not to lie to each other."

"Yes. Yes, we did." She flashed him a weak smile.

"Then you see that you have nothing to worry about. However, before we can focus on any of that, you and I have a job to do. We need to bring about justice for another young man's unfortunate death. Fingers didn't deserve to die either. And right now, we have the best chance of finding his murderer first, and I don't want to walk away from this case until it is solved."

"Nay, he didn't deserve to die. He was only here to try to help us reunite with Adrian. And since that happened, I agree that we owe it to Fingers, and also to his brother Mouse, to find his killer."

"Fingers cared a lot about Mouse and he'd be happy to know you are taking him under your wing. He also said he was friends with Adrian. If he hadn't cared a lot about your brother, he never would have come to the ship to give me information about him in the first place."

"I am glad that Adrian at least had good friends like Fingers and Mouse."

"Me, too. Unfortunately, someone else didn't agree with that. His friendship with Adrian must have been a threat to the killer. He must not have wanted us to know whatever information Fingers was about to give us, and for that, the poor lad lost his life."

A look of horror washed over her face and her bottom lip trembled. "Am I to blame for the death of Fingers? Did it happen because of my selfish desire to find Adrian again and be with him? The young man risked his life to help me...and because of it, he died."

She looked even worse now than before and seemed as if she was going to start wailing with lament. He had to do something fast.

"Nay, Vivienne, it is no one's fault. Things always happen for a reason, even if we don't know what that reason is. I think Fingers was about to tell me who sold Adrian to Adder."

"What?" That took her interest and pushed her out of her self-pity. "Fingers saw the man who kidnapped Adrian seven years ago and then sold him into thievery?"

"Yes. That's what he told me on the street. However, he never gave me a name. But he did say he'd remember the man if he ever saw him again."

"Then he did see him," said Vivienne. "And the man who sold Adrian to Adder knew this and wanted to shut him up before he was discovered."

"It almost seems that way. However, you know that we can't come to any real conclusions before we have all the facts."

"Yes. Yes, of course. You're right. We need facts."

With a quick gaze one way and then the next, he realized no one aboard the *Falcon* was really paying attention to them. Bear and Isaac were up on the sterncastle with Stitch in the middle of a conversation. Ramble was up in the lookout basket, and the rest of the crew were scrubbing the decks or hiding in the shade playing cards. He grabbed her by the shoulders and pulled her to him, giving her a big hug. He felt her rapidly beating heart against his chest. Then he quickly released her again and stepped back, trying to avoid the slap he figured would follow. To his surprise, she grinned instead.

"Thank you, Sheriff," she said. "I really needed a hug right now. You always seem to know what I need."

"You're...not mad at me then?" He still approached the issue cautiously. "It was just a friendly hug, that's all. I didn't mean anything by it." After last night, he was thoroughly confused and wasn't sure if she even felt attracted to him anymore even though he was still very attracted to her.

"I won't be slapping you again if that's what you mean."

"You won't?" He hoped she meant that in a more-than-friends way.

"Nay. After all, that's what friends do. Help others when they need it."

"So I helped you? With a hug?"

"Aye. It comforted me and helped me to snap out of my gloom. I know now exactly what I need to do."

"And what is that?" He ran a hand through his hair, confused by her words and not knowing what to expect next.

"I need to give Adrian time, of course. I have to be patient with him. And love him for who he is, even if he can't love me back. Yet."

"Oh. Yes," he said, seeing they were no longer talking about them, but back to speaking about her brother again. "That's a good attitude to have."

"He'll remember me and everything. In time. Just like you said. I just need to get him away from this horrible place. Once he's back at Mablethorpe Castle, I am sure he'll change."

"I hope so," said Zachariah. "But you said he doesn't want to go."

"Not yet, he doesn't. But I'll think of something to make him change his mind." Her spunk was back and he rather liked it. So she wasn't giving up after all. His little talk had done some good.

"I'm happy about your decision, but right now, we need to talk to Adrian about the murder of Fingers. Mayhap he'll be able to shed some light on the situation and help us catch the poor lad's killer."

"Yes. I agree. Let's go question him together, Sheriff Fitch."

Zachariah was proud of Vivienne for gathering herself together so fast. He was also happy that he could be the one to help her find that thread of hope once again. He opened the door to the cabin and let her enter first, following right behind.

"Red, Sheriff Fitch and I would like to ask you some questions," Vivienne told her brother.

"Vivienne," Zachariah said softly. "You don't need to keep calling him Red since you now know he is really your brother."

"Red is my name," said the lad, having overheard him.

"It's all right," Vivienne told Zachariah. "Until his memories return, it will be easier for him if I call him by the name he's been using for the past seven years."

"Well, I need to get back to the galley," said Nairnie, heading for the door. "Buzzard is goin' to be screamin' for a meal, and I'm not in the mood to listen to him right now." She left the room, closing the door behind her. Grunt ran to the door wagging his tail.

"She's still upset with Bear, I see," mumbled Zachariah, taking a seat at the table across from Adrian. Grunt started to bark.

"Mother, I think Grunt wants to go out on the deck," said Martin.

"Can you take him out there to sniff around? But stay away from the side rails and don't go on the upper decks without me," Vivienne told Martin.

"Sure. Come on, Mouse." Martin ran to the door and started to open it.

"Nay. Mouse needs to stay here," said the sheriff. "I have some questions for him as well."

"But Mouse wants to come with me," complained Martin.

"Martin, do what the sheriff says, please." Vivienne kissed her son atop the head. "And don't get in Nairnie's way if she's cooking."

"Yes, Mother," said Martin, somberly leaving the room with the hound and without his new friend at his side.

"Mouse, come join us," said Vivienne, holding out her hand for the child. He seemed scared and backed away. "Or if you want, I'll sit on the pallet with you instead." Vivienne picked up the hem of her skirt and sat on the pallet, right on the floor. Mouse gingerly seated himself next to her. She slipped her arm around the boy's shoulder, pulling him closer.

Zachariah smiled inwardly. Vivienne truly was a good mother. Even if Mouse wasn't her child, she still showed care and kindness toward him. Zachariah could see now that her heart was full of love, and that she wanted every orphan to feel this kind of importance and acceptance. However, if she kept it up, soon the castle would be overridden with strays that she'd brought home. That was definitely her weakness, though an admirable one at the same time.

"When can I leave this ship?" asked Adrian impatiently.

"We're going to have a good meal soon," said Vivienne, before the sheriff could answer.

"I'm not hungry." The lad's stomach growled, proving him a liar.

"Red, the food is really good," said Mouse, rubbing his belly with one hand and licking his lips.

"Well, mayhap I could stay for a while," Adrian finally agreed. "But not long. I need to get back to town."

"Good, I'm glad you decided to stay for a while," said Vivienne. "And if you'd like, I could get you a barrel of water to wash up in too."

"Why?" Adrian jumped up. "Are you saying I stink?"

Zachariah could smell the stench on the young man from across the table. Plus, since Adrian came from the tannery, he was sporting a few scents that no human should ever have to endure.

"Sit down," he told the boy. "There is no need to get so defensive. Lady Vivienne is only trying to make you comfortable. You should thank her for it, since none of the men of this ship would be so accommodating with you."

"I'm comfortable without her help," he spat. "I like it in my pit back at the tannery."

"Red, this pallet is really warm and soft." Mouse slipped out of Vivienne's hold and lay down, hugging a pillow. "They even have blankets and pillows. I slept so good that I feel I'm on top of a cloud. You should try it."

Zachariah saw Adrian's longing to do just that as his gaze wandered over to the pallet and stopped on the pillow that Mouse hugged. It had to look like heaven compared to a hard, smelly pit for a bed at the tannery. Zachariah knew the look of want in someone's eyes, and this lad certainly had it.

"We can talk about all that later," said Zachariah. "Right now, we need your help in trying to identify Fingers' murderer."

"I don't know who did it. It wasn't me."

"No one thinks it was you, Adrian," said Vivienne, getting a nasty look from the lad. "I mean...Red."

"Do you know anyone who might have wanted to kill your friend?" asked the sheriff.

"You mean besides Whitstable's sheriff and Adder?" asked Adrian.

It was no surprise to hear that the sheriff was a suspect, since the man seemed to hate all the boy thieves. But Zachariah needed to know more about Adder.

"I thought you all worked for Adder and that he was somewhat of a...father to you," said Zachariah.

"Well, he was. At first." Adrian removed his hood and looked down at his dirty hands that were clasped together atop the table. "Adder never really liked me, but he adored Fingers."

"My brother was nice to everyone," said Mouse. "He especially liked Adrian. The three of us were like brothers."

"Yes. I felt like their brother, though I know I really wasn't," admitted Adrian.

"So, if that's true that Adder liked Fingers so much, then why would you think Adder would want to kill him? I thought he was Adder's best thief," continued the sheriff.

"My brother was the best at picking pockets, that's true." Mouse sat up and seemed to want to help now. "Adder always said he liked Fingers better than any of the other boys. I heard him say it."

"If so, then why would you say Adder might want him dead?" Zachariah looked back at Adrian, hoping for an answer that might at least give him a clue as to solving this case.

"I don't know," said Adrian, finishing off the wine in his cup. "It's just a feeling I get. I never trusted Adder. That's why I stopped bringing him the things I stole. I have been hiding from him for years now."

"And Fingers was going to tell us where to find you," said Vivienne.

"Actually, he was going to tell me all about you. Including about the man who sold you to Adder when you were only nine," said Zachariah.

"What?" Adrian looked at each of them as if in disbelief. "So I was sold to Adder when I was a child. I didn't know that. No one ever told me. I just thought I was an orphan and Adder took me in."

"Yes, you were kidnapped and sold to Adder. And it happened right after you disappeared when the bandits attacked us on the road. Don't you remember?" asked Vivienne. "Think really hard. Who was it who took you to Adder?"

An odd expression darkened the lad's face. Then he shook his head and it showed that frustration inside him was growing.

"I...I don't know. I can't remember. My head hurts." He swiped at the cup, sending it skidding across the table and hitting the floor. With both hands he hid his face.

"Mayhap if you lay down and rested for a little while it would help." Vivienne shot to her feet and so did Mouse. "Come, lie on the pallet."

"Do it, Red," said Mouse. "It's real nice. I'll stay with you, so you don't need to be scared."

"Who said I'm scared?" Adrian jumped up. "I'm not scared. I'm the bravest person you'll ever meet."

"We believe you," said Vivienne calmly, leading the lad to the pallet. "Just lie down and close your eyes for a while. Mouse will stay with you. The sheriff and I will be back soon."

Once Adrian was comfortable, Zachariah and Vivienne left the room together, closing the door to the cabin behind them.

"What do you think?" asked Zachariah.

"I think my brother needs a little attention and a lot of love, and that is exactly what I'm planning on giving him."

"Vivienne, he doesn't seem to know anything. I'd like to talk to Mouse again, though, since he was actually here when the crime was committed."

"Not now," she told him. "It is important that my brother trusts us. Also that he is made to feel at ease, happy, and satisfied while he's here. But we don't have much time to do that. If we can't bring him around to agreeing to go to Mablethorpe with us by the time Bear has to go on his next mission for the King, we might never see him again."

"So, then. You're not planning on kidnapping him and bringing him home, even against his will, are you?" Zachariah felt apprehensive waiting for her answer. "No lies, Vivienne. Remember our promise."

She smiled and chuckled. "Of course not, Sheriff. My

brother needs to make decisions for himself, and I won't get in the way of that."

"Good. All right, I'm going back to the dock to question the workers. Some of them say they thought they saw someone in a hooded cloak coming from the ship that day, but then again, most of them are drunken sailors, so I take that confession lightly."

"All right. Let me know what you find out. I'll stay here and see to the comfort of Adrian and Mouse."

The sheriff walked away just as Nairnie walked up, looking over her shoulder at him. "Did I hear ye say ye're goin' to let Adrian stay in Whitstable if he decides he doesna want to return to Mablethorpe with ye?"

"Did I say that?" She purposely blinked several times and smiled again. "If so, I must have forgotten."

"Lady Vivienne, you're plannin' on kidnappin' the boy, even though ye promised the sheriff ye wouldna."

"Nairnie, I made a promise to the sheriff, and I cannot break it."

"Then ye're really goin' to let Adrian stay in Whitstable?"

"Nay. Of course not. I will not lose Adrian again. He is my brother and I want him back, no matter if he remembers me or not."

"And how are ye goin' to do that without forcin' the lad or lyin' to the sheriff?"

"I'm...not sure yet. I'm going to have to just figure something out."

"Like what?"

"Well, I still have a little time yet. I guess I'm just going to have to talk to Adrian and do everything in my power to make him remember before this ship sails back to Mablethorpe without him."

"And if he doesna remember? What will ye do if he wants to stay in Whitstable?"

"That is not going to happen if I can help it."

"But it might, lassie. The boy doesna even ken his own name."

"Then we have a lot of work to do quickly, don't we?"

"We?" she asked. "Och, dinna get me involved in this. Bear and I are already at each other's throats and he willna like me bein' deceptive."

"Nairnie, you have to help me. I can't break my promise to the sheriff, but you didn't make one."

"I willna kidnap the lad if that is what ye're hintin' at."

"You don't want to see me lose my brother again after having searched for him for seven long years, do you?"

"Nay, of course no'." Nairnie looked over at her husband who was staring at her from the other side of the ship. "And I really dinna want to lose Bear either, but some things just canna be helped. We must think of what is best for us all, I suppose. And I just hope what is best for us all will also make all of us happy."

Chapter Fifteen

Another day was nearing an end, and Zachariah was no closer to solving the murder of the lad named Fingers than he'd been several days ago.

"I think it was Adder who killed the boy," said Bear, sitting up at the sterncastle, leaning back against the bulkhead with his feet propped up.

"He is suspicious, I admit," said Isaac, "but we still have no real proof it was him." He stood up, holding on to the tiller and looking out at the water, probably pretending he was captain of the ship.

"That's not exactly true," said Zachariah.

"What do you mean?" asked his brother.

"Well, I wanted to wait for Lady Vivienne to join us to discuss this, but she seems to have locked herself away in the cabin, so we'll have to move on without her."

"I think she's just wanting to stay close to her brother," said Bear.

"Yes. Although it might be better if she didn't at this point."

"So did you find out something, Sheriff?" asked Bear.

"I think so," said Zachariah. "When we were talking with

Adder, he referred to Fingers in the past tense when I questioned him about the lad. However, we never told him that Fingers had died."

"That proves he knew about it. And probably did it," said Isaac, nodding his head.

"He could have heard about the murder from the wharf rats," suggested Bear. "After all, word spreads fast on the docks."

"I'm here," said Vivienne, climbing the steps and coming to join them. "And I heard what you said. I am not convinced Adder killed Fingers, although I think he probably knew about it, or mayhap was involved somehow."

"That could be true," said Zachariah. "However, Adder never could have hoisted Fingers up to the yardarm by pulling him up with a rope. The man has no thumb on one hand and part of his first finger is missing as well."

"I noticed that," said Isaac. "And he seemed to have a hard time just getting up off the ground."

"The boys are still both very afraid of Adder," Vivienne told them. "Adrian wants nothing to do with him, especially since he heard that he was sold to Adder like livestock."

"What about Mouse?" asked Zachariah. "Have you gotten him to talk yet? He seems to clam up around me."

"Mouse hasn't said a lot yet." Vivienne leaned her back against the railing of the ship with her arms out to the sides, holding on. She turned her face turned upward to the sun with her eyes closed. Damn, thought Zachariah, if she didn't look like a goddess with the wind blowing her loose hair up in the air and her gown billowing around her, making her seem so ethereal. "However," she continued, "I think he must have seen something or someone the day that his brother was killed, but is just too frightened to tell us."

"He could be our key witness," said Zachariah. "If he did

see who killed his brother and can identify him, we'd have a closed case by now."

"What about motive?" asked Isaac, catching on fast how to be a detective. "Who would have good cause to want the boy dead?"

"Well, I think he was killed because he was going to tell me about Adrian and bring me to him," said the sheriff.

"So the key part of the murder has to do with Lady Vivienne's brother then?" asked Bear.

Vivienne's brows dipped in worry. "Nay. Please don't say that. Because if that is true then my brother's life could be in danger."

"We need to find out for sure, Vivienne," said Zachariah. "Whatever you do, don't let Adrian or Mouse off this ship. Without them, we may never catch Fingers's killer."

"I WANT to go question the workers on the docks with you," Vivienne said to Zachariah later that day, just before sunset. They were still on the ship which was docked in Whitstable. Bear planned on leaving tomorrow but they still hadn't caught the killer.

"Nay, my lady. It's not a safe place for you to be." Zachariah looked over to his brother, raising his hand in the air. "Isaac, are you ready to go?"

"Sure thing, Sheriff," said his brother, raising a bottle of whisky to his lips. Zachariah's hand shot out to take it from him.

"What did you do that for? If you want a drink, just ask," said Isaac.

"Nay, I don't. We need to keep a clear head while we're questioning potential suspects."

Peg Leg Pate and Coop trudged past, and Zachariah handed Pate the bottle.

"Why thank you, Sheriff." Pate grinned ear to ear. "I could do with a drink."

"So could I." Coop snitched the bottle away from Pate just as the man was about to drink.

"That's my bottle," sneered Pate, taking it back. "The sheriff gave it to me."

"Well, it's mine now," complained Coop, pulling the bottle back his way.

"I think it really belongs to me." Bear snatched it away from him and raised the bottle, sucking down the liquid.

"Quit drinkin' like that or ye'll be hobblin' around the ship like Pate with one good leg," said Nairnie, reaching up and grabbing the bottle away from him. When she did, Bear tried to get it back and it ended up falling, broken on the deck with the remains of the golden liquid seeping down through the cracks into the hold far below.

"Now look what ye've done, ye old fool," said Bear. "Ye're wastin' good whisky."

"Ye dinna need the drink. And how many times do I have to tell ye no' to call me old?" She gave his long beard a good yank, causing Bear to grimace and let out a loud groan.

"I think this is our cue to leave," Zachariah told his brother, as they headed toward the ladder to go to shore.

"Clean up this mess," commanded Nairnie.

"Ye clean it up since it was yer fault." Bear crossed his arms over his chest. "And while ye're at it, go down into the hold and get me another bottle of whisky to replace that one."

"Ye are more daft than I thought if ye really expect me to make my way down those steep stairs into that black hole." Nairnie was furious, and their argument was once again out of control. Most of the crew slunk off in different directions aboard the ship, just to get away from them.

"I'll get a new bottle of whisky for you, and I'll clean up the mess when I return," offered Vivienne, heading for the door leading to the hold. She really didn't want to go down into that rat-infested damp, dark space, but knew Bear wouldn't calm down without his whisky, and that Nairnie wouldn't be happy until the mess was cleaned up, since she seemed to like to run a tight ship when she was here.

Grunt followed alongside her as she went over and yanked open the door leading down to the bowels of the ship. The sun was getting low on the horizon and it was dark down in the hold.

"Afraid to go down there alone, my lady?" Peg Leg Pate stood behind her. "I'd go down for you, but unfortunately..." He held up his wooden leg that looked like naught more than a broom handle to her.

"Nay, Pate. I wouldn't expect you to attempt these steep stairs. Not in your condition," she told him.

"Let me escort you down into the hold," said Scythe, eying her up as if he wanted to eat her.

"Nay, let me do it. I'd be honored to escort a lady into the dark." It was Goldtooth, the biggest of the ex-pirates, besides Bear. He held up a lit lantern and his gold front tooth seemed to glitter in the firelight. "Here, I brought a lantern we can use." He hung it on a post next to the open door.

Suddenly, she was surrounded by most of the crew. Her heartbeat picked up and she felt bile rising to her throat. They all wanted to take her down in the hold and, she was sure, try to have their way with her too.

"Nay, I don't need any help, thank you." Grunt growled lowly, showing his teeth as the men got closer to her. Now Vivienne wished she had gone to shore with Zachariah, because she wasn't feeling safe at the moment at all. Her hand grabbed for her weapons, but she cursed herself when she realized that she'd left her weapon belt with her dagger and sword back in the cabin.

"What's the matter with all of ye? Get away from the lassie, because ye are gettin' me angry." Nairnie fought her way through the group of men, her ladle in one hand and her iron pan in the other as she swung at the men, managing to hit a few of them along the way.

"God's toes, Nairnie, put that pan away," yelled Jax, ducking as it went right over his head.

"Use that ladle for scooping soup, not bruising us," complained Stitch, hurrying back up to the sterncastle to escape her.

"Go on! Scat!" shouted Nairnie, until the last of the crew had finally left.

"Thank you, Nairnie," said Vivienne, letting out a deep breath. "I was wondering how to handle that."

"What are ye doin' goin' in the hold? That is no place for a lady."

"I told Bear I'd get him a new bottle of whisky, and I didn't want you to have to go down there."

"He doesna need the drink. Besides, he's busy cleanin' up the mess." She nodded to show Vivienne that Bear was doing just that. But when they looked, Bear was leaning his back on the railing while he watched Ramble down on his knees mopping up the spilled whisky and picking up the glass.

"Buzzard! I told ye to do it, no' the boy." Nairnie threw her hands up in the air. "Do ye ever listen?" She waddled over to Bear and the two of them started arguing once again.

"Well, Grunt, I guess we'll go back to the cabin to escape all this noise." She heard the clicking of nails on wood and turned to see her hound barreling down the steep steps, barking at something in the hold. "Grunt? Grunt, nay. Get back here.

Don't go down there. Please." It was too late. The hound had disappeared into the dark hold, and now she was going to have to go after him.

Vivienne looked back, but realized she didn't want the crew to help her fetch her dog. And Nairnie and Bear were in the middle of a heated discussion, so she didn't want to intervene. Isaac and Zachariah might not be back from questioning sailors for hours yet, and she wouldn't leave her hound down there in the dark that long. Her gaze traveled over to the cabin next. Should she ask Adrian to help her? Nay, she decided. Mouse and Martin were also in there. Knowing her son, he'd probably purposely want to visit the hold, since he liked dangerous adventures. She didn't want the boy down there at all.

"Grunt, come," she called down the steps once more, but now the dog was silent. She had no choice but to go and retrieve him herself, taking the lit lantern that Goldtooth had left her. Slowly, she descended into the dark, scary space, leaving the door to the hold open. She clutched on to the side rope that served as a hand rail as she took the narrow steps one at a time. She had to keep her feet turned sideways since the steps weren't even wide enough to hold her entire foot in the normal position. As she made her way lower, the sound of dripping water filled her ears. Dim slits of light shone down from the spaces in the boards of the deck above her head. When she got to the bottom, she realized there was at least a foot of water down there!

"Grunt? Where are you?" She held the lantern up, screaming loudly when a large rat brushed past her hand as it hurried across one of the crossbeams. She covered her chest with her hand as her heart beat rapidly in her chest. "I hate rats. Grunt, stop chasing rats and come here right now," she scolded, still not able to see him.

That's when she spotted a crate with full bottles of whisky sticking out of it. She was about to reach out to get a bottle for

Bear, but Grunt's barking started up again from behind her. And this time it had that sense of urgency that meant there was trouble. She knew she had to go to him right now, but dreaded doing so.

Bravely walking in the murky water that she could not see through, she trudged toward the sound of her hound's barking, really wishing she had at least had her dagger with her right now. But she wouldn't take the time to go back to get it. Not when her dog might be in trouble. Nay, she wouldn't leave Grunt there alone.

"What's the matter, boy? Did you find something?" she asked, moving closer toward the sound. That's when she saw her dog standing atop a barrel. Grunt barked, looking down into the water on the floor. Moving her lantern to what took the hound's attention, the scant light fell across something floating on the water just up ahead, but she couldn't tell exactly what it was. She moved closer, and that's when she realized just what she was looking at, and it was the last thing she wanted to see right now. There, in the water on the floor of the hold was a dead body!

Chapter Sixteen

Vivienne screamed loudly, seeing the body floating face down in the water. It looked to be a man with his arms out to his sides. He was one of the crew she surmised by the way he was dressed. Grunt continued to bark from atop the barrel. Vivienne still stood in the water, so scared that she couldn't even move. She'd been around dead bodies before, but the sheriff had always been with her. She had never had to encounter one on her own. And in such secluded and scary surroundings. For all she knew, the man could have been murdered. And if he was...she could be next if the killer was still lurking in the shadows of the hold.

"What the hell is going on down here?" Bear barreled down the steps with Stitch and Ramble right behind him. "Lady Vivienne, I heard your scream. Are you all right?"

"I am...but he isn't." She pointed a finger, her eyes still fixated on the poor, dead man.

"God's eyes! Who is it?" asked Stitch from behind him.

"Come on, we need to get him out of here." Bear waded through the water, flipping the man over. That's when she saw that it was Tyne. With a knife stuck in his chest.

"It's Tyne!" shouted Ramble to the crew members at the top of the stairs, who were watching and wondering what happened.

"Nay!" screamed Scythe, Tyne's best friend. He pushed his way through the crowd and ran down the stairs to join them, nearly falling in the process. "Who would have done this? Why?" he cried, dropping to his knees in the water, reaching out to give his dead friend a hug.

"We'll leave that to the sheriff to figure out," said Bear. "Men, get his body up on deck. Quickly, before the rats find him."

"Yes, keep him away from the rats," said Vivienne, with a quaver in her voice. She couldn't stop thinking about the murder on Rotten Row and what the rats had done to that poor, dead woman.

"Lady Vivienne, come with me," said Bear, holding out his hand. "You're a lady and shouldn't be down here."

"Gladly," she said, handing the lantern to Stitch, and taking Bear's hand as he led her to the steps. "Come, Grunt. Good boy," she told her hound, realizing that once again her dog had led them to a body. That is, right into the heart of more trouble.

"Lady Vivienne, are you all right?" Zachariah pushed his way through the crew members to get to her aboard the ship. He and Isaac had been on the docks, but saw Ramble motioning to them from the lookout basket and hurried back, thinking there might be a problem. They had just returned to the ship when Ramble informed them that Tyne was dead and had been murdered.

"Zachariah!" Vivienne ran to Zachariah, giving him a tight hug. He could feel her body shaking beneath his touch. Neither of them cared that everyone witnessed their display of affection for each other. In times like this, it was a necessity, not a frivolous act.

"How did it happen?" he asked, looking over Vivienne's head to see Tyne spread out on the deck. Scythe was down on his knees next to his friend.

"Grunt found Tyne, dead in the hold," she told him.

"We've got another murder on our hands, Sheriff." Bear nodded to the body lying prone on the deck. Zachariah saw the dagger sticking in the man's chest, having been stabbed right through the man's heart. Releasing Vivienne, Zachariah hunkered down and inspected the body closer. "Whose dagger is this?" he asked, removing the blade and taking a good look at it. He was sure it looked familiar, but he could not remember where he'd seen it before. It had a black handle with a lot of notches carved into it.

"It's not Tyne's. I've never seen it before," said Scythe, looking more than distressed about the situation.

"No one leaves the ship without my permission," said Zachariah, needing to get to the bottom of this quickly. They were sailing back to Mablethorpe tomorrow, and now they had not one, but two murders to solve.

"Shall I fetch the sheriff and coroner?" asked Bear. "Or doesn't it even matter, since the Sheriff of Whitstable doesn't seem to care."

"Isaac will do it," said Zachariah, still inspecting the knife. "And yes, it matters. Tyne wasn't a thief from his town, so the sheriff should take a better interest in this death."

"Sure, I'll go," said Isaac, hurrying off to get them.

"Now, I want to know if anyone heard or saw anything suspicious," continued Zachariah.

There was silence. The crew members all looked at one another but none of them said a word.

"Someone had to have seen someone go down into the hold. Didn't anyone even see Tyne go down there?"

"What was he doin' down there in the first place?" asked Nairnie, watching from the back.

"I didn't tell anyone to do any work in the hold or to fetch any of the cargo," said Bear.

"He went to get us some whisky," admitted Scythe. "We wanted a drink."

"No one gets whisky without my approval, and you know it," Bear reprimanded the man.

"I know," said Scythe. "We were only going to sneak out one bottle. We saw them down there when you made us sleep there, and figured we deserved it. We didn't think anyone would notice it missing. Sorry, Cap'n."

"How long was Tyne gone?" asked the sheriff.

"Mayhap half an hour," said Scythe with a shrug. "Perhaps an hour. Mayhap more."

"That long and you didn't think it was a little odd that he hadn't returned? Why didn't you go looking for him?" asked Zachariah.

"I was trying to keep the rest of the crew from noticing. I thought it was a little long, but sometimes Tyne stopped to snitch an apple or some salted herring from the barrels down there." Scythe lowered his head as if in shame.

"So you were stealing whisky all this time and not telling anyone about it?" asked Jax.

"Nay. Not all the time. Just sometimes," Scythe answered.

"I knew those two couldn't be trusted," snapped Goldtooth. "I told the Cap'n not to take them on as part of the crew in the first place."

"He probably killed his own friend," shouted another of the crew members.

"I don't have to stay here and take this abuse." Scythe

jumped up and pushed through the crowd as he headed for the shuttle boats.

"The sheriff said not to leave," Coop shouted after him.

"Tyne was my friend and I'm not going to just sit here. I'll find the killer since no one else seems able to do so." Scythe kept on going.

"Shall I bring him back, Sheriff?" asked Bear. "I'd be happy to use force on that one."

"Nay, he won't go far." Zachariah shook his head. "We'll get him soon, but first, I want to know if anyone saw anyone suspicious aboard? If so, it would clear the names of all the crew."

"I did," came a little voice from the shadows. Zachariah looked up to see Mouse creeping slowly toward them.

"You did?" asked Zachariah, putting down the knife. He got up and headed over to the boy. "Are you saying you saw someone come out of the hold?"

Mouse nodded. "It was right before Grunt and Lady Vivienne went down there."

"Who was it, Mouse?" asked Vivienne. "And why didn't you tell anyone about it?"

Zachariah saw the boy flinch. He didn't want Vivienne to ruin things for him since Mouse was finally opening up to him. This could be the important lead they needed to solve mayhap both of the cases.

"Vivienne, please. I'll handle this," he told her.

"Sheriff, I am part of this investigation too, if I must remind you."

"You just had a bad scare and the bottom of your gown is soaking wet. Why don't you go back to the cabin and change into something dry?"

"Sheriff Fitch, I do not appreciate the way you are trying to get rid of me. Please stop ordering me around."

"Lady Vivienne, the sheriff is right. It's for the best if ye let him handle this," said Bear. "That is, let the men handle it since Tyne was one of the crew."

Zachariah heard Nairnie snort as Vivienne stormed away with her dog following.

"All right, Mouse. Now tell me what or who you saw. Don't be frightened." All the crew stood around watching and waiting to hear what the little boy had to say.

"It was a man in a cloak with his head covered by a hood. I saw him sneak out of the hold."

"Did he seem familiar?" asked the sheriff.

"Aye. He was wearing the same cloak as the man who killed my brother."

Now they were finally getting somewhere. "So you did see who murdered your brother."

"I was up there and scared so I stayed hidden." Mouse peered up to the lookout basket. "A man in a cloak hit Fingers over the head and he falled down."

"Was he by himself?"

"Aye," said Mouse. "He was big and really strong. He threw the rope over the yardarm and then put it around Fingers' neck and hoisted him up all by himself. I wanted to help my brother, but I was too scared to even move."

"It's understandable," said Zachariah, putting his hand on the boy's shoulder. "You were too frightened. Besides, you couldn't have helped him, since you are just a small child. If the killer had seen you, then he would have most likely murdered you as well."

VIVIENNE STORMED TO THE CABIN, yanking open the door and going inside. Martin was sleeping on the pallet and Adrian was peering out the portal.

"That man makes me so furious!" she said through gritted teeth. Grunt barked, waking up Martin.

"Mother? What's the matter?" Martin sat up yawning, and reached out to pet the dog.

"Someone killed Tyne, that is what's the matter," she told her son, not wanting to keep the truth from him. "He was stabbed with a black-handled dagger right through his heart and left floating in bilge water in the hold."

"What?" Adrian turned around, seeming surprised. "Did they catch the killer?"

"Nay. No one knows who murdered him." Vivienne sat down on the bench taking off one soggy shoe and pouring out some water. "Scythe left the ship and I am going after him." She decided to put the shoe back on, and stood up and grabbed her weapon belt.

"So someone else really died?" asked Adrian in concern.

"Yes. And I'll bet it was the same man who killed Mouse's brother." She looked around the room. "I need to get Mouse back in here. I can't leave him out there with those men." She turned to go back out to the deck.

"It's all right, Missy. He's out talkin' to the sheriff." Nairnie stood in the open doorway with her ladle swinging from her belt. "Are ye plannin' on goin' somewhere with that?" Nairnie's eyes settled on the weapon belt in Vivienne's hand.

"Nairnie, don't even try to stop me, because it won't work." She strapped on the weapon belt and then headed over to a hook on the wall to get her cloak. "I am going out to find and follow Scythe. I think he knows more than he is letting on, regarding the murders."

"I'll come with you!" Martin jumped up.

"Nay. You'll stay here where it's safe," she told her son.

"The sheriff isna goin' to like ye leavin' the ship by yerself," warned Nairnie.

"I don't care." She finished fastening her cloak. "Did you hear how the sheriff just dismissed me out there? We are supposed to be a team, working on this investigation together."

"Aye, I saw and heard," Nairnie answered. "And how about the way Bear said to let the men handle things. It was despicable."

"If you want something done correctly, then let a woman do it," said Vivienne, heading toward the door. "Nairnie, will you please cover for me?"

"If I wasna so angry with Bear, I'd say no. But in this case, I will agree with ye. However, I think ye need to at least bring a man with ye. It's dangerous out there for an unescorted female. I dinna want to see anything happen to ye."

"I can't ask any of the crew to go against the sheriff's orders. He told them not to leave the ship," Vivienne told her, honestly feeling like she would appreciate having someone with her this time since her legs were still shaking from what just happened in the hold.

"The sheriff didn't tell me that," said Adrian, walking over to join her. "I'll go with you, my lady. I have a dagger and know how to use it." He patted the knife attached to his belt.

"Nay, I couldn't ask you to do that." She smiled fondly at her brother, reaching out and cupping his cheek in her hand. To her surprise, he didn't back away, but let her do it. The Adrian from the past had always wanted to be with her, so his offer touched her heart. Since Adrian had been the only son, he had thought it was his job to protect Vivienne, even though she was quite a bit older than he.

"I want to help," he told her.

"I don't want to risk losing you again after last time," she answered.

"But I think I know where Scythe went."

"Where?" she asked him. "Please tell me."

Adrian crossed his arms over his chest and smiled smugly. "I won't tell you, but I'll show you. That is, if you let me come with you."

"Och, the boy is too much like ye, my lady," said Nairnie, throwing her hands in the air. "Bein' stubborn and connivin' seems to run in yer family's blood."

"All right. You can come with me," she finally gave in. "But Martin, you and Grunt will have to stay here."

"You can't leave Grunt behind," protested Martin. "He's a good protector. Better than anyone."

"I'll protect Lady Vivienne," said Adrian, making Vivienne's heart just about burst to hear her brother say this aloud, let alone call her Vivienne. Even if her brother didn't remember her or even who he was, he was still willing to put his life on the line to watch after her and keep her safe. That action said more than any words ever could. Yes, this truly was the brother she knew and loved after all.

"I'd be honored to have you join me, Red," she told him.

"Lady Vivienne?"

"Yes?"

"You can call me...Adrian if you really want to," said her brother, looking down to the floor.

"All right...Adrian," she said with a smile. "Let's go find out who killed your good friend before the man strikes again."

Chapter Seventeen

After talking with the Sheriff of Whitstable, Zachariah released Tyne's body over to the coroner for now, since this was a murder and it was part of the procedure for the coroner to inspect the body too. The crew was sad and quiet, and even Bear and Nairnie's arguing had momentarily stopped. This was the second murder on the *Falcon* and it really bothered him that they hadn't seen either of the murders happen. It basically happened right under their noses, and yet they were all oblivious to who could have done it.

Zachariah decided to take a moment to talk to Vivienne. He'd been short-tempered with her, and it hadn't been right. But honestly, this case was wearing on him. He knew they had a time constraint and he still didn't feel any closer to finding answers than before. They really didn't even have any clues to go on. It made him feel like a weak sheriff. Mayhap it was because he was away from home and not back in his own town. There he felt more comfortable and more in control. Not to mention, even walking down Rotten Row with all the rats wasn't half as difficult as having to climb down a rope ladder and take a shuttle boat every time he wanted to go somewhere.

All Zachariah wanted was to solve this case...both the cases, and get back home where he belonged.

"Sheriff, I've been thinking," said Bear.

"What about?"

"I really don't think any of my crew are killers."

"We haven't been able to prove that yet."

"But there is no evidence that any of them did it."

"True, and even without evidence, I have to admit that I feel the same way as you," said Zachariah.

"Do you have any feelings who it might have been?"

"I have some suspicions. After having heard Mouse say that there was only one man who killed Fingers, I realized it couldn't be just anyone. This killer was strong. And he knew how to maneuver the lines and get the body up to the mast quickly just by hoisting him up with a rope. Not everyone could do that."

"I suppose ye're right," Bear answered. "It would have to be someone from the docks. Or a sailor of some kind, I agree."

"Sailor," repeated Zachariah, suddenly remembering where he'd seen that black-handled dagger before. "God's eyes, Bear, I remember where I've seen that dagger that we found in Tyne's chest. And you are right. It belongs to a sailing man. Come with me, because I want to tell Lady Vivienne at the same time who I suspect is the killer. She is supposed to be investigating the murders with me, but I'm afraid I haven't been very easy to work with lately. It is time I start including her."

"Where is she?" asked Bear.

"I believe in the cabin." They made their way over to the cabin and he knocked. Martin flung the door wide open. Mouse was inside the small room and so was Grunt, but he didn't see anyone else. The dog barked a lot, almost as if he were trying to relay some kind of message to Zachariah.

"Martin, where is your mother?" he asked, scanning the

room but not seeing her anywhere. "I need to talk to her about the murders."

"She's not here," Martin answered.

"What? Where did she go? Is she in the galley with Nairnie then?"

"Nay. She left to go look for the killer. Uncle Adrian went with her." One thing about Martin that was different from his mother was that he never hesitated to blurt out the truth, no matter what it might be.

"What do you mean?" he gasped. "Why would she do such a foolish thing? What the hell is the matter with her?"

"She left because the two of ye dinna seem to hold a bit of respect for her, or even me, for that matter." Nairnie approached, looking more than angry with both of them.

"Mmph. Nairnie," grunted Bear. "Ye knew Lady Vivienne left the ship along with the boy thief, and yet ye let them go? Even against my wishes as well as the sheriff's orders?"

"Aye. That's right," she answered with a sniff. "And it is exactly why I agreed to her plan. I think the two of ye have been actin' like pompous asses lately."

"Watch that sharp tongue of yers, Nairnie," warned Bear. When it looked like they were about to argue again, Zachariah broke in.

"Whether that is true or not is beside the point, Nairnie," said Zachariah. "We're dealing with a killer here. Lady Vivienne and Adrian are both in a lot of danger. They never should have left the ship, especially not this late in the day."

"Then go after them instead of standin' here givin' me a tongue lashin'," she said with a wave of her hand.

"Where did they go?" asked Bear.

"I dinna ken. Adrian said he could lead her to where Scythe went, and then they left the ship together."

"I think I know where they went," said Martin, jumping up and down. "I bet they went back to that mean man, Adder."

"God's eyes, I certainly hope not," Zachariah ground out. "If that's the case then they certainly are in danger. Bear, will you join me? We'll grab Isaac on the way out."

"Of course, Sheriff Fitch. My muscles might be needed. And I'm more than willing to use them on that no-good scally-wag, Adder."

"I'm comin' with ye," announced Nairnie. "I willna let Lady Vivienne face that horrible man alone."

"Nay. Ye'll stay here, old woman," commanded Bear. "Lady Vivienne is not going to face Adder alone, because me and the sheriff will be there too. Didn't ye hear us?"

"On second thought, I'll take Isaac only," said Zachariah. "Bear, you can find the Sheriff of Whitstable and tell him every-thing we know. If Martin is right and they went to find Adder, we're going to need all the help we can get since we have no idea where to find him." Zachariah felt like this was the right deci-sion. After all, the last thing he needed right now was for Bear and Nairnie to be squabbling in his ear while he was trying to save Vivienne and Adrian, and at the same time bring down a killer.

"This is where Adder normally stays during the daylight hours." Adrian led Vivienne down a dark alley, ending up outside a door that led into the back of the whorehouse.

"I can't go in there," said Vivienne, stopping and shaking her head.

"Why not?" he asked.

"Because I'm a lady and that is...it's a—"

"A whorehouse," said Adrian. "Can't ladies even say the name of it aloud?"

"It doesn't matter. I don't want to go inside."

"Then I'll go in by myself and you can wait for me here," said Adrian.

"Nay, wait." She grabbed his arm as he started to open the door. "I'll come with you. I don't want you going in there without me at your side."

"I'm capable of taking care of myself," he told her. "Besides, it's not like it's the first time I've been in a whorehouse." He chuckled, but she didn't find it amusing.

"Adrian, you are too young to be visiting this kind of a place."

"You're not my mother, so stop telling me what I can or can't do," he said in a snide manner.

"Nay, I'm not your mother, that is true. However, I am your older sister, and I feel I am responsible for your safety."

"I don't have a sister," he said, just about breaking her heart once again. "Besides, I can defend myself. I don't need any girl to protect me."

"Adrian, if I would have protected you better seven years ago, then mayhap I never would have lost you in the first place. This time, I won't make the same mistake again. I'm coming with you, like it or not."

"My name is Red. And even though I told you it's all right if you want to call me Adrian, I still don't know what you're talking about with all this seven-years-ago crap. But if you really want to go in there, then follow me."

She didn't really want to go in, but neither did she want her little brother stepping inside without her. So she followed Adrian into the back of the whorehouse, then up the stairs and down a long corridor. It smelled like whisky, danger, and sex in there. Every room they passed by, she heard sounds of coupling.

Moans and screams of passion floated through the air. She even heard the knocking of bed frames banging up against the walls. Part of her always wondered what went on in the upstairs of a place like this, but now she decided that she would really rather not know after all.

The thought of her little brother possibly having bedded one or more of these whores was sickening to her. She had to work hard to push the thought aside and stay alert, since she didn't know what to expect. She held her father's sword in both hands, continuously scanning the area, hoping not to be noticed. Finally, Adrian stopped at the room at the end of the corridor and nodded.

"Adder's in there."

"Are you sure? How do you know?" she asked.

Adrian held up a finger, and leaned his ear toward the door, listening. "Shhh," he told her. "Listen."

She cocked her head to listen and heard the voices of two men arguing inside the room.

"You killed my friend. You bastard!" shouted one of the men.

"That sounds like Scythe," she whispered to Adrian.

"Calm down. I did no such thing," said the second man.

"And that's Adder's voice," Adrian whispered back. "I told you he'd be here."

"I know you had something to do with Tyne's death. Just admit it, you worthless fool," said Scythe.

"All right, I admit it. I did what I had to do. Just like you did seven years ago when you brought me the whelp who has since proven to be nothing but trouble."

Vivienne's heart jumped into her throat. Could they be talking about Adrian, she wondered.

"Speaking of that whelp I sold you, you still owe me money for the boy," said Scythe. "Don't think I didn't notice that you filled the coin bag half with rocks when I handed him over to you, and then you conveniently disappeared."

"You're not getting another penny from me. The boy is lazy, he doesn't listen, and had I known he was noble, I never would have taken him in the first place. If his family discovers the truth, we're both going to die. You do know that, don't you?"

Vivienne gasped, but quickly covered her mouth. She couldn't believe what she was hearing.

"That's why you had Tyne killed, wasn't it? You somehow knew I was going to come clean and tell the sheriff everything, didn't you?" asked Scythe.

"You saw what happened to Fingers when he was about to snitch, didn't you?"

"What does that boy's death have to do with me?"

"I heard on the docks that you were back and ready to spill your guts."

"From who?"

"I had one of my men follow you. He even stopped to play dice with you and Tyne, but you didn't know it." Adder laughed, obviously thinking he'd been so cunning. "I thought that little message I sent with Fingers swinging by his neck from the yardarm would have worked."

"The death of that boy was a message for me?" asked Scythe.

"Now, you get it." The sound of Adder slapping his palm against his head could be heard. "If you had figured it out the first time, your friend Tyne would still be alive today."

"I don't understand. I didn't tell anyone but Tyne about wanting to come clean."

"And Tyne talks a lot when he's full of whisky," said Adder. "You'd better choose your friends more carefully from now on."

Vivienne felt ill hearing all this. How could she and the sheriff have been so preoccupied that they hadn't picked up on any of it? That boy never should have died, even though there was nothing they could have done to stop it.

"Sadly for you, Scythe, now you're going to have to die too. Because I can't risk you telling anyone else that you've had a change of heart." Adder laughed uncontrollably. "You even thought you'd make a new life hitching up with pirates. What a bad decision, you dolt!"

"They're not pirates. And we work for the King!"

"Not for long you don't."

"Just try and kill me. I won't let you." The sound of a struggle came from within the room. "I'll slit your throat before you can even touch me. You're no threat to me, Adder. You're not even a good thief."

"Stay in Whitstable and work for me then, and I'll let you live," said Adder, trying to make a deal with Scythe.

"Why would I do that?" asked Scythe. "I don't fear you."

"Mayhap you don't feel I'm a threat, but you might not feel the same way about my henchman. Scoop! Get in here."

Vivienne gasped, hearing him calling to the oyster-seller that Bear, Isaac, and the sheriff had met with in the tavern, thinking the man was a friend. So it seemed Scoop was a killer after all! Although she'd not personally met him, she had heard he was a big, strong man. She realized she could never fight him off alone. This man had killed two people already, not to mention how he hoisted a dead lad up to the yardarm by a rope all by himself. That thought truly frightened her. Even with her father's sword in her hands, and with Adrian at her side, they really didn't stand a chance. "We need help, Adrian," she whispered to her brother. "We'd better go back and get Bear, Isaac, and Sheriff Fitch right away, and tell them what we know."

"Now, now, I think it's a little too late for that, my pretty little lady." A man came out of another room, catching them listening at Adder's door.

"Leave us alone!" she cried, holding her father's blade up to the stranger. Just then, the door to Adder's room swung open.

"Dammit, Scoop, get in here. Oh, it's that pesky lad. Who do you have with you, Red? She's alluring and looks like a whore that I'm really going to enjoy bedding."

"Adder, leave her alone," cried Adrian. "She's not a whore, she's a noblewoman."

"She's that lady from the *Falcon*, I'm sure of it," Scoop told Adder. "I saw her going to the hold of the ship just as I was climbing down the rope ladder."

"Red, you should have stuck with me, because joining the wrong side is only going to bring you trouble," said Adder. He then focused on her. "So you're Lady Vivienne who I've heard so much about from the wharf rats," said Adder with a chuckle. "You've seemed to create quite a stir here on Rook Row."

"I am she," said Vivienne, holding up her sword. "My uncle is Lord Mablethorpe, and this is my brother, Adrian. I am also King Edward's daughter, so I warn you not to harm us."

"Don't try to threaten me, because it won't work and you don't scare me, even with that blade in your hands," said Adder.

"I promise you, I know how to use it."

"You're a damned wench! And the King is not here, so he can't protect you."

"Nay, but Sheriff Fitch from Mablethorpe is here in Whit-stable, and he'll have your head if you or any of your men even try to hurt us."

"Oooo, I like a feisty wench," said Adder, not seeming at all worried that she had a sword in her hand and was ready to use it. "Bring them in, Scoop." Adder retreated back into the room.

"Get in there," growled Scoop, pushing them both into the room. From the man's brute force, Vivienne stumbled and lost her balance. She dropped her father's sword trying to catch herself when she fell.

"Boy, are you going to come back to me or die with her?" asked Adder, gripping the back of Adrian's tunic. "It's your choice. But I won't be deceived again."

"Don't trust the lad. He's a no-good liar," said Scythe. "Here, let me kill him for you, Adder. Then you can see I'm on your side and that you don't need to kill me after all." Scythe gripped his dagger and raised it up, heading for Vivienne's brother.

"Nay! Leave him alone." Vivienne reached for her sword, but Scoop's foot covered her hand, pressing down and keeping her from getting to it.

She heard a groan and her attention flashed over to the other men once more. Scythe hadn't killed her brother like he said he was going to do, but instead he had stabbed Adder. Adder, in turn, pushed Scythe into Adrian and the two of them fell to the ground.

"Dammit. Kill him, Scoop! Kill them all," shouted Adder, staggering backward and collapsing atop a table. He had Scythe's knife embedded in his side and blood flowed freely from the fresh wound.

"Nay, I'm done killing people for you," snapped Scoop. "I've paid off my debt to you, Adder. I killed the boy and that scurvy pirate. Killing boys and pirates is one thing, but I never agreed to kill a noble, and especially not a woman."

"So you were the one to kill both Fingers and Tyne?" asked Vivienne, pulling back her hand from under Scoop's foot. She already knew the answer, but needed to hear the man confess.

"Yes. I only did it because I owed Adder." Scoop kicked her sword away from her and it slid across the floor. "If I had known I'd be in so deep that I'd never get out, I never would have agreed to Adder's plan."

"A debt? What kind of debt?" she asked, trying to stall for time and also get more crucial information out of him. This would be all the evidence they needed to lock the man away for good.

"Scoop lost everything gambling, including his captain's ship," said Adder, struggling just to speak. "Then he killed his captain, and took over the fishing boat, thinking that would work, but it didn't," Adder went on through even worse ragged breathing. "I saved him from prison by lying to his crew and also the town sheriff. I covered it all up beautifully, but Scoop still owes me for all I did for him."

"Well, you still owe me money for bringing Red to you," said Scythe, pushing up to his knees.

"I knew it! And you just confirmed it twice. You and Tyne were the ones who kidnapped my brother seven years ago. And then you sold him to Adder to be a thief, didn't you?" asked Vivienne, the anger inside her only growing stronger.

"That's right," said Scythe. "We found him on the road, and he was so stupid that he didn't even know his own name. He was perfect for what we had in mind to make a little money. We knew Adder had a thieving ring and bought boys to do his stealing for him. We were promised good money for him, but Adder tricked us!"

"You did that? You really kidnapped me and sold me to Adder?" asked Adrian sounding stunned and seeming to try to understand or perhaps even remember this horrific event.

"Don't cry, boy," said Scythe. "We did you a favor. You were dumb and all alone and wouldn't have survived a day by yourself. You'd be dead years ago if it weren't for us."

"Scythe, when you said you wanted to come clean, you weren't going to confess to the sheriff that you had kidnapped and sold my brother to Adder, were you?" asked Vivienne. "You just wanted to tell them where Adder was so he would be arrested. You wanted him punished just because he cheated you out of money that you were promised. Isn't that right?" She couldn't see a man like Scythe ever confessing to something that would land him behind bars.

"Well, you have a brain after all, and not just pretty looks," said Scythe, making Vivienne wonder how she could have ever felt bad for Scythe when his friend died. "I waited a long time, but had my perfect opportunity when I joined Bear's crew and found out we were coming to Whitstable. You see, I knew Adder resided here. Then, when Fingers was found swinging from his neck, I figured I'd be able to put the blame on Adder, no matter if he had been the one to do it or not. It was all so perfect."

"How can you say that? An innocent boy died for nothing. You men all make me want to retch. Scythe, I cannot believe Bear ever trusted you and Tyne enough to take you on as part of his crew," said Vivienne. "He should have been able to see right through you."

"Pirates don't know nothing about trust," said Scythe with a chuckle. "That is why I knew it was exactly where Tyne and I needed to be."

"Scoop, shut him up," demanded Adder on a choked breath. "Do something to help me, don't just stand there! Kill him."

"Give me your knife, boy," commanded Scythe, ripping Adrian's dagger from his side. In the meantime, Vivienne quietly reached for her own dagger but unfortunately, Scoop noticed.

"Nay, you don't, you sneaky wench," said Scoop, ripping her dagger out of her hand just as Scythe got up and lunged at Scoop with Adrian's blade in his grasp. Scythe seemed to want everyone to pay for Tyne's death and being cheated out of what he was owed. Plus, he didn't want to die and would lie or kill anyone just to stay alive.

"Dammit, I don't want to kill you too, but you give me no

choice." Scoop stabbed Scythe through the heart with Vivienne's dagger and the man fell dead to the ground. Vivienne was starting to think they were doomed. How in the world were she and Adrian ever going to get out of here alive? She now regretted not waiting for Zachariah, or even telling him where she was going. God's eyes, if she had a chance to change things, she would do things differently and not let her emotions get in the way.

"Scoop, help me," said Adder, holding his hand over the wound but he was getting more and more weak from the loss of so much blood. "I'll get you out of this like I did before," promised Adder. "Just kill the girl and Red. We can't leave witnesses or we'll both hang."

"Bid the devil, this keeps getting worse," snarled Scoop. "And how much of a debt will I owe you this time, you rotten swindler? Mayhap I should just finish you off instead."

"Nothing. You'll owe me nothing, I swear," said Adder, starting to beg. "We'll call it even. Please. I'll even give you whatever jewelry or money we take off their bodies, but just get them out of the way and help me."

"Fine, but if you're lying, I'll have your head." Scoop ripped the dagger out of Scythe's chest and turned with it in his grip, coming for Vivienne next. She screamed. Being on the ground, she struggled to get up, not wanting to die now that she'd finally found her brother. She also didn't want to be killed by her own blade.

"Nay!" she cried. "Adrian, help me." She called for her brother, seeing him on his knees behind Scoop. "Don't let me die the way Mother and Father did. Please, help me, Brother. I'm sorry I wasn't able to protect you before, but now I need you to protect me."

"Shut up, wench!" snarled Scoop. "He's not going to help you because he's just a mindless, stupid boy who can't even make a decision on his own." Scoop swung his arm up over his head, stepping closer as he prepared to stab her to death.

Feeling frozen in fear, Vivienne closed her eyes, knowing she was about to die. Without a weapon, she couldn't fight him. She could try to kick at him...if she was able to move. But for some reason, she could do nothing but sit there waiting to die. Now, she knew the immense fear her brother must have lived through the night he watched his parents being murdered. So much fear must have encompassed him that it forced him to forget everything and everyone he knew and ever loved. Fear was a powerful thing. But then again, as she was about to find out...love was even stronger.

"Nay! Don't touch my sister, you bastard!"

Vivienne's eyes sprang open when she heard her brother's voice. Instead of being stabbed to death with her own dagger as she expected, Adrian had come to her rescue after all. She saw Scoop above her, frozen in motion, his hand in the air with her dagger still in his grip. But then she noticed that blood dripped from his lips. And as her gaze traveled a little lower, she discovered the tip of her father's sword sticking out from the man's chest. Scoop dropped her dagger and started to fall. She rolled to the side, just getting missed by his heavy body. Then she saw Adrian, standing tall and proud, using his foot against Scoop's backside as he pulled her father's blade out of the man's back and held it up high in a triumphant salute.

"Adrian?" she asked, her jaw dropping. She wondered about so many things right now that it made her head spin.

"I remember, Sister." Adrian reached down with one hand and helped her to her feet, all the while still gripping the bloody sword with his other hand. "I remember everything. Who I am, who you are, and even our parents. And Father's sword," he said, raising the tip of the sword and nodding toward it. This was Father's blade, and you tried to protect us all with it the night the bandits attacked us on the road and murdered them."

"Yes. Yes, that's right, Adrian," she said, in a shaky voice, barely able to speak. Was this truly happening right now? Could it really be that the boy who didn't know her a moment ago had just had his memories come flooding back into him, just like Zachariah had told her it might happen?

"I'm sorry I didn't know you at first sight, but now I remember that you are the best sister in the whole world," said Adrian, not able to stop smiling.

"It's a miracle," she cried, falling into her brother's arms, hugging him and kissing him, and feeling like she'd just been given the most precious gift of all. First, finding her son Martin was a miracle. Now, after searching for seven years and thinking he was dead, her brother Adrian returned to her, and best yet, he finally remembered everything that he'd forgotten. Yes, this truly was a second miracle, and she felt like the luckiest woman in the world.

Vivienne heard the sound of Grunt barking through the partially open door. Then she heard Zachariah's voice too.

"Grunt is telling me they're in here," Zachariah told someone, pushing open the door, holding his sword at the ready. "Good God, what happened here? Are you all right, Vivienne?" he asked, stepping over the dead bodies in a hurry to get to her.

"I am more than all right," she told him, smiling at her brother.

"What happened?" Isaac entered next, followed by Bear.

"It's that no-good Adder," said Bear, making his way over to the wounded man. "I'm going to strangle him with my bare hands."

"Don't hurt me," pleaded Adder. "I'll tell you everything, but please just let me live."

"Zachariah, Scoop killed Tyne and Fingers," Vivienne blurted out.

"We know. I figured it out when I remembered that I saw him with the black-handled dagger shucking oysters in the Blue Mermaid the last time we were there. I told the others, but we couldn't get here fast enough," said Zachariah, lowering his sword and reaching out to take her hand. "Are you hurt, sweetheart?"

"Nay, I'm fine. Adrian killed Scoop and saved me just as I was about to die." She smiled at her brother.

"I remember everything now, Sheriff Fitch," said Adrian. Zachariah noticed Adrian gripping Vivienne's bloodied sword. "I think seeing my sister in danger and also recognizing Father's sword is what jolted me enough to make my memories return. I remember everything that happened that night seven years ago as if it just occurred yesterday." Tears filled Adrian's eyes. "Sheriff, I confess, I killed a man tonight." He slowly lowered the sword. "Will I go to prison now because of it? I really don't want to lose my sister after we were finally reunited after so long."

"It was done in self-defense. To save me from being killed by a mad murderer," said Vivienne, looking over to Zachariah for help. "Please tell me Adrian won't be arrested for that."

"It's not his choice, it's mine," said the Sheriff of Whitstable, standing in the open doorway with his constable at his side. Nairnie peeked around them from behind.

"I heard what ye said, Lady Vivienne," said Nairnie, pushing her way between the men and focusing on the sheriff. "Sheriff Whitstable, ye wouldna arrest a young lad who no' only saved a noblewoman's life, but brought down a murderer and broke up a thieving ring, would ye?" Nairnie's hands went to her hips.

"This boy is a thief," said the sheriff, entering the room. His constable walked in as well. "We've been trying to catch him for years."

"A reformed thief, mayhap," said Nairnie, following them inside. "He didna ken who he was but his actions prove he's got a good heart." She gave the sheriff as well as the constable her evil eye.

"I ask you not to arrest the lad," said Zachariah. "And we'll be taking him back to Mablethorpe with us, so he'll be gone from Whitstable and no longer be a burden to you."

"What about all that he's stolen through the years?" asked Sheriff Whitstable.

"I'll pay you back whatever he's stolen from the people of Whitstable," said Vivienne. "Just please, let my brother come back home with me where he belongs. He saw his parents killed seven years ago, and then his memories were gone and he was sold to Adder like a slave. He was trained to steal and didn't know any better at the time. You can't blame him. He was a victim of horrible circumstances. He's a noble, Sheriff Whitstable. He's my brother. Please, just pardon him and let him leave here peacefully at my side."

"Well, I...I'm sure we can discuss this. I mean, I'll figure this out with Sheriff Fitch, that is," mumbled the Sheriff of Whitstable, his gaze flashing back to Nairnie when he spoke.

"Sheriff Whitstable, you have to agree that it is nice that the thieving ring will be brought down now, and no longer will be active in Whitstable," said his constable. "And the murderer is dead now, so there isn't much we have to be concerned with any more."

"Yes. Yes, I know that," said the Sheriff of Whitstable, looking a little frightened of Nairnie if Vivienne wasn't mistaken. It made her smile. "I said, we'll work things out before Sheriff Fitch and the Harlowes leave town. I think we can come to some sort of agreement."

"Did you hear that, Adrian?" asked Vivienne. "Before you know it, we'll be home at Mablethorpe Castle with Aunt Ellen and Uncle Gilbert once again."

"Yes, Sister, I heard," he said, putting his arm around Vivienne. "And you know the best part about all this?"

"That you won't have to sleep in an old tanning pit anymore?" asked Bear. That made them all smile.

"Or that you'll finally get a bath to clean you of your stench?" asked Isaac.

"Isaac, please. That wasn't very nice," scolded Vivienne.

"Nay, it's all right, Sister," laughed Adrian, not seeming at all to mind their insults. "He's right. I do stink." He sniffed his armpit making them all laugh. Then he bent over and petted Grunt on the head. "The best part of all this is that I found you, Vivienne, and that I have my memories back. I swear I won't let anyone take them away from me again. I also won't let anyone take me away from my sister, my nephew, or even Grunt, now that I've met him." That made them all smile, and the dog howled, giving his opinion too.

"Neither will I ever let anyone or anything get between us, Brother," said Vivienne, her heart soaring with happiness. "I promise you, Adrian, that from this day on, we will never be separated again."

Chapter Eighteen

The next day, Vivienne traveled with the others aboard the *Falcon*, returning to Mablethorpe after they'd attended a quick funeral for Fingers and Tyne, too. Zachariah had made a deal with the Sheriff of Whitstable and he'd agreed to let both Fingers and Tyne be buried just outside the church graveyard, even though the priest wasn't happy about it at all.

Vivienne had mixed emotions about things, since she'd almost died and needed time to think over all that had happened. She also wanted to ponder the kiss that had so surprised her with Zachariah, as well as the agreement they'd made to keep things professional between them.

She was ecstatic to not only have found Adrian, but that his memories had all returned. They'd stayed up half the night talking...remembering...laughing, and discussing their parents and things from their childhood, some of them that he'd remembered but she'd actually forgotten over the years. It was so good to have her brother back in her life again. She had thought she'd lost him forever, but thankfully she was wrong.

Adrian also loved spending time with Martin and getting to know him, and that did her heart good, too, since Martin really liked his uncle. Grunt loved Adrian, too, and the three of them were constantly together now.

Then, as if the voyage passed in an eye-blink, the ship docked, and they all started to disembark, having to take several shuttle boats to get them all back to the wharf. Vivienne's boat arrived there first.

"Mouse, you'll come to live with us now at Mablethorpe Castle," Vivienne told the little boy. He was still very scared and quiet...like a mouse. But being around Martin seemed to make him a little more outgoing over the past few days. Plus, Mouse felt more comfortable since he had already known Adrian and had been friends with him his entire life.

"Yes, Lady Vivienne. Thank you. I would like to live at the castle with all of you," said Mouse, being quite polite for a young boy who had been raised as naught more than a thief.

"Martin, Martin!" came the shout of Starah as she stood up in the back of the wagon that her uncle and aunt drove to the dock when they'd heard the ship had returned. The little girl waved her hand high over her head. Maleine and Wymond were in the back, and Maleine held on to Starah so she wouldn't fall out.

"Come on, Mouse. I see my friend Starah. I want to introduce you to her."

"Oh, you mean the pretty girl," said Mouse, tamping down his hair as if he actually cared about his appearance.

Grunt barked, jumping up on Martin. "You come too, Grunt. We have to tell Starah how we helped to catch a killer." The two boys and the hound headed down the pier to be with Starah.

"Oh, I see Aunt Ellen and Uncle Gilbert." Vivienne called out to them. "Hello. I'm back. And you won't believe who is with me." She put her arm around Adrian. "You remember your aunt and uncle, don't you?" she asked.

"Of course, I do," said Adrian with a big smile. "I told you, I remember everything now, Vivienne."

"Then let's go see them together."

"I can't wait to tell Uncle Gilbert that I finally figured out the answer to his riddle after all the years of him teasing me about it."

"Yes, you do that," she said, remembering how much Adrian enjoyed playing games with their uncle. They had always been jesting and laughing and being silly when they were together. Vivienne had often thought it was because Gilbert's own sons had died, so he considered Adrian as a son, in a way. He always used to spoil her brother, giving him not only lots of attention, but everything he could have ever wanted.

"Adrian? Is that you?" His aunt saw Vivienne's brother and held her hand to her mouth as tears fell from her eyes. "It's a miracle! You're alive! Gilbert, help me out of the wagon so I can hug him." Her husband helped her get out, and she ran to meet them, throwing her arms around Adrian and giving him a big hug. Then she proceeded to kiss him all over his dirty face.

"Vivienne," said her uncle, following her aunt over to them. "Is it true what I heard about someone being murdered on the ship? I told you not to go with those pirates. Now do you see why you should have listened to me?"

"Two people were murdered on the ship, actually," said Adrian, but hearing that only seemed to make her uncle even more cross.

"God's teeth, will this ever end?" asked her uncle.

"Gilbert, the children are alive and fine, so stop being so grouchy," said Aunt Ellen.

"I'm not a child anymore, Aunt, in case you haven't noticed," said Adrian. "I'm now a man."

"A young man," Vivienne corrected him, knowing in her mind and heart Adrian would always be nothing but her little brother. "Everything is fine, Uncle Gilbert, so don't worry," she told him. "The murderer has been apprehended, and Adrian saved my life."

"You almost died?" growled her uncle. "What the hell happened out there?"

Vivienne immediately regretted telling him that part.

"Gilbert, we'll talk about things when we get home," said Aunt Ellen. "Right now, you need to greet Adrian, since he's been found after all these years and you've yet to even acknowledge him."

"Uncle Gilbert, I'm back," said Adrian, with a big smile.

"Yes. Welcome back," said her uncle, with little expression at all.

"Uncle," said Adrian, looking happy and excited. "I know the answer now."

"We're glad you are alive, boy. That is wonderful." Her uncle patted Adrian on the back instead of picking him up in a big bear hug like he used to do when Adrian was a child. Vivienne found it a little cold of him not to welcome Adrian home in a more inviting way. Then again, it had been seven years since Adrian had disappeared. And Adrian wasn't that same little boy anymore that her uncle had once loved. She supposed that the time and distance between them was what most likely was making things awkward between them.

"Uncle, I know the answer to your riddle," said Adrian once again. "Even though it did take me seven years to figure it out."

"Huh? What is that you say?" he asked.

"The riddle about what walks on four legs in the morning, two in the afternoon, and three at night. I know the answer now."

"I'm afraid I don't know what you're talking about," said Lord Mablethorpe.

Adrian's face darkened. The joy and excitement he'd had a moment ago all seemed to suddenly wash away.

"Adrian, a lot has changed since you've been away," said Vivienne. "I'm sure Uncle Gilbert's memory is lacking a little too."

"But it was our favorite thing to do together," said Adrian. "Surely, he couldn't have forgotten about that."

"I'm afraid Vivienne is right. My memory isn't what it used to be," said their uncle. "Well, let's get home, shall we? I have a lot to do." He turned and headed back to the wagon.

"Give it some time, Adrian," their aunt tried to console him. "Gilbert has been though a lot as well, with the death of your parents and your disappearance, and also Martin's. He hasn't seemed the same since that awful night."

"But we always used to laugh together. He prided himself on his stupid riddles that I never understood. Until now."

"I know, but I am sure things will return to normal now that you're back," said the woman, with a kind and caring tone to her voice.

"Hurry up, I'm ready to go," called out Uncle Gilbert from the wagon.

"Things will be better in time. You'll see." Aunt Ellen kissed Adrian on the cheek, not hurrying in the least.

"I suppose," said Adrian, looking so forlorn that his uncle didn't remember about the riddle, even if it had been seven years since he'd last told it to him.

"Adrian, how would you like a nice bath once we get back to the castle?" asked their aunt.

"Yes, that would be nice," he said shyly. "I know I'm dirty and I really stink."

"Aunt Ellen, can we give Adrian his own room?" Vivienne asked her.

"Of course, we can, dear. He can have his old room that he

used to sleep in as a child when you came to visit." She held out her arm. "Let's go to the wagon before your uncle gets more impatient. He doesn't seem to have the same calmness about him that he did in prior years, but you'll get used to it in time, just like I did."

"What about Mouse?" asked Adrian.

"Who is Mouse?" she asked.

"I'm Mouse," said the little boy, as he and Martin had just run back to them with Grunt. Now Starah was out of the wagon and with them as well. Their uncle saw the children leave the wagon and started back after them.

"Mother, will Mouse be sleeping in our chamber with us?" Martin asked Vivienne.

"Vivienne, please tell me you didn't bring home another orphan," complained her uncle, walking back up to them.

"Yes, I did," she proudly admitted.

"This has got to stop," he continued. "We don't have room to house them all."

"Don't be silly, of course we do, darling," said his wife.

"Martin, Mouse can't stay with us in our chamber," Vivienne told her son. "We already have Maleine in our chamber and it is getting quite crowded."

"Then Mouse and Martin can stay with me," suggested Adrian. "In my room. After all, I don't need much space. Remember, I'm used to sleeping in a tanning pit."

"A tanning pit?" asked her uncle, his brows dipping down, making the crease in his forward more severe. "Vivienne, what is this all about?"

"We'll tell you all about it later," said Vivienne. "Go on, boys, climb in the wagon so we can get back to the castle. We have a lot to do."

"Come on, Grunt," said Martin, as the boys ran back to the

wagon, but Starah's eyes were on her father, who had taken the second shuttle boat to get to shore and was just unloading.

"Starah. I missed you." Zachariah stepped out of the shuttle boat and ran over and scooped his daughter up in his arms, giving her a big hug and kiss and making her giggle.

"I missed you, too, Father." She kissed him back.

"Hey, what about me?" Isaac got off the shuttle next, and walked over and stuck his face close to the little girl. "Didn't you miss your handsome, witty Uncle Isaac?"

"Nope," she said, making them all laugh.

"No?" Isaac made a sad face and Starah giggled.

"Yes," she said now.

"Come here, you little teaser." Isaac took Starah from Zachariah and walked off talking to her and carrying her to the wagon.

"Vivienne, while we have a second alone, I wanted to apologize." Zachariah seemed like he wanted to say more, but wasn't sure how to do it."

"For the kiss?" she whispered, smiling and wiggling her eyebrows.

His head jerked upward and he cleared his throat. "Well, yes. I suppose I should apologize for that as well, but I meant I should have included you more on this investigation. Now I regret that I didn't."

"It's all right." She gently laid her hand on his forearm. "It all turned out fine in the end, so no harm done. Plus, I found my brother."

"I am so happy that Adrian is home again. And that his memories have returned as well."

"He's not that little brother I remember any more, Zachariah."

"Nay? What do you mean?"

"I mean that Adrian is a man now. A man who even killed someone to protect me and save my life."

"Vivienne, I'm sorry about that too. I should have been there to protect you. You could have died in Whitstable."

"Well, that is something that I need to say I'm sorry for, I guess. I never should have left the ship without you to then go courting sure trouble."

"Aye, that's true. You don't need to look for trouble since trouble always seems to follow you wherever you go."

"Hurry up, or I'm leaving without you," Gilbert impatiently yelled from the wagon.

"We're coming. But we have to wait for Nairnie," Vivienne called back to him, then turned again to Zachariah. "I'm so glad Adrian is home now."

"Me, too. And I'm sure he will make a fine knight someday," said Zachariah.

"Yes, he will. If he wants to be a knight, that is. I haven't even talked to him about that yet. I'm not sure what he wants to do."

"Get away from me, ye old Buzzard," came Nairnie's shrill voice as the last shuttle boat docked at the pier and Bear helped her disembark.

"Uh oh. Nairnie and Bear are at it again," said Vivienne. "I don't like what's been happening between those two."

"Neither do I," said Zachariah. "But you have to admit that Nairnie hasn't been very pleasant to Bear lately."

"What?" Vivienne's mouth fell open. "It's Bear that hasn't been very kind to her."

"Now, Vivienne, before you say another word, I want to tell you that I don't care to get involved in their disputes."

"You're right," she said. "And neither do I."

"Well, Sheriff, I'm ready to go back to town." Nairnie walked up with her big bag of cooking supplies shoved into a burlap sack that she carried slung over her shoulder. Her ladle and the handle of the frying pan stuck out the top.

"Let me take that for you, Nairnie," offered Zachariah, removing the bag from her shoulder so he could carry it for her.

"Thank ye, Sheriff. It's nice to ken that someone still has some manners." There was no doubt she was saying that her husband didn't have any.

"Did you want to invite Bear and his crew for dinner before they leave?" asked the sheriff. "Because, now that I've gotten to know them all, I wouldn't mind at all."

"Nay," she said, not even looking back at the ship. "Bear and I...are finished with each other. It's over, so just let him go do what he has to do for the King."

"Nay, Nairnie, please don't say that. You two seemed to be so much in love. I saw it on both your faces the day Bear showed up at the sheriff's house," said Vivienne.

Vivienne turned to see Bear getting back into the shuttle boat while giving instructions to Ramble, who was rowing. Most of the crew hadn't even gotten off the ship.

"Is Bear really leaving already?" asked Zachariah. "I had hoped they'd at least stay until tomorrow."

"Aye, he's leaving. As always." Nairnie sounded spiteful. Vivienne knew it was because her husband was always sailing instead of being home with her like she'd prefer.

"It's his job, Nairnie," said Zachariah. "You need to under-stand that his work is important." His daughter called to him from the wagon then, and he turned to go to her, carrying Nairnie's big bag over his shoulder.

"I'm sure he'll be back soon and then you two can talk and make amends," said Vivienne, trying to make Nairnie feel better.

"Nay, he willna. I told him no' to bother to return. Ever. He's no' comin' back, my lady."

"Oh, Nairnie, don't be that way. I'm sure you could work things out if only you tried."

"Nay, lassie. I told ye, it's over. Now let's get on that wagon before yer uncle starts spittin' curses at us next."

Vivienne's heart went out to the woman since she knew how important family life was to Nairnie. Even though Vivienne told Zachariah she wouldn't get involved, she had to do something to help the poor woman. The only problem was, she wasn't sure what she could do that would make a difference and help to get Bear and Nairnie back together again.

"Och, look at those strumpets that just got off that ship. I think they're Winchester Geese," said Nairnie. "Ye can tell since they are wearin' striped hoods on their cloaks. Blethers, it's disgustin' the way they're showin' their faces here now instead of stayin' back at their own stew in Southwark."

Vivienne looked over her shoulder to see two scantily-dressed women meandering down the dock, shaking their hips as they walked. One of the dockworkers whistled and the girls smiled, as the men all started following them down the pier, sniffing them out like they were dogs in heat.

"I think it's time to go," she said, turning to go back to the wagon, but stopping when she heard someone call out her name.

"Lady Vivienne? Is that you?" came a woman's voice.

She turned around to see one of the whores actually waving to her.

"Please dinna tell me ye ken that goose," said Nairnie. "No noblewoman should be anywhere near someone like her."

"Cassandra?" Vivienne's eyes opened wide and she smiled and waved back. "Yes, I do know her, Nairnie. Don't worry, she's a very nice woman. Actually, we used to be friends at one time. I am glad she's here because I haven't seen her in years and I've missed her greatly."

"Ye'd better tell me what ye mean, because I'm no' likin' the sound of this, my lady."

"Don't take it the wrong way, Nairnie. I've never been a...a you know what," she said. "If that is what you're thinking, just put your mind at ease right now."

"Vivienne, Nairnie, come on," said Zachariah, coming back to get them, having left Nairnie's bag on the wagon. "Your uncle is extremely impatient and wants to return to the castle."

"Zachariah? Is that you?" said the same whore.

Nairnie's eyes opened even wider. "Blethers, dinna tell me ye're friends with the goose too, Sheriff," spat Nairnie. "Or do ye ken her in a...different way?"

"What in heaven's name are you talking about?" asked Zachariah, turning to look to see who had called out his name. "Oh, bloody hell, you've got to be jesting," he ground out. "Please don't tell me it's true."

"Zachariah, we need to go over and greet Cassandra," said Vivienne, taking his arm.

"Who is this goose named Cassandra and how do ye both ken her?" Nairnie demanded answers.

"Well, Nairnie, all I can say is that I'm not proud to admit that I even know her," Zachariah answered, as the two women walked up and bent over to put down their bags, giving them all a good show down their bodices at their half-naked breasts as they leaned over.

Zachariah groaned and quickly looked the other way.

"Zachariah, come here. Let me give you a big kiss," said the one named Cassandra, reaching out to grab his face, but he held up his hand and backed away from her.

"Don't even," he warned her, his head down and his jaw clenched tightly.

"Oh, stop it," said Vivienne, hitting the sheriff on the arm. "Don't act that way. What is the matter with you?"

Nairnie cleared her throat, crossing her arms over her chest. "I'm waitin' for an explanation."

"Sheriff, if you won't introduce them, then I will," said Vivienne. "Cassandra, this is Nairnie. She is the nursemaid for Zachariah's daughter, Starah. And, Nairnie, this is Cassandra. She is Zachariah's youngest sister."

"God's teeth!" said Nairnie, her eyes about popping out of her head. "The sheriff has a sister who is a Winchester Goose!"

Zachariah let out a deep breath, and looked directly at his sister. "Cassandra," he said, finally acknowledging her. "Whatever you are here for, I'm not interested. And whatever you want from me, the answer is no."

"But, Brother, you haven't even heard what I have to say yet."

"Yes," agreed her friend. "We've traveled here just to see you. Please don't turn us away."

"I would have rather you stayed back in your London stew," Zachariah ground out. "There is nothing here for you in Mablethorpe anymore, Cassandra."

"Who are ye?" asked Nairnie, eyeing up Cassandra's friend from head to toe.

"Oh, I'm Cassandra's good friend. My name is Frances, but back at the stew I'm known as Feathered Fanny." She flipped back her striped hood that was the marking of a Winchester Goose, and showed Nairnie the feathers she'd pinned in her loose hair. "I have feathers somewhere else too. Want to see where?" She started to pull up the hem of her gown.

"Nay!" both Vivienne and Zachariah said at the same time, trying to stop her. The men on the wharf still watched closely with interest.

"Feathered Fanny, huh?" asked Nairnie, now looking back over to Cassandra. "And what are ye called in the stew?"

"Oh, she's referred to as Lady Longneck," said Fanny,

covering her mouth with her hand as she giggled. "However, it's not always her neck that is the long one, if you know what I mean."

"Enough!" Zachariah ground out. "No one cares to hear any more about your vulgar profession."

"What are ye two doin' here in Mablethorpe?" asked Nairnie, continuing with her questions. "Yer stew is in Southwark. Ye dinna belong here."

"I whole-heartedly agree," said Zachariah. "So go back to where you came from and leave us alone. Come on, Vivienne, Nairnie, we need to go." The sheriff took each of them by the arms and turned to head back to the wagon, but stopped dead in his tracks when he heard what his sister had to say to him next.

"Fanny and I have decided to take a week or so off work to come here and visit you, Brother.

"Please tell me I'm only having a nightmare," grumbled Zachariah.

Vivienne looked up to see Zachariah's eyes closed. She was sure he was about to explode with anger. He already had his ex-mercenary brother staying with him, and he certainly wouldn't want his daughter exposed to women of this profession. She almost felt a little sorry for him. Then again, this would be the perfect opportunity to make amends with his estranged sister.

"We were counting on staying with you since we have nowhere else to go," said Cassandra.

No one said anything, and Vivienne couldn't stand the silence a moment longer. Cassandra was part of Zachariah's family, and had even been her friend while growing up. She decided she needed to help Zachariah make amends the way he did with his brother Isaac, and his other sister, Magdalena. Vivienne couldn't stand to see this feud continue a moment longer.

She broke free of Zachariah's hold and turned around and smiled, reaching out her arms in a most accepting way. "Well, that sounds wonderful, Cassandra. I'm sure the sheriff wouldn't mind having you and Fanny as his guests during your stay. Welcome home!"

She heard a snort from Nairnie and a deep and low groan from Zachariah. Suddenly, she was more than a little apprehensive to turn back around.

Somehow she just knew another wild adventure was upon them.

From the Author:

I hope you enjoyed **Murder on the High Seas** and will take a moment to leave a review for me. As I am sure you know by now, this is an ongoing series with a main thread of a mystery that continues throughout each book.

At the same time, each book has a new murder that is solved by the end of that story. The next book in my **Harlowe & Fitch Historical Mystery Series** is called **Murder of a Winchester Goose.** As you've already seen, Zachariah's estranged sister has come home to Mablethorpe, and as you've probably already guessed, that means nothing but trouble for poor Zachariah.

The Winchester Geese back in medieval times were named thus because of the Bishop of Winchester. He owned land, and stews or brothels, and ended up legalizing prostitution there so he could charge rent, hand out fines, and also tax the harlots and make a profit off them and their work. You'll find out a lot more regarding this, in the next book.

It is best to read the books in this series in order, or else there will be many surprises ruined along the way. Still, each book can stand on its own.

I always like pulling in existing characters from some of my other series, and giving them guest appearances in the new books. Nairnie, for example, was first seen in my ***Seasons of Fortitude Series***, as handmaid to the four sisters, Spring, Summer, Autumn and Winter. She appears again in my ***Pirate Lords Series***, as the grandmother of the pirate brothers, Tristan, Mardon, and Aaron. The book called ***Aaron*** is where you will also find out about Bear and his background. These are all historical romances, but you will find a few murder mysteries as well along the way.

Stay tuned for more adventures and more mysteries and murders in medieval times. A small-town sheriff and a lady and her dog investigate murders to bring about justice, revealing that which is hidden, but needs to be unveiled.

Until next time,

Elizabeth Rose

Also by Elizabeth Rose

Mystery Series:

Harlowe & Fitch Historical Mystery Series

Murder at Mablethorpe Castle

Murder on Rotten Row

Murder at Maltby le Marsh

Murder at the Joust

Murder on the High Seas

Medieval Series:

Below the Salt

Legendary Bastards of the Crown Series

Seasons of Fortitude Series

Secrets of the Heart Series

Legacy of the Blade Series

Daughters of the Dagger Series

MadMan MacKeefe Series

Barons of the Cinque Ports Series

Holiday Knights Series

Highland Chronicles Series

Pirate Lords Series

Highland Outcasts

Medieval/Paranormal Series:

Elemental Magick Series

Greek Myth Fantasy Series

Tangled Tales Series

Portals of Destiny

Contemporary Series:

Tarnished Saints Series

Working Man Series

Western Series:

Cowboys of the Old West Series

And More!

Please visit http://elizabethrosenovels.com

About Elizabeth

Elizabeth Rose is an award-winning, bestselling author of over 100 books and counting. She writes medieval, historical, contemporary, paranormal, and western romance. Her books are available as EBooks, paperbacks, and some audiobooks as well.

Her favorite characters in her works include dark, dangerous and tortured heroes, and feisty, independent heroines who know how to wield a sword. She loves writing 14th century medieval novels, and is well-known for her many series.

Elizabeth loves the outdoors. In the summertime, you can find her in her secret garden with her laptop, swinging in her hammock working on her next book. Elizabeth is a born storyteller and passionate about sharing her works with her readers.

Please be sure to visit her website at **Elizabethrosenovels.com** to read excerpts from any of her novels and get sneak peeks at covers of upcoming books. You can follow her on **Twitter, Facebook**, **Goodreads** or **BookBub.** Join Elizabeth's **newsletter** so you don't miss out on new releases or upcoming events.

9 798900 430119